The Touch of Sage

ଓଡ ଓଃ

by

Marcia Lynn McClure

The Touch of Sage
Copyright ©2007 by Marcia Lynn McClure

This is a work of fiction. All characters are fictional and any resemblance to persons living or dead is purely coincidental.

Published and Distributed by:

Granite Publishing and Distributions, LLC
868 North 1430 West
Orem, UT 84057
98010 229-9023 Toll Free (800) 574-5779
www.granitepublishing.biz

Cover Photo by Denise A. Kelly
Cover Design by Tammie Ingram
Page Layout and Design by Myrna Varga, The Office Connection, Inc.

ISBN: 978-1-59936-014-0
Library of Congress Control Number: 2007933220

First Printing: August 2007

10 9 8 7 6 5 4 3 2 1

Printed in the United States of America

To My Mother,
Patsy Christine . . .
You are the truest heroine!
Thank you for giving me life, joy, and love . . .
and for making everything a beautiful adventure!
I love you!

And
To My Friend,
Patricia "Patsy" Maureen . . .
For gifting me one of the most
serene and peaceful memories of my life . . .
For our moments together in Ruth's pasture.

෮ ෴

Prologue

"Rummy! I win!" Rose Applewhite announced, laying her cards face-up on the table. "Rummy, rummy, rummy!" Pushing her chair back, she jumped up and began prancing about the parlor like a proud, gray-haired pony. "Rummy, rummy, rummy!" she sang.

"For pity's sake, sit down, Rose," Mary Anne Farthen grumbled. "It's *one* hand."

"Oh, let her dance, Mary," Livie Jonesburg chuckled. "She so rarely wins," she added under her breath.

"Rummy, rummy, rummy!" Rose sang again, swishing her skirts this way and that like a French can-can girl.

"I can see all the way to yer knees, Rose," Mary scolded. "And they're as wrinkled as an ol' elephant's."

Rose Applewhite quirked a once-blonde eyebrow. Her blue eyes sparkled brightly with mischief just as they had at age eighteen some forty years before. Smiling, she continued, "Rummy, rummy . . ." and turning her back to Mary shouted, "Rummy!" as she whipped her skirts and petticoats high over her back, revealing the seat of her lacy, ruffled bloomers.

"For cryin' in the bucket!" Mary moaned as Livie burst into giggles. "The girl has no shame."

Eugenia Smarthing smiled. She knew Mary delighted in Rose's antics as much as she and Livie did. However, Mary was a well-weathered, leathery old woman and used to guarding her smiles like a rare treasure. Still, Eugenia wondered how anyone could resist smiling at the sight of Rosie Applewhite's brazenly displayed bloomer ruffles.

"And you quit eggin' her on, Eugenia!" Mary demanded, pointing a withered index finger in Eugenia's direction.

Eugenia bit her lip to stifle another giggle as Rose returned to her seat at the parlor table. Leaning over to Mary, she whispered, "Rummy!"

"Oh, for cryin' out loud," Mary mumbled. She gathered up the cards and began reshuffling.

Eugenia chuckled, purely delighted with her friends. What a blessing it was to have one another—four elderly widows living together at Willows' Boarding House. A blessing indeed, and Eugenia pondered each of them for a moment as Mary dealt the next hand.

◌℥

ROSE "ROSIE" APPLEWHITE had been an actress, a golden-haired song lark in San Francisco where she had caught the eye of a wealthy young silver miner from Leadville. Johnny Applewhite married his "Silver Rose," as he called her, sweeping her away to a life of fanciful privilege in Denver.

Now, Rose was in her mid-fifties, a fine and respectable age to obtain. Even though her darling Johnny had been gone for nearly ten years and her own hair was as ashen as granite, her blue eyes still sparkled as brightly as the heavens, as did her spirits.

Mary Anne Farthen led a far different life than Rose. She had married an older man of nearly thirty at the innocent age of fourteen. Archibald Farthen was married twice before, both wives having died in childbirth. He was left with three small children and a painfully demanding farm in Oklahoma. He needed a wife, and when Mary Anne's parents were both taken with a fever, Archibald married the young orphan. To become an instant mother at such a young age, Mary, out of necessity to survive, became stern and guarded.

Archibald was good to Mary Anne, and they had three more children of their own. He worked hard, too hard for his heart, and Mary Anne had been a widow for more than sixteen of her sixty years. Yet, she was a good, caring, old woman, even if her perpetual frown and rather ratty-gray hair caused folks to think otherwise.

At fifty-three, Livie was the youngest of the widows who boarded at Willows' Boarding House. Olivia "Livie" Jonesburg, the third of Eugenia's dear companions, was a cheerful, white-haired old gal. Her husband, Clive, died only the previous spring; Eugenia knew how cruelly Livie still struggled with the loss. The feelings in her heart blatantly showed on her face quite often.

Clive had come from Europe and fallen madly in love with Livie, a society girl, a debutante of the highest caliber, in New York. Upon meeting Clive, Livie had forsaken her family, abandoned her home and its luxury to spend her happy life with her beloved husband on his bean farm in Cortez. Life had been grand, full of happiness and loving . . . until last May when Clive was kicked in the head by a frightened foal and died from the trauma.

Eugenia's husband, a local cattle rancher named Buck Smarthing, also passed on the previous year. He was the friend and lover of Eugenia's dreams. Together they raised four children and enjoyed life to its fullest. She mourned to the very depths of her heart and soul when he was lost. She had been very thankful for her children, for the comfort they gave her, for their support in allowing her to remain independent and live in the boardinghouse she now shared with her friends. She had a good life with Buck—a wonderful life. Though forced to be without him, she was thankful for the good and happy life she shared with the other ladies of Willows' Boarding House.

ೞ

EUGENIA SMILED AS she watched Mary and Rose bicker over Mary's dealing of the cards. Livie was grinning, amused at the antics of the other two. Yes, these were the best of women, true friends, the kind of companions any widow would wish for in her later years. And, she was ever thankful for the entertainment they lent to her life.

"Who's winnin'?" Sage asked as she entered the parlor and set glasses of sweet lemonade in the middle of the table.

"Well, Livie's winnin' all around, but Rose just won a hand," Mary stated.

"Miss Rosie!" Sage exclaimed. "You won?"

"Why, of course I did," Rose boasted with a smile.

"Well, good for you," Sage giggled.

"Ya missed the victory dance, Sage," Mary grumbled. "Thank yer lucky stars ya didn't have to sit through *that* parade of nonsense and lace bloomers."

Sage glanced at Eugenia who winked, indicating Rose's display had been quite entertaining.

Sage pulled up a chair, planted her elbows firmly on the tabletop, resting her chin in one palm.

"What've you been up to this afternoon, Sage?" Livie asked.

Sage shrugged her shoulders and sighed. "Oh, I got the bread baked and the hens fed. Worked on my quilt a bit. Thought I might take Bullet for a walk in a while."

"That dog," Mary growled. "Ya know . . . that's why they geld horses, Sage . . . calms 'em down. That dog could use a good . . ."

"Oh, now, Mary," Eugenia interrupted. "Bullet's a good dog. Just needs some direction through his pup years."

"Hmph," Mary breathed. "Ya shoulda made Karoline take that pup with her when she married Joel."

Sage shook her head. "No, Karoline is too busy with a new husband. She doesn't have any time for a spoiled puppy."

❧

EUGENIA STUDIED SAGE Willows. Her young friend seemed too youthful to have the responsibilities of running a boardinghouse heaped so heavy on her shoulders. Sage should be somewhere being adored by a good-looking husband and raising babies of her own. But life had dealt her a hard hand. Like Mary, responsibility came early to sweet Sage.

Matt and Susan Willows died in a tragic accident when Sage was only sixteen. Their wagon had lost a wheel and plummeted into Raven's Canyon, and Sage suddenly found herself responsible for three younger sisters.

Rose was already boarding at the Willows' house when the accident occurred. It was with Rose's help Sage was able to keep the house running, thereby providing a way of life for herself and her sisters.

As often as it went with older daughters who found themselves rearing their siblings, all of Sage's time and efforts were put into providing for her sisters' care and then seeing them happily married. This left Sage with little or no time to consider her own future, let alone chase after it.

As a result, with her three sisters wed and moved away, Sage sat at the table in the parlor, twenty-three years to her name, unmarried and watching four old widows play rummy.

Eugenia smiled as she considered the girl. What a pretty little thing she was. Her hair was the color of an acorn's lid, soft, silky, and unusually long. Most of the time the length went unnoticed, for she wore it in a rather spinsterly knot at the back of her head. Sage had green, almond-shaped eyes, guarded by thick, black lashes, which curled up to meet her sweetly arched brows. Though her eyes were her most striking feature, the rest of her face was pleasing as well. A small nose, somewhat heart-shaped lips, and high-set cheekbones combined to make a very lovely girl. Her frame was average in height and her figure properly curved as to attract the admiration of the men in town.

Yes. There seemed no reason on the face of the earth for Sage Willows to remain unmarried and unhappy. Yet, Eugenia knew very well why Sage remained unattached. The poor child had married off the only decent men in the county to her sisters. Those left were rather ancient widowers and tattered undesirables—men who had fewer teeth in their heads than Primrose Gilbert's new baby, or who were, perhaps, younger, but ugly as mud fences with temperaments and dispositions to match. Old Forest Simmons had proposed marriage to Sage several times. Forest was just that side of fifty, bowlegged, and smelled of whiskey and mule apples. Sage hadn't reconciled herself to the slop bucket yet . . . thank the heavens.

Still, it was wrong . . . unfair. And it troubled Eugenia that such a darling girl should be left with such a lot. It had troubled her so much that, in weeks past, she had spent quite a lot of time trying to fix on a remedy for Sage's dull, hopeless, and romance-less situation.

But now . . . now Eugenia grinned impishly. For a possibility, an answer had presented itself just that very morning by way of a telegram she received from her niece in Santa Fe. The idea had set her mind aflame, burning with mischief and pompous pride at having hatched such a brilliant scheme.

Yes, she thought. It was time to address her niece's request.

⚃

"LADIES," EUGENIA ANNOUNCED, rising from the table. "I'm out."

"Out?" Rose and Livie exclaimed simultaneously, as Eugenia laid her hand face down on the table.

"Ya can't be out. We're not finished," Mary scolded.

"I know. But I've somethin' to do. I need to answer Bridie's telegram," Eugenia explained.

"I'll play your hand, Miss Eugenia" Sage offered, slipping into Eugenia's chair.

"You do that, sweetie," Eugenia said with a smile. "You do just that."

Chapter One

෨ ෬

$\mathcal{S}$age gently poured water from a bucket onto the dry ground at the base of the little rosebush.

"There now," she said. "Your roses should take to bloomin' in just a few weeks, Ruthie." Crouching down in front of the small tombstone, Sage reached out, letting her fingers tenderly trace the roughly engraved letters of little Ruth's name. "I'm bettin' they'll be smellin' like heaven itself this year."

She rose to her feet, smiling at the tiny marker once more, before stepping through the weathered picket gate and latching it securely behind her. "I'll be back in a few days," she said, more to the air than to anyone else, for in reality, there was no one else anywhere near to hear her. And she preferred it.

Sighing heavily, Sage strolled away from the tiny, lonely little gravesite, closed her eyes and inhaled the fresh, sweet fragrance of the pastures. Oh, she knew some folks might not call these rather plain grazing fields pastures, but to Sage Willows, they were the most beautiful and serene place on earth.

Reaching back, she pulled the pins from her hair, letting its length fall down about her shoulders and back. The breeze played among the silken tresses, cool and soothing. Sage smiled. She could hear nothing but the soft breeze around her, the faint trickle of the creek just over the hill, the quiet hum of soothing bug music in the grass.

Inhaling deeply, Sage caught the scent of piñon trees, of dry soil and sagebrush. The fragrances of the pasture filled her senses with serenity, joy, and an odd feeling of freedom. This was Sage's pasture, the one near where the creek ran, the one where Buck Smarthing's cattle had once grazed, the one where little Ruth States had rested in heavenly peace for over forty years. How she loved the space and dreamed of it in moments of despair. She was thankful her father had kept his grazing lands, choosing to rent them to local ranchers when their family moved into town to run the boardinghouse. She was filled with gratitude that the pastures were now hers, that she could continue to visit little Ruth, tend to her solitary grave, and find rare moments of joy and serenity in the quiet expanse of the pastures.

With a heavy sigh, Sage opened her eyes and began walking toward the creek bed where she had tied Drifter's reins to a small piñon tree. The late spring rain was past due and the creek ran low, but Drifter seemed contented enough with one final drink from its refreshing water. Sage hooked the bucket handle over the saddle horn and mounted.

"Creek's a bit low, isn't it, Drifter?" she said to the buckskin, leaning forward to stroke his jaw. "But you wait and see, the rain will come soon. Then you can get good and wet, and I can have a good cry."

Pausing to twist her hair into a bun once more, Sage clicked her tongue twice, nudging Drifter's belly with her stirrups to urge him toward home. As melancholy as the moment left her, Sage couldn't help but smile, wondering what in the world the ladies at the boardinghouse had been up to during her absence.

She loved the widows! All of them, even cranky old Mary. Sage often wondered what she would do without them—not simply because the money for their board at Willows' was her one source of financial means, but because they were her friends—her true, loving and faithful friends. Oft times it felt to Sage as though she had four darling grandmothers to love and care for. And now, now that her youngest sister, Karoline, was married, the ladies at Willows' would be her only company. Gifts of heaven they were, and Sage was grateful for them.

ℭℛ

"YA SIMPLY CANNOT deal that way, Livie," Mary was scolding as Sage entered the boardinghouse by way of the parlor back door.

"I can so if I want to, Mary," Livie argued. "It doesn't matter how the cards are dealt."

"It does too!" Mary argued. "If ya go and deal 'em that way, they don't get mixed up enough. Ya have to give one to me, one to Rose, one to Eugenia and one to yerself. Then start it all over again. That's how it goes, Livie and ya know it! They don't get mixed up proper if ya don't deal 'em that way." Reaching for the deck of cards, Mary tried to take them away from Livie. "Give 'em to me if ya ain't gonna deal 'em right. I'll do it."

But Livie pulled hard, too, attempting to retain possession of the deck. "I'll do it, Mary! It's my deal and I can do it whichever way I see fit!"

"What's the matter, ladies?" Sage asked, smiling at the scene before her. Her four friends sat around the parlor table, apparently engaged in a heated afternoon of cards. As Rose sat, twisting a stray lock of hair around one finger, Eugenia read a telegram she was holding in her hand. Mary and Livie were ready to tear each other's hair out over a difference of opinion as to how the cards should be dealt.

"She ain't dealin' 'em proper, Sage!" Mary stated. "Ya know they don't get mixed up good if ya don't deal 'em right."

"I can deal them however I see fit! Can't I, Sage?" Livie retorted. Sage shook her head. As usual each woman made a legitimate point.

"Why not let her deal the cards the way she wants, Mary," Sage suggested. "Maybe the lack of proper mixin' up will turn out in your favor."

"She's spoilt rotten, Sage. That's all there is to it," Mary grumbled. Still, she let go of the deck of cards and sneered at her friend when Livie stuck her tongue out and continued to deal.

"They've been squabblin' like children ever since you left, Sage," Rose sighed. "It's a plain miracle that we've managed to play even four hands."

Sage smiled, amused by Rose's relaxed manner. She sat, one arm draped over the back of her chair, lounging indecorously, legs crossed and ankles showing for all the world to see. Though an older, widowed woman, the traits of the relaxed proprieties of the stage were still often very apparent in Rose Applewhite's mannerisms. Sage loved Rose's free spirit, for it gave her cause to feel free and somewhat rebellious herself, if only by proxy.

"I've had another telegram from Bridie," Eugenia announced.

"Oh?" Livie asked, still dealing seven cards to each player instead of one card to each alternately.

"Reb has agreed to take over the ranch," Eugenia said. Sighing, she folded the telegram and tucked it into her apron pocket.

"Are you sure that's what you want, Miss Eugenia?" Sage asked. Sage knew that, since the death of her husband, Buck, Eugenia had struggled with what to do concerning their large cattle ranch outside of town. "If ya sold it, you could make a mint of money."

Eugenia sighed again. "Oh, don't I know it, Sage," she admitted. Her eyes twinkled as she looked to the young girl. "But some things are worth so much more than money, sweetheart. And . . . and I want to see Reb happy. He's such a good and deservin' man. I want the ranch to be a success again, too. Buck worked so hard to see it to what it was."

"I still think it was might smug of that niece of yers to write and even ask such a thing," Mary grumbled. "Offerin' for her son to take over runnin' Buck's business," she said, shaking her head in obvious disapproval. "She's just a hopin' you'll drop off and leave the ranch to him 'stead of to yer own children."

"Mary!" Livie exclaimed.

"I'm just sayin' . . . it was a purty arrogant thing to ask," Mary grumbled.

But Eugenia smiled. "Reb is a wonderful boy," she explained. "He's had some misery of his own of recent, and I've always favored him. I'm glad to help him out and let him help me if he's willin'."

"Is he handsome at all, Eugenia?" Rose asked.

"For the love of Pete, Rose!" Mary exclaimed. "He's a boy!"

"Don't matter if he's a boy or not," Rose said. "I still prefer to look at the handsome ones more than I do the plain ones." Sage giggled, delighted by the women's banter.

Smiling, Eugenia said, "Yes, he's handsome, Rose. I expect you'll have quite a nice time lookin' him over.

"When's he comin', Miss Eugenia?" Sage asked. She wondered if Eugenia would have him stay out at the ranch right away, or if she had it in mind for him to board at Willows' for a time.

"I don't rightly know," Eugenia answered. "Bridie's still havin' a bit of trouble convincin' him all the way. But she's confident she will. She's told him how important the ranch is to me and all."

"Do you want me to prepare the extra room for him?" Sage asked.

Eugenia seemed thoughtful for a moment, finally saying, "It might be a good idea. I haven't been out to the ranch house in so long, and I'm sure it's just crawlin' with critters."

Sage smiled, for Eugenia seemed very excited about the possibility of having her favorite nephew close by. Eugenia deserved happiness and Sage was glad for her.

"I'll get lunch on, take Bullet for a walk, and then get right into that upstairs room, just in case," Sage said.

Eugenia reached out and took one of Sage's hands in her own, squeezing it affectionately. "You're too good to us all, Sage," she said.

"Rummy!" Rose giggled as she spread her cards on the table, revealing her instant win.

Mary threw her cards to the table's surface with angry indignation. "I told ya, Livie! I told ya! Ya have to deal 'em out proper!"

Sage smiled as Rose leapt from her chair and began performing an elderly lady's version of the can-can. "Rummy, rummy, rummy!" she sang as she danced.

"It don't count a wit, Rose," Mary told her. "The cards weren't dealt proper."

"Rummy, rummy, rummy," Rose continued to sing, swishing her skirt and petticoats this way and that as she danced.

"Well, why don't we just throw a sign out on the front door." Mary grumbled. "Willows' Saloon and Dance Hall . . . neked knees and ankles a flyin' ever'where."

Sage laughed, amused, not only by Rose's scandalous behavior, but by Mary's predictable response as well.

"I'll get us some lunch," Sage said, smiling.

"Oh, lunch can wait," Eugenia said. "Come play a hand or two with us, Sage."

"Yes, Sage," Livie begged. "Please do."

"All right," Sage agreed, pulling a spare chair up to the table. "just one . . . maybe two."

With a contented sigh, Rosie returned to her seat, only to hear Mary grumble, "It would serve ya right, Rose Applewhite, if the Reverend Tippetts hisself walked in here to see ya dancin' around like a heathen."

"You know as well as I do, Mary," Rose began, "that Scarlett Tippetts was a dance hall girl in Leadville before Reverend Tippetts married her. I 'spect he wouldn't be a bit undone." Rose picked up the deck of cards and began to shuffle.

"One at time, Rose. Ya just be sure ya deal 'em one at a time," Mary mumbled, irritated with being one-upped.

Sage looked at the faces of her friends, delighted for their company. Still, the familiar, painful pinch of regret pricked at her heart, reminding her of what she didn't have . . . of what she knew she never would have. Oh, she loved these dear ladies, it was true, but they did nothing to fill the loneliness, the gaping void in her soul, which longed for a life of wonder with a loving husband and a family all her own. The sting of buried resentment began to well up in her, but she fought it, painfully tucking it away and trying to concentrate on the cards in her hand.

Reminding herself she was blessed, that she was happy for her sisters and their blissful lives, Sage smiled, however half-heartedly, when Mary said, "Now ya see, Livie? Proper dealin'—it's important."

"I feel a win comin' over me," Rose giggled.

"Well, I just hope the Reverend Tippetts is in time to see it," Mary grumbled.

"Maybe he just will be, Mary," Rose said as she drew a card. "Then me and Scarlett Tippetts can both start into kickin' up our heels."

"That would be a sight!" Mary exclaimed, discarding a card. "A sight indeed."

&

EUGENIA GLANCED AT the sweet young woman at her side. One look at her nephew Rebel Lee Mitchell, and the girl would be lost. Or, perhaps found, whichever way Eugenia chose to look at it. It was, in fact, dangerously daring, quite meddling in reality, but Eugenia felt warm and excited inside, happier and brighter than she had felt since Buck passed. Reb's soul was damaged, it was true, but he wasn't completely unrecoverable. There was a heart in him yet. There had to be! And Eugenia could only hope Sage would be the one to find it.

Again Eugenia studied Sage, her sweet and lovely features, the smile she forced, attempting to mask her profound loneliness. If only the girl knew what was about to arrive on the front porch step of Willows' Boarding House. If only she knew.

&

"HUSH, BULLET!" SAGE scolded, eating a piece of biscuit dough off her finger. "We'll go out as soon as I get these in." Hurriedly, Sage arranged the biscuits in a pan. It was obvious by the dog's unceasing barking for the past five minutes he needed to go out.

Sliding the pan into the oven, she said to the sandy-colored dog, "Ya know, if you'd just quit chewin' through your rope and consortin' with Mr. Simmons lady dog, I could let ya out on your own." Quickly, she untied the rope tethering the dog to the table leg and wrapped it around her wrist several times to secure it.

At the prospect of the outdoors and some semblance of freedom, the dog instantly began to pant, excitedly jumping up and down, attempting to thankfully lick Sage's face. Bullet was only a puppy, just one and a half years old, but he was already enormous! A big dog with a puppy's mind was, indeed, a handful. When Karoline married Joel Evans just before Christmas . . . well, somehow Sage inherited the handful.

"Come on, boy," Sage giggled as the dog smiled at her in relief. "Let's take you out back."

However, at that very moment, a loud, solid knock sounded at the boardinghouse front door. Sage sighed, slightly irritated at the interruption, and led Bullet toward the front door instead.

"I guess we'll go out front this time, boy," she told him. "But just this once. Do you hear me?" The dog seemed to nod in agreement as he bounded happily toward the door.

"Settle down, Bullet. Settle down," she said, wrapping the rope around her wrist again in an effort to shorten the slack.

Pasting on a friendly smile, Sage opened the door to greet whomever she might find on the other side. Her smile vanished instantly, however, as astonishment washed over her.

Standing there on the front porch of Willows' Boarding House, was as tall a man as Sage had ever seen. He wore a black front-flap shirt.

He removed his weathered, black hat to greet her with a deep, "Mornin', miss." Sage saw that his hair was as black as the shirt he wore, as were the finely groomed mustache and goatee he smoothed with an index finger and thumb as he greeted her. Other than the fact that the color of his eyes was nearly dark as his pupils, Sage only had time to notice one other thing—he was so extraordinarily handsome. She was left with her mouth gaping open.

Her awe of the stranger at her door was cut short when Bullet began jumping about in excitement. He jumped, planting both front paws firmly on the stranger's stomach and licked the front of his shirt.

"Down, Bullet!" Sage scolded. "Down!" Bullet obeyed long enough for Sage to utter, "I'm sorry, sir. He . . ." Instantly the dog squeezed himself between the stranger's knees in an effort to escape. The rope around Bullet's neck was still anchored securely around Sage's wrist as he managed to break between the stranger's legs. Sage went with him, hitting her face solidly on the man's knee as he raised one long leg to let the dog through.

Bullet was desperate. He continued pulling against the rope in an effort to escape. Sage, flat on her stomach on the porch, shouted, "Bullet!"

The dog kept pulling. Her arm was so outstretched with the dog's pull on the rope, she could not even begin to lift or right herself.

"Here, boy!" she heard the stranger command with a shrill whistle. "Bullet! Here!" Sage looked to see the dog immediately cease his barking and his attempted escape. He straightened his ears as much as they would straighten and looked to the stranger.

"Here, Bullet," the stranger repeated, his voice deep and commanding. As the dog came toward the man, the rope slackened. Sage's hand quit turning purple. Sage felt the stranger's strong hands, one at her elbow and one at her waist as he helped her to her feet.

"You all right, miss?" the stranger asked.

"Yes. I . . . I . . ." Sage stammered. Perhaps, it was the sound of Sage's voice, or perhaps, the fact the dog was incapable of remaining calm for more than a few seconds—whatever the reason—Bullet suddenly bolted round one of the stranger's legs and through his knees again. This retightened the slack in the rope. Furthermore, the rope was now entwined around one of the stranger's legs as well. Before Sage could utter another word, she felt her body slam into the solid mass of the stranger's, his chin meeting brutally with her forehead. Horrified, embarrassed beyond description, Sage looked up into the stranger's handsome face.

"Mighty unruly pup ya got there," the stranger mumbled a moment before Bullet's tug on the rope sent the man stumbling backward, taking Sage with him. Sage heard herself scream as the man lost his footing and fell flat on his back, pulling her down on top of him.

"I'm so sorry," she began to apologize as she watched the stranger grimace. No doubt the fall, coupled with the weight of Sage's body on his, caused him great discomfort. To make matters worse, Bullet now stood over them, happily licking the man's face. The man did not explode with anger, simply reached to his side and pulled a knife from his boot. Awkwardly, he reached down and cut the rope that was twisted around his leg.

Once he had unwound the rope from about his leg, the man tossed it at the dog and said, "Take care of yer business, boy." Bullet bounded off as happy as any dog could be.

"Oh, no, no, no!" Sage argued. "He'll go off and find Mr. Simmons' lady dog and then . . ."

"Then Mr. Simmons will have a new litter, won't he?" the stranger stated, smiling as he looked at Sage. Sage was enchanted by his charming smile for a moment before realizing she still lay tangled up on the porch with a strange man. Gasping, she struggled to her feet, brushing a stray strand of hair from her cheek as the man slowly stood. Sage removed the rope from her wrist, wishing she could simply disappear and not have to face such an uncomfortable situation. She had never been so physically intimate with a man, let alone a complete stranger! The humiliation of it all was as ripe as a late summer tomato.

"Ya busted yer lip there, miss," he said. "Probably when ya hit my knee fallin' down so hard."

Embarrassed and thinking the situation couldn't possibly get any worse, Sage touched the corner of her mouth with her fingers. Yep. She was bleeding. She pressed the wound with the hem of her apron.

"I'm so sorry about all this, Mr . . . Mr . . ." she stammered.

"Mitchell," the man answered, still frowning at her.

"He's just a pup and he gets so excited," she explained.

"Ya sure yer all right, miss?" the man asked.

"Oh, yes. I'm fine. Thank you." Feeling very self-conscious as the stranger stared at her disbelieving, she ventured, "How 'bout you?"

Mr. Mitchell smiled, chuckled a bit. "Oh, I'm just fine, ma'am."

"What can I do for you, Mr. Mitchell?" Sage ventured, blushing under his gaze.

"Well," he began, studying Sage from head to toe, his amused grin broadening, "the sign says this is Willows' Boardin' House."

"Yes, sir. I'm Sage Willows."

"Oh. Then I'm pleased to meet ya, Mrs. Willows." Mr. Mitchell offered a hand to Sage. As she took it, she instantly wished she hadn't accepted his friendly greeting of a handshake. As he grasped her hand firmly, it seemed as though some strange unseen source of heat traveled from Sage's hand, up the length of her arm and into her bosom.

"*Miss* Willows," she corrected him, releasing his hand as quickly as she could.

"Oh," he said. "Pleased to meet ya, *Miss* Willows." The man stooped to pick up his hat, which had fallen to the porch during the ruckus with Bullet. "I'm lookin' for Eugenia Smarthing."

"Oooh!" Sage exclaimed. "You must be her nephew up from Santa Fe." Sage smiled. "She's been so excited about your comin'. All we've been hearin' for weeks now is Reb this, and Reb that. She'll be so glad you're here!"

The man chuckled, his eyes twinkling with a hint of mischief. "Well, I'm mighty excited to see her, too."

Sage looked at him, finding it rather difficult to breathe regularly. "So . . . you're Eugenia's nephew?"

"Yep. My mother is Bridie Mitchell, Eugenia's niece," he explained.

"Well . . . come on in," Sage said. "I'll run up and tell her you're here."

Reb Mitchell nodded, but as Sage turned, expecting him to follow her into the house, he caught hold of her right hand. Once again startled by his touch, Sage stopped and looked back at him.

"That there's one nasty rope burn, Miss Willows," he mumbled as he inspected the red chafing on Sage's wrist.

"Oh," Sage said. Having been distracted by the man's presence, she hadn't been aware of the pain of the wound until that very moment. "It . . . It'll be fine," she stammered, slowly pulling her hand from his grasp. "I'll take care of it as soon as I've fetched your aunt." He was intoxicatingly handsome, this nephew of Eugenia Smarthing's. Sage felt a tremor of jealousy travel the length of her body at the thought of the way all the young girls in town would instantly take to fawning over him like a new puppy.

"I didn't telegram her I was on my way," he said as he stepped into the house, hanging his hat on the hat rack near the front door. "Figured I'd just surprise her. I hope ya don't mind, miss."

"Not at all, Mr. Mitchell," Sage said. "And please, call me Sage."

"All right, Sage. And *you* can call *me* whatever ya want," he said. Sage turned around, astounded more by the flirtatious intonation of his voice than by the implied intimacy of his words. Further, her mouth gaped open slightly as he actually winked at her and added, "As long as it ain't, Mr. Mitchell."

Sage was completely unsettled. The man had the manners of a saloon hound! No amount of good looks gave a man leave to be so improperly forward.

Still, Sage was so undone by his flirtation, by his pure attractiveness, she was at a loss as to how to reprimand him. She could only gesture toward the parlor and say, "Please have a seat and . . . and I'll let your aunt know you're here."

⚘

REB MITCHELL SMILED as he watched the young woman run up the stairs. He had unsettled her and enjoyed observing the consequences. Chuckling, he stepped into the parlor of Willows' Boarding House. The room was cozy with a happy atmosphere. He was pleased his great aunt had found a haven after her husband's passing. It was definitely a room meant for ladies, all ivory lace and doilies, framed photographs, and fringed curtains.

Reb's curiosity was peaked. How had a young girl such as Sage Willows come to be the proprietress of this house? She seemed a pleasant girl, and was unusually pretty. Yet, Reb knew all about women, especially the pretty ones. Like every other man on the face of the earth, he had been the victim of their catty, vindictive ways, and he would ride clear of Miss Sage Willows.

Still, he couldn't stop the chuckle rising from his throat as he thought of the chaos the dog created at the door. Tangled up in the rope, lying on top of him out on the front porch for all the world to see—what a sight it must have been to anyone watching. No doubt she would wring the dog's neck when he came home. Reb felt guilty for finding amusement and pleasure in Sage Willows' obvious embarrassment. Not guilty enough to stifle another chuckle, however.

"Well, hello!" came a voice from behind him. Reb turned to see three older ladies, each sweet, elderly face beaming with an impish smile.

"Look who's come to visit, gals," the shorter one said. Reb thought she had too much color in her cheeks for her age.

"That ain't a visitor, Livie," another said. "That there's dessert!"

Holding her skirt and petticoats, Sage hurried up the stairs to the second floor, all the time shaking her head, as embarrassment from the display at the front door began to envelope her. How mortifying! That dog! What a sight she must've been to Eugenia's nephew, answering the door covered in flour, Bullet taking her to the porch boards. A bleeding lip, for pity's sake! It could not have been a worse introduction. And why hadn't Eugenia told her about her nephew's . . . appearance? It certainly would've helped to have been forewarned. Then maybe she could've stopped staring at him, her mouth hanging open like a trout!

Sage had reconciled herself long ago to the fact that, if ever she did marry, it would be an older man, perhaps a widower—certainly not a handsome young man the likes of whom just stepped into the boarding-house. Still, an attractive man entirely unnerved her, whether or not she saw such a man as out of her reach.

"Miss Eugenia," Sage said, knocking on the woman's bedroom door.

"Yes, dear?" came Eugenia's sweet voice. She opened the door to her bedroom and gasped as she saw Sage. "Oh, my dear!" she exclaimed, reaching out and taking Sage's chin in her hand to study the wound at the side of her mouth. "What on earth happened?"

Shaking her head, indicating the wound was of no consequence, Sage said, "Your nephew is here."

Instantly, Eugenia's eyes lit up. "Reb?" she squealed, clapping her hands together. "He's here already?"

"Yes, and . . ." Sage began.

"Land's sakes! Why didn't he send a telegram first?" Eugenia said, taking hold of Sage's hand and pulling her along behind as she fairly scampered down the stairs. "Oh, I can't believe he's actually here!" Pausing, Eugenia looked to Sage, an impish smile curling the corners of her mouth. "Isn't he the handsomest thing you ever did lay eyes on, Sage?"

Sage couldn't help but smile at Eugenia's pride in her nephew. After all, such an attractive relative was worth being proud of.

"Yes, Miss Eugenia," Sage admitted. "He's very handsome."

Eugenia giggled like a schoolgirl and returned to her descent of the staircase. "And we better get down there before Rose has him cornered and kissin'!"

Sage stumbled once as Eugenia pulled her down the stairs and into the parlor. The scene which met them there was nothing less than comical! Instantly, Sage felt sympathy for Mr. Mitchell as she saw him backed up against one parlor wall, Mary firing questions at him with the speed of a rifle, Rosie toying with the button of one of his shirtsleeves, and Livie clasping his free hand adoringly. She couldn't stop a quiet giggle from escaping at the surprised look on the man's face. Eyebrows raised, eyes wide, Reb Mitchell had obviously never dealt with the likes of the Willows' Boarding House widows.

"How old are ya then, boy?" Mary was asking, a characteristic frown of suspicion wrinkling her already wrinkled forehead.

"Twenty-six, ma'am," Reb stammered a moment before liberation arrived in the sound of Eugenia's voice.

"Reb!" Eugenia exclaimed. "Rebel Lee Mitchell! You angel! Why didn't you send a telegram and let me know you were comin'?"

Sage giggled again as she saw the man exhale, relieved as the other three women in the room stepped away from him, allowing his aunt to capture him in a loving embrace.

"Thought I'd just send myself instead, Auntie," the man chuckled.

"I see you've met my friends," Eugenia said, once they ended their embrace.

The thought traveled through Sage's mind, *How wonderful it must feel to hug him.* But clinching her teeth tightly, she quickly drove the notion from her mind.

"Well . . . in a manner of speakin', I guess," Reb chuckled.

"Then, let's be proper," Eugenia said. Pointing to Rose, she said, "Mrs. Rose Applewhite, my nephew, rather my grand nephew, Reb Mitchell."

Rose curtsied saying, "A pleasure, Mr. Mitchell."

"Ma'am," Reb said, nodding a greeting.

Eugenia smiled and gestured to Mary, "Mrs. Mary Farthen, Reb Mitchell."

Mary reached out and gripped the man's hand in a firm shake. "Reb," she mumbled.

"Mrs. Farthen," Reb said, returning her firm grip.

"I'm Livie Jonesburg," Livie interrupted, too impatient to wait her turn. Taking the man's hand, she added, "And I'm delighted to have you with us."

"I'm glad to be here, ma'am," Reb chuckled.

"And I guess you've already met our Sage," Eugenia said, pushing Sage forward.

"Miss Willows," Reb said, nodding. Sage smiled and took the hand he offered, shaking it firmly. Still, the heat from his hand again traveled the length of her arm, pooling warm and sweet in her bosom.

"Met the dog, too," he added, smiling at Sage. "He gave Miss Willows here a bit of a run fer her money."

"That why yer lip's bleedin', Sage?" Mary grumbled. "I wondered what on earth all that racket was a minute ago. Where's that mutt now?"

Sage sighed. "I suspect he's out visitin' Mr. Simmons' lady dog," Sage told them.

Mary chuckled as Rosie and Livie shook their heads. "Well, then, I suppose ol' Forest will be over any minute now to propose marriage to ya again." Sage blushed furiously as Reb looked at her, one eyebrow arched with curiosity.

"Again?" Reb asked.

Sage felt her fingers fiddling nervously with her collar button as he looked at her, waiting for an explanation. But her mouth was dry, her face hot, and she couldn't say a word.

"Ol' Forest Simmons has less teeth in his head than a gray gander and he's always lookin' for a reason to propose to Sage," Eugenia explained.

"Biscuits are ready," Sage announced abruptly, thankful for the aroma of hot biscuits which gave her an excuse to change the subject. "Have you had breakfast yet, Mr. Mitchell?" she asked.

"Call me Reb," he instructed. "And no. I haven't."

"Well, then . . . you have to have some of Sage's biscuits! They're divine!" Rosie told him, taking his arm and leading him from the parlor and toward the kitchen.

Sage smiled as Livie took his free arm and added, "And with a little bit of honey, you've never tasted anything so sweet."

"Oh, for Pete's sake," Mary grumbled, following the others to the kitchen. "You all quit a slobberin' over the boy. Ya look like a pack a hungry hounds."

"Oh, you hush, Mary," Rosie told her. "There's enough of this boy to go around. You'll get your turn."

Sage looked at Eugenia who was smiling, too amused to do anything else.

"I never thought he'd cause such a fuss," Eugenia said.

"He probably feels like he's stumbled into some saloon girl's grave-yard," Sage whispered, trying hard not to giggle out loud.

"The one where all the saloon girls go when they're old and gray," Eugenia added, also stifling her giggles. "Well, it's a good thing we've got you here to give him somethin' young and pretty to look at." Sage felt her smile fade and she felt extremely self-conscious all at once. She knew good and well she was no kind of young and pretty type woman to catch the eye of such a man. She was almost irritated with Eugenia for saying she was.

But as the smiling faces of her friends and the handsome face of Reb Mitchell met her as she entered the kitchen, Sage pushed thoughts of loneliness and despair to the back of her mind. Or, at least, she tried to. However, as the man's dark eyes seemed to follow her during each task of serving breakfast, she found nervous perspiration gathering at her temples, a slight trembling in her hands, and she knew he was dangerous, this nephew of Eugenia Smarthing. This was the kind of man who left a trampled trail of broken hearts in his footsteps and Sage Willows had no desire to feel the heel of his boot. She would have to strengthen her defenses, avoid him as much as possible.

For pity's sake! she thought suddenly. She didn't even know him! Reb

Mitchell was a complete stranger to her. Why was her mind lingering on how to keep from falling in love with him anyway? The very notion was ridiculous! And so, determined to purge her mind of even the idea of any silly schoolgirl daydreams about a handsome stranger, Sage sat down to breakfast.

"Whatcha got in mind fer the ranch there, Reb?" Mary asked, buttering a steaming biscuit.

"Well, I got me a purty big herd rounded up and waitin' down in Santa Fe," Reb answered. "I figure there's probably some fence that needs mendin' out on the ranch. That right, Auntie?" Eugenia nodded as she took a bite of her biscuit. "So," Reb continued, drizzling honey over a biscuit with his fork, "I'll patch up any fence troubles, then have my partner, Dugger, run the herd out here for me."

"Are you . . . uh . . . unattached as yet, Mr. Mitchell?" Rosie asked. Reb looked up at Sage and smiled when he heard her fork fumbled to the table. Sage scolded herself silently. She was a mess of nerves and she couldn't seem to simmer down.

"Yes, ma'am," Reb answered. "As unattached as they come."

"Well, that's nice!" Rose exclaimed. "Ain't that nice, Sage?"

Sage wanted to simply curl up and die as Reb chuckled, all too wise to the woman's inference.

"Yes," Sage said. "Milly Michaels and all the other girls in town will be pleased as petunias to hear that."

"I don't plan on spendin' much time in town," Reb said. "Besides, I plan on stayin' unattached, Mrs. Applewhite."

"You call me, Rosie, hun," Rosie told him. "And unattached is fine by me."

Sage felt her face go as hot as the coals in the oven. Did these women have no manners at all? She had never seen them so forward.

"Yer indecent, Rose," Mary scolded, slathering a biscuit with butter. "He's Eugenia's nephew for Pete's sake!"

"Yes, he is," Rose admitted, "and he knows a little harmless flirtin' never hurt anybody. Don't ya know it, Reb?"

Sage couldn't even take a bite of the biscuit sitting on her plate. In reality, she had seen the widows do this kind of thing before, flirt, tease, flatter in their playful and friendly manner. But for some reason, it was causing her great discomfort this time.

"Yes, ma'am," Reb answered with a smile. "Ain't nothin' wrong with a little flirtin'."

"I like this boy, Eugenia," Livie giggled. Eugenia smiled, obviously delighted with the goings on.

"How 'bout sparkin' then?" Rosie asked. "You think there's anythin' wrong with a little sparkin'?"

"Mercy sakes!" Sage exclaimed fairly leaping from her chair. She couldn't sit still any longer. All the talk of flirting and sparking with Reb Mitchell in mind somehow completely disconcerted her. He hadn't been in their company for fifteen minutes and already they were asking the most personal, flirtatious questions a body could ask!

"Nope," came Reb's chuckling answer. "Ain't nothin' wrong with a little sparkin' neither."

Sage went to the sink and worked the pump, filling the sink with water. She had no reason for doing so, save she needed something to distract the others from her nervous condition.

"You see, Mary," Livie said. "He's game for a little sparkin' here and there, too."

"Well, he ain't a plannin' on sparkin' with you two, so let the man eat his biscuit 'fore Sage drops dead in the sink," Mary grumbled.

At that moment, Sage wondered if in fact dropping dead in the sink would be better than enduring the teasing of her friends. She knew darn well they were trying to embarrass her, attempting to discover whether or not Reb Mitchell might be a candidate for saving Sage Willows from spinsterhood. But good intentions often led to disaster, and Sage had never been more thankful to hear a familiar pounding on the boarding-house front door.

"Well, there he is," Eugenia said, pushing her chair away from the table.

"And here it comes," Livie added, pushing her chair back as well.

Sage took a deep breath, dried her hands on her apron, and started for the front door.

"I'll take care of it," she said as Eugenia and Livie started after her. "He's my dog, after all."

Bullet was a sweet dog, but he had caused Sage a lot of grief, especially where Forest Simmons and his precious lady dog were concerned. As much as she liked the troublesome pup, she wished Karoline and Joel had taken him with them, for he was obviously too much for Sage to handle. At the memory of being wrapped up and lying on the porch with Eugenia's nephew, Sage sighed. *Yep! Far too much for me to handle,* she thought as she brushed a strand of hair from her cheek and drew in a courageous breath. Forest Simmons had a very distinctive manner of knocking on a door. Two knocks in succession, a pause and then four knocks. No doubt he had found Bullet consorting with his lady dog and was crazier than a fox in a henhouse.

"Hello, Mr. Simmons," Sage said, opening the door to see Forest Simmons glaring at her. The scruffy old man held Bullet's rope tightly in one hand, the truant mutt wagging his tail and panting happily.

"This dog of yers is on his last leg, Sage!" the man nearly shouted. "I don't want me no pups! I done told ya that last time!"

"I . . . I know, Mr. Simmons," Sage stammered. "It was an accident. He just . . ."

"This would be my fault, sir." Sage felt the hair on the back of her neck tickle at the sound of Reb's voice behind her. Stepping in front of her, Reb offered his hand to the man and said, "I own the dog now. Miss Willows gave him to me just this mornin' and I guess I just didn't tie him up proper while I was in for breakfast."

"And who are you?" Mr. Simmons asked.

"I'm Reb Mitchell, Eugenia Smarthin's nephew," Reb explained. "I've come up from Santa Fe to get the ranch runnin' for her again. I do apologize for the dog, sir."

"Forest Simmons," the older man said, eyeing Reb suspiciously. Sage watched his eyes move to her, traveling the length of her body and back, and she resisted the urge to sneer at him.

"Well," Mr. Simmons grumbled. "You just keep this mutt off my property. I don't like puppies. I drown 'em."

"I'll watch him a might closer, sir. I thank ya," Reb said, taking Bullet's rope from Mr. Simmons. "Thank ya again," he said, closing the door in the man's face.

Sage smiled, relieved to be rid of Mr. Simmons and delighted in the way Bullet put his front paws on Reb's stomach, lapping at the man's arms affectionately as Reb scratched the dog's chin and ears.

"Did I earn myself a dog here, Miss Willows?" Reb asked, chuckling. His smile was like nothing Sage had ever seen, white, bright, and dazzling. Reb was obviously pleased with the dog and the dog was obviously pleased with Reb.

"If you're really willin' to take him on, Mr. Mitchell. He's a terrible handful," Sage said. Bullet was far too restless and needed more training than Sage could provide. He was meant to be a man's dog and she was happy to see him as such.

"Then I thank ya for the gift and for the breakfast, Miss Willows," Reb said, turning and striding to the kitchen, new best friend in tow.

Sage watched him walk away, noticed the way his Levi's fit him so perfectly, the way his shoulders rocked back and forth as he walked. An odd, long-absent flutter filled her bosom and she frowned. It had been a very long time since any man had caused her to have butterflies in her stomach, merely by being in his presence. She wasn't comfortable with the sensation, and besides, Reb Mitchell had made it very clear he intended to stay unattached. He had come to help his aunt run her ranch, and Sage could sense he had no other agenda. It would be bad enough to dream of a man who would soon be the object of every woman's fancy, but to dream of such a man who had no interest in attaching himself to anyone . . . well, that would be just plain ignorant.

Sage returned to the kitchen and gathered up the plates from the table. The others were already involved in a light-hearted discussion, and Sage felt somewhat irritated when she noticed the way Bullet sat obediently at Reb's feet. After all the grief the dog had heaped upon her, it was exasperating to see him give his loyalty over so quickly.

"Reb says he'll play rummy with us, Sage," Livie announced. "Are you up for a game?"

Sage looked to Livie, but couldn't keep her eyes from wandering to Reb. He sat, grinning, and winked at her unexpectedly.

The gesture unnerved Sage and she said, "Oh, I don't think so. I need to get some things finished and start the pies for dinner." Turning back to the sink, she added, "You be careful Mr. Mitchell. They cheat."

As every other woman in the room erupted into defense of themselves, Sage glanced out the kitchen window. Several dark clouds had moved in from the west and she could only hope and pray for the rain to come. Oh, how desperately she needed it now, with her heart in danger of being distracted by Eugenia Smarthing's attractive nephew.

⟡

EUGENIA PAUSED IN bantering with her friends. Something in Sage's eye had caught her attention, and although she was happy to see it, her heart understood the battle beginning within the young woman's heart and mind. She was a bit anxious where Reb was concerned, too. Oh, he was friendly enough, as playful and kind as he had always been. Yet, something was missing from his countenance. Was it trust, compassion? Eugenia couldn't quite grasp the difference in her nephew, but it did worry her. She had the best intentions for both Sage and for Reb. But what if . . . what if what was said about good intentions proved to be true? Still, she was hopeful. Something had led Eugenia, prompted her to write to Bridie and allow Reb to come run the ranch, and if the road to hell was paved with good intentions, well then, she would just trot on down it and give the devil a piece of her mind!

Chapter Two

ಐ ಲ

*S*age stretched her arms out at her sides and turned her face up to the blanket of gray clouds in the sky. The rain mingled with the tears on her face. Cool and refreshing, the early summer rain washed over her, soaking her hair, her clothing, helping to purge the heartache she had secreted in her soul so long. It seemed months since the last rains had come, months since she had been able to cry freely, to release the deep sobs of misery. She allowed emotion to wrack her body as her soul ached, surrendering to the reality of loneliness.

The clouds had gathered throughout the morning. Sage watched them collecting as she prepared breakfast for the ladies at the boardinghouse and she had prayed those clouds would bring rain. She needed it desperately, as desperately as the new crops the farmers had planted needed it. Since Eugenia's nephew arrived, since the very moment he entered her life, Sage's misery, her feelings of despair, hopelessness and loneliness had increased ten-fold.

Reb Mitchell, so strong, handsome and friendly, yet unobtainable, had brought great unrest and distress to Sage. Each time he entered a room or glanced at her, the hair on the back of her neck tickled, her arms erupting into tiny goose bumps. She was certain he had the same effect on every other woman in town, married or not, for she had seen Milly Michaels blush clear to her toes when he tipped his hat to her that very morning. Oh, certainly it helped some when he took to staying at the ranch house the day after his arrival. Yet, he was in town quite often and always stopped in for a visit with his aunt and her friends before heading back.

Reb's manner was so relaxed, so comfortable, and it had caused Sage to loosen her guard far too many times. He was dangerous to a woman's heart, especially a woman like Sage, still young enough to dream of romance with a handsome cowboy, but too old to be blessed with it. Reb's presence was scarring her heart and she knew it. Visions of him haunted her dreams, both night and day. Part of her wished he would leave or that he had never arrived. Yet, he brought such joy to Eugenia and the others. His presence drew people like ants to honey, and Sage was not immune to his wiles. Only a month after his arrival, Sage Willows' heart was already damaged, and she knew only the rain could offer comfort and reprieve.

Sage cried at her parents' funeral, but she had never cried in front of anyone since. With the death of her parents, necessity had dictated Sage become strong, responsible and seemingly void of deep emotion. With three young sisters to finish raising, to provide for, there had been no time for the happy drama and emotions of youth. She took to saving up her pain, despair and fear, secreting it within her soul, never letting it out, never crying when anyone could see. Still, Sage knew guarding too large a cache of withheld sorrow and emotion could destroy a person, and eventually she had found a way of purging her pain: the rain.

Rain sent most people indoors, leaving a world of privacy outside, especially in Ruthie's pasture. The isolated pasture where little Ruth States rested in peace had become Sage's venue for tears, her space of privacy where she could sob, releasing bitter tears of heartache. And on this day, her tears were plentiful as well as painful.

The drops of rain became fewer and fewer as the day wore on, and Sage hoped she had cried enough, released enough sorrow and frustration to last until the rains came again. Lifting her skirt, she tugged at a layer of dry petticoats. Raising it to her face, she wiped the last bit of moisture from her cheeks.

"Well, Ruthie," she sniffled. Turning to the tiny grave, she said, "You've got a few weeds croppin' up here." She knelt down and pulled the little sagebrush sprouts out of Ruthie States' soil blanket. "Thank goodness for the rain; these little devils are comin' up easy enough today."

"Did ya know her?"

A startled scream erupted from Sage's throat. She lost her footing and sat down flat in the wet grass. She looked up to see Reb Mitchell standing just outside the fence, rain dripping from the brim of his hat as he looked at her. What a sight she must be, dripping wet and red-faced from crying.

"Um . . . um . . . no. I didn't," Sage stammered struggling to her feet. "I just . . . I just tend to her . . . whenever I can." Sage pushed back the wet strands of hair sticking to her cheeks and forehead, trying to appear unruffled as she stood.

"Sorry I scared ya, there," Reb said, stepping over the fence to stand next to her. "Got caught in the rain, huh?"

"Uh huh," Sage said. He removed his hat and studied the tiny gravestone. Sage was touched by his gesture of respect and a smile spread across her face.

"*Ruth States*," he read. "*Beloved daughter and sister. Born September 18, 1834, died October 22, 1840.*" He shook his head. "Just a little one, huh."

"Yes," Sage said, as she nervously smoothed her drenched skirt. Oh, why had she worn a white shirtwaist? No doubt he could see clean through the light, wet cotton all the way to her corset strings!

"How'd she die?" Reb asked.

Sage felt her fingers begin to fiddle with her collar buttons. "The story goes, that after losing her husband, Ruth's mother moved out here from Ohio, bringing her five children with her." He looked at her and nodded, a gesture she should continue.

Drawing a deep breath, Sage continued, "It seems her mother had a sister whose husband was homesteadin' out this way. Anyway, Ruthie's mother had to go back to Ohio—something to do with her husband's business—and she left the older children to care for the little ones. Little Ruth came down with typhoid. The oldest boy walked for miles to the nearest homestead to get help. The only person he found was a kindly older lady and she came back with him. She tried her best to help—nursed the little girl as well as she could. But . . . Ruth was too sick and she died."

Reb released a heavy sigh. "Does she have any family left 'round here?" he asked. Sage shook her head.

"No. Her mother was so devastated she loaded the rest of the children in a wagon, cursed the day she'd left Ohio, and headed back." Sage sighed. "I used to be angry at Ruthie's mother for leavin' her and goin' back to Ohio. Still, I can imagine how, when the mother returned, seein' the little grave on this lonely hill—her little six-year old girl—how it just caused her to die inside and want to run back to the things, the places and people familiar to her. Ruthie's in heaven, after all. It's just her earthly self restin' here."

Reb's eyes narrowed as he looked at Sage. "Yet, ya tend this grave regular. I can tell just by lookin' ya spend a lot of time out here with little Ruth."

Sage was uncomfortable under his gaze. What a sight she must be! Still, she answered, "Well, it's a pretty, peaceful little spot and maybe Ruthie's spirit comes along once in a while to see if anyone remembers she was here once. My guess is none of her brothers and sisters have ever been out this way and I just want to make sure . . . to make sure . . ."

"That she don't get lonely," Reb finished for her.

Sage smiled. "Yes," she admitted, mesmerized by his insight and understanding of her feelings.

Reb looked around the gravesite. He seemed to note every flower and plant. Reaching down to a space near his foot, he broke a leaf off a small plant.

"Did you plant this?" he asked, folding the leaf and putting it to his nose.

Sage nodded, delighted that he pinched the leaf and inhaled its fragrance in the same manner she always did. "To remind her of me . . .

just in case she ever really does stop by," she answered. Reb smiled and inhaled the scent of the sage leaf again.

"Nothin' like a bit of sage to improve the flavor of any pan of gravy," he chuckled.

Sage blushed. "Nothin' like it," she agreed, smiling. Reb tucked the sage leaf into his shirt pocket. He glanced at the gravestone for a moment before stepping over the fence and replacing his hat.

"Well," he sighed looking up at the sky for a moment. "I was out checkin' the fence, and since Aunt Eugenia mentioned that Uncle Buck once rented this acreage from yer daddy, I hope ya don't mind me ridin' out here to look around," he said.

Sage left the gravesite by way of the small gate, latching it carefully behind her. "Of course not," she said.

"I 'spect that's yer horse down by the creek with mine," he said.

"Mmm, hmm," Sage confirmed. She smiled and began walking toward the creek. Reb stepped aside so she could precede him.

"I was wondering, would ya consider rentin' yer acreage out to me when my herd gets up here?" he asked.

"Oh!" Sage exclaimed. His question was quite unexpected. "I don't see why not."

"I think I'd want to put up another fence 'round little Ruth here, though," he said. "Wouldn't want to risk the cattle chewin' up yer pretty flowers and gravy fixin's."

Sage smiled, again delighted by his charm. It was impossible to keep her heart from fluttering madly in his presence!

"I'd certainly appreciate you doin' that for her," Sage said.

"It's a nice piece of land ya got here, Miss Willows," he said, looking around as they walked. "Nice and peaceful."

"Yes," was all she could think to say.

Far too soon, or rather not soon enough, they had reached the creek. Drifter stood sheltering near a piñon tree. Sage smiled as she noticed Reb's black gelding near another.

Again, Sage's heart fluttered as Reb took hold of Drifter's reins and walked him over to her. He reached out, holding the stirrup steady to assist her in mounting. Smiling at him, she settled into the saddle.

"Thank you," she said.

Reb nodded, touched the brim of his hat and said, "Yer welcome." As he walked to his own horse and mounted effortlessly, he said, "Aunt Eugenia invited me to supper tonight. Is that all right with you?"

In actuality, it wasn't all right. Sage wasn't sure she could endure any more wonderful minutes in his presence. Still, she nodded and said, "Supper's at five thirty . . . roasted chicken and potatoes."

He smiled and rode his horse over next to hers. "Any chance of there bein' some chicken gravy with just a touch of *sage* in it, too?" He chuckled. Taking the sage leaf from his shirt pocket, he waved it under his nose.

A natural, sincere smile spread across Sage's face. The feel of it surprised her. "I'm sure sage gravy can be arranged, Mr. Mitchell."

"Reb," he corrected, holding the sage leaf out to her. She smiled. Taking the leaf from him, she hoped he didn't notice the way her hand trembled as her fingers brushed his.

Pinching the leaf with her fingers, Sage inhaled its familiar fragrance and said, "Very well, supper will be at five-thirty, Reb."

He smiled at her, smoothed his mustache with one index finger, touched the brim of his hat and said, "Five-thirty it is, Sage Willows." Clicking his tongue, he said, "Let's go, Ned."

Sage smiled. She couldn't keep from smiling! All the way back to the boardinghouse she smiled. What a handsome measure of a man Reb Mitchell was! Polite and kind, too. At the same time, he was tougher than nails and a hard worker, the very stuff of any woman's dreams, and Sage could not help dreaming of him. She would make him some sage gravy, all right. Cornbread stuffing, too, the like he had never tasted!

♲

REB PULLED NED to a stop just beside Ruth States' grave. How strange it had been to step over the hill and see Sage standing out in the rain, letting the moisture freely fall on her face and body. In those first moments she had seemed so free, yet wholly sad at the same time. Reb had watched her for a few moments, waiting until she had knelt before the tiny grave and begun plucking weeds from the soil before he had approached.

It was obvious she was startled to see him there, and he hadn't been able to discern whether her face was red from the rain or from something else . . . tears perhaps. Still, Reb smiled as he thought about her. He liked this Sage Willows, this young woman who had resigned herself to spinsterhood at such a young age. For one thing, she offered no threat of pursuing him. Reb Mitchell had no time for a woman, no desire to waste his life romancing some fickle filly, who would end up wanting to own him like some stray dog and treating him worse. It was one reason he chose to spend his social time with his aunt and her friends; the old ladies weren't about to start dreaming of marriage and babies with him. Further, though they were sweet little women, they held no attraction, no temptation for him. They were perfectly delightful and perfectly safe.

Still, Reb could see how their pretty, young proprietress could be a danger if she had any intentions toward him, which she did not. In fact, she seemed rather indifferent to him at times, leaving the room when he was visiting with his aunt and the others, never talking much to him. Sage had made her own way, whether out of necessity or choice, and she seemed as resigned to a singular life as he did.

She was dang pretty, though. He thought of the way her green eyes flashed when she was amused at Rosie Applewhite's rummy antics. He wondered how long her hair was, how she would look with it down instead of strapped back in such a tight widow's knot at the back of her head.

Yep, Reb thought. *She could be dangerous . . . if she had a mind to be.* But she didn't. Reb knew he could show up for supper at Willows' Boarding House later that night and not be in danger of having to side-step any flirtatious females. Well, any his own age, that was.

Still, for a moment, as he urged Ned toward home, he was a bit bothered by Sage's apparent disinterest in him. Maybe he was getting ugly, losing his charm. Yet, thinking of the way Rose and Livie lit up when he paid them any attention, the way that pestering Milly Michaels smiled and batted her eyelashes at him—well, surely not every scar his soul wore showed through on his face. Did it?

❦

SAGE QUICKLY BRUSHED Drifter, set a bucket of oats in his stall, and hurried toward the house, pausing at the old rain barrel by the back kitchen door. The old barrel was filled with dirt, abundant with rosemary, thyme and sage plants. Sage pinched a large branch from one of the sage plants. Folding one of the leaves and rubbing it with her fingers, she drew the herb branch up to her face, caressing her lips with the soft leaves and inhaling their wonderful aroma. Oh, how it reminded her of her mother! It always had, and she wondered if that was why she had always loved the fragrance and flavor of sage so very much. There was her kinship with the plant to be considered, too, being named after it as she was. Whatever the reason, the sweet scent of sage always cheered her and when it came to cooking with it, any woman Reb Mitchell had ever known before had certainly met her match in Sage Willows.

Smiling, Sage entered the house to start supper. There were a few extra things to do before Reb arrived, and for the first time where the man was concerned, Sage wasn't afraid of her happy thoughts. After all, God had His reasons for creating dreams, and who was she to deny one of heaven's greatest gifts.

❦

"YA'LL CATCH YER death of pneumonia out in that rain, Sage," Mary grumbled. "For Pete's sake . . . yer hair isn't dry yet!"

"Oh, hush, Mary," Livie scolded, shuffling the deck of cards in her hand. "I think it very . . . very eccentric of Sage to slosh about in the rain."

"Eccentric?" Mary exclaimed. "Runnin' through town with a white shirtwaist on, wet to the skin? It's pneumonia and scandal just awaitin' to settle in."

Sage smiled and gathered her cards as Livie counted out seven to her. "Thank you for caring, Mary," she said. "But I'm fine. Summer rain is warm and refreshin'."

"I still can't believe you saw Reb out there, Sage," Rosie said, fanning herself with the cards in her hand, plucking one out and tucking it into a new spot in the arrangement. "How romantic!"

"Romantic?" Mary growled. "Stuff and nonsense." Leaning toward

Sage, Mary lowered her voice and said, "I could see clean through yer shirtwaist when ya come in, Sage." Mary shook her head. "I'm sure Reb Mitchell saw more'n the pasture out there today." Sage blushed, knowing Mary was probably correct, but hoping she was wrong.

"Oh, it's nothin' the boy hasn't seen before, I reckon," Eugenia said, rearranging her own hand of cards.

Mary was aghast. "What? Why Eugenia Smarthin'! What kinda thing is that to say?" she exclaimed.

"Reb's plenty old enough to have seen a saloon girl or two while walking down the street, Mary," Rosie told her.

"Humph," Mary grunted. "He's a seein' one ever' time he comes in here."

"Thank you, Mary," Rosie said, smiling. "I'm glad to see you can admit I'm still attractive."

"You forgot to discard, Rose," Livie interjected.

"Oh. Silly me," Rosie said, laying down a card. "Well, all I know is Eugenia's nephew is the prettiest boy I've ever seen."

"Why thank you, Rose," Eugenia said, giggling. "He is rather pleasin' to the old eyes, isn't he?"

"Oh, my yes!" Rosie said. "Don't you think he's the prettiest thing, Sage?"

Sage felt her cheeks begin to pink-up. "Of course, Miss Rosie." But Rosie sighed, her shoulders sagging with disappointment.

"Oh, come on, Sage. Will you just up and admit it for once? Reb Mitchell is a walking dream!" Rosie said.

Suddenly, all sets of eyes at the table were intent on Sage. "Well . . . well . . . of course he's . . . he's handsome," she finally stammered.

"There it is, Eugenia!" Livie exclaimed. "She's admitted it, at last!"

"I've admitted it before, Miss Livie," Sage told her, giggling. "You four make me admit it every time we sit down to play cards."

"Well, personally, I like to think on what kissin' him would be like," Rosie mumbled under her breath.

"Rose Applewhite!" Mary exclaimed. "That there's just pure nonsense!

Not to mention immoral. Reverend Tippetts would drop down dead as a rolled-over rodent if he heard ya sayin' such a thing. Yer turn, Sage."

"I agree with Rose," Livie announced, picking up the card Sage discarded. "Why, if I were Sage's age, I'd be at him like a bee to a buttercup!"

ℭ℥

"AFTERNOON THERE, LADIES," Reb said, stepping into the parlor. He was immediately puzzled, for every woman in the room went pale, their mouths dropping open in astonishment as they looked at him. "What kind of evil doin's are you girls up to today?" Reb sat down on a large, soft chair near the fireplace, his mischievous nature aroused. Each woman, especially Sage, looked as if she had just been found gossiping by the preacher, and Reb knew exactly how to find out what was going on.

"Miss Mary," he said. "Why does everyone look like they been caught with their knickers around their knees?" He smiled as Mary straightened in her chair, the perpetual look of disapproval on her tight lips.

"Oh, nothin' too much to speak of, Reb," she said. "They was all just talkin' about kissin' on ya."

"For Pete's sake, Mary!" Livie scolded. Reb was quite surprised, yet likewise flattered. He knew how picky elderly women could be about handing out compliments. Furthermore, the look of pure mortification on Sage's face was absolutely amusing.

"Were they now?" he chuckled. He liked the old widows who boarded at Willows'. He liked the young proprietress, too, and he wasn't one to pass up an opportunity to tease. "Well? Who's first, then?" he asked, stretching his arms out, beckoning for an embrace. The four older women erupted into delighted giggles, even his Aunt Eugenia who knew what a little imp he could be. Sage, however, looked as if she literally might be ill. Sincerely worried for the young woman's health, Reb directed his attention at a less unsettled victim and said, "Miss Rosie?"

He chuckled when the gray-haired lady blushed and said, "Go on with you, Reb, ya little devil!"

He shrugged his shoulders and looked to Mrs. Jonesburg. "Miss Livie?

Wanna do a little sparkin' with me here?" She likewise blushed and shook her head playfully.

"Miss Mary?" Reb said, looking to the more serious-minded one of the group. "Ya gonna turn me down, too?"

"Oh, for Pete's sake, boy," the old woman grumbled. "I ain't a ninny like the rest of them," she said, scowling at him. Reb saw the uncharacteristic blush warming her cheeks all the same.

Reb sighed, feigning disappointment. "Well, Auntie, they've all brushed me off like last Sunday's crumbs," he said. She smiled and winked at him, all too wise to his ways as he stood and pretended to stretch.

Taking a quick step forward and placing one arm across the back of Sage's chair, he leaned down and said, "Unless yer willin' to give me a try, Miss Willows." He could sense her fear and anxiety and let his pride swell, knowing he had entirely unnerved her.

"Rummy!" Sage choked, dropping her hand of cards to the table and fairly flying out of her chair and toward the kitchen.

"Sage Willows! You ain't got rummy!" Mary called after her. "Ya ain't even got a set!"

Reb couldn't help himself. He had to chuckle out loud as the other women burst into snickering, delighted over his utter undoing of their young friend. Oh, he could definitely see how Sage Willows could amuse him, in one way or the other. It was a dang good thing he was beyond being dumb enough to fall victim to any feminine charms, not that Sage used hers in any intentional manner the way other young women did. But if she chose to, Reb was confident in his immunities against them.

Still, an odd something akin to sorrow pricked in his chest for a moment. Sage was a sweet little gal. She was nice, smart, pretty and kind. It was a sad thing to think on: the possibility she might be lonely later in life, having chosen not to marry. A vision of Sage standing in front of Ruth's little gravestone, gazing up into the cloudy sky with the summer rain bathing her in its refreshing moisture, traveled through Reb's mind and he wondered—why hadn't she ever married?

Well, it was certainly no concern of his, so sitting down in Sage's recently vacated chair, he picked up her hand of cards and said, "Who's turn?"

"It ain't yers, purty boy," Mary told him, drawing a card from the pile in the center of the table.

ℭℛ

SAGE BUSIED HERSELF in the kitchen, thickening gravy, whipping potatoes, and removing the stuffing from the roast chickens before cutting them up. Her heart still hammered wildly from the scene in the parlor. How unlucky could five women be? To have the very subject of their rather silly conversation step in upon them the way Reb had just done? It had been completely humiliating! Sage could not believe Mary had actually told Reb what kind of thoughts Rosie and Livie were sharing about him. The woman could be so infuriating at times. Sage closed her eyes and caught her breath for a moment as goose bumps erupted over her body again—the same goose bumps which spread over her like a warm rain when Reb teased her in the parlor. His teasing her about sparking with him had nearly undone her completely, for in her dreams, she had done just that—sat on the front porch swing, sharing kisses with Reb Mitchell. Sage sighed and tried to chase the dreams from her thoughts.

Using her apron to open the oven door, Sage saw the crusts of her bread loaves were perfectly golden. Looking around and being unable to find a bread cloth, she once more used her apron to protect her hands and removed one loaf without any trouble. By the time the second one was out of the oven, however, she was hopping around, waving her slightly singed fingers in the air.

"Ya all right?" Reb asked from the doorway. Instantly, Sage quit jumping around like a happy rabbit and smoothed her apron.

Humiliated to be found in yet another ridiculous situation, Sage nodded and said, "Yes. Fine. The bread pans were just hot."

"Did ya burn yer fingers?" Reb asked, walking toward her and taking one of her hands in his. He raised her hand to his face, frowning as he studied her fingers. "They look all right," he mumbled. Then he smiled and held her fingers very close to his mouth, just under his nose. "Mmmmm. We havin' sage in the gravy, Sage?" he asked.

Sage swallowed the lump of delight budding in her throat at being so near to him and nodded. For a moment, the deep brown of his eyes, the way his hair fell across his forehead so carelessly, the flecks of auburn among the dark whiskers of his mustache and goatee distracted her, distracted her enough she almost forgot what he had asked.

"Yes. And . . . and in the stuffin'," she stammered.

"Stuffin'?" he exclaimed, dropping her hand and clapping his together. "I do love stuffin'!" he added, rubbing his hands together with delighted anticipation.

"That's nice," Sage said. "Now . . . now why don't you run along and entertain the ladies while I finish up." He made her far too nervous. She was sure she would end up ruining supper somehow.

"Well, all right," he said. "But yer missin' out on all the fun." With a quick wink and a smile, he turned and rather sauntered from the room. Sage breathed a heavy sigh, relieved to have the kitchen to herself again. Her respite was short-lived, however, for no sooner had she turned her attention back to the bread, when she heard a knock at the front door.

"Howdy, there Reverend, Mrs. Tippetts," she heard Reb say. "Afternoon, Winnery."

"Oh, for cryin' in the bucket," she mumbled, quickly slathering the bread crusts with butter. "Doesn't anybody have anythin' better to do today than to show up for supper half an hour early?"

Reverend "Whipper" Tippetts, his wife Scarlett, and Joss Winnery joined the residents at Willows' for supper every Tuesday evening. Whipper Tippetts, a shorter man with light-colored hair, had been one of the greatest lawman in the territory, until a bullet through his left leg had left him with more than just a limp. However, to hear the reverend tell the story, the wound to his body saved his soul, for it had given him a vision of heaven and he had turned in a Texas Ranger's star for a bible.

His wife, Scarlett, had been a fair-haired dance hall girl before she met and married Whipper. In Mary Farthen's opinion, Scarlett wore far too much red on her cheeks and in her clothing to be a proper preacher's wife. Still, she was genuinely kind and compassionate. A woman would have to be to put up with Reverend Tippetts' friend Joss Winnery.

Joss Winnery preferred to be called simply "Winnery," and was the tallest man in town. Dark-haired and broad-shouldered, Winnery hardly ever spoke a word. He and the reverend had been saddle pals for years, and when Whipper Tippetts became a preacher, Joss Winnery followed. Oh, he wasn't the type of preacher Reverend Tippetts was, for Joss was shy and soft-spoken, but he could raise the roof for any congregation with his fine scripture reading and nice singing voice.

Tuesday evenings at Willows' were always something to look forward to. Sage and her lady boarders thoroughly enjoyed sitting in the parlor after supper, swapping stories with Reverend Tippetts and his companions. Therefore, normally Sage enjoyed cooking supper on Tuesdays more than any other day. But today was different because Reb Mitchell would be there, too.

Arranging the stuffing in a pretty bowl, Sage hurried to finish preparing the meal. What if Reb didn't like her stuffing? What if he didn't like her gravy or chicken or potatoes? The thoughts caused a strange sort of trembling to begin in her bosom. And why did she care so much? He was just Eugenia's nephew. What did it matter whether or not he liked her cooking?

"Hi there, Sage," Scarlett Tippetts said, entering the kitchen.

"Good evenin', Mrs. Tippetts," Sage greeted, smiling.

"Anythin' I can do to help?" Scarlett asked.

"Oh, no. I'm nearly finished and then we can sit down to supper," Sage told her.

"Mmmmm! It all smells divine!" Scarlett sighed. "I swear you're the best cook in town, Sage."

"Oh, I doubt that," Sage told her.

"Maybe that handsome nephew of Eugenia's will be so smitten with your cookin' that he'll just have to carry you away to his own kitchen," the woman teased. Sage couldn't be angry at Scarlett, for she knew her friend meant well, even if Sage did get terribly tired of the reverend and his wife trying to marry her off to every new cowboy who rode through town.

"Maybe," Sage said, smiling. She knew the subject would die off more quickly if she just appeared to encourage Scarlett rather than argue with her. "You can take that plate of chicken and the stuffin' into the table if you'd like, Mrs. Tippetts. I'll herd everyone into the dinin' room."

"You bet," Scarlett said, picking up the plate of chicken. "Mmmm! It really does smell delicious, Sage."

Sage smiled and untied her apron strings, tossing the apron onto the counter by the sink. Smoothing her skirt and taking a deep breath, she walked to the parlor.

Even after seeing Reb fairly often over the past month, Sage still could not believe the entirely unsettling effect he had on her. As she entered the parlor to see Reb sitting in a chair on one side of the room, Reverend Tippetts and Mr. Winnery on the sofa across the way, she shivered a little when he looked at her. It was a delightful shiver, but a shiver all the same. *He's so handsome!* she thought releasing a heavy sigh.

"Everyone ready for supper?" she asked.

"Miss Sage," Joss Winnery said, standing and offering his hand to her. "Thank ya for havin' me to supper."

Sage smiled and took his offered hand, shaking it firmly. "Thank you for comin', Mr. Winnery," she said.

"I could smell that chicken when I stepped up to the porch outside, Sage," Reverend Tippetts said, smiling and patting his belly. "And if I ain't mistaken, yer blessin' us with some of that sage stuffin' I like so well."

Sage giggled, amused by the man's smiling eyes. "Yes, sir," she said. "Potatoes and gravy, too."

"Well, then," Reverend Tippetts said, patting his belly again with delighted anticipation. "Let's get to eatin'!"

"Cards face down, girls," Mary instructed as she stood.

"Well, just remember, it's my turn when we get back," Livie said. "You're always cheatin' me out of my turn, Mary."

"I am not always cheatin' ya outa yer turn!" Mary argued.

"Supper smells wonderful, Sage," Eugenia said, walking between Livie and Mary, thereby interrupting their argument.

Sage smiled and nodded as each person left the parlor for the dining room. However, when it came Reb's turn to exit, he politely motioned for her to precede him. Sage nodded and stepped in front of him, walking into the dining room adjoining the kitchen.

Everyone sat down around the table and Reverend Tippetts offered up a blessing before passing the food around.

"I hear that new baby of Primrose Gilbert's is just a tub of lard and cute as a bee's bonnet," Rosie said.

"Oh, yes!" Scarlett exclaimed. "That little boy is just the sweetest thing you ever did see. Whipper and I were out to the Gilbert place just this mornin'. Isn't that right, Whipper?"

"Yes, indeed," Reverend Tippetts said. "That's a darlin' little bundle they got out there."

"And how's your heifer doin', Mr. Winnery?" Eugenia asked. Everyone in town knew one of Joss Winnery's favorite heifers had taken ill. "I hear she was bloatin' somethin' awful."

"Yep, but she's fine now," came his answer. "Thank ya fer askin'."

"Mmmm! Mmm! Mm!" Reb hummed, suddenly. Everyone looked over at him as he said, "Sage Willows, this here's the best stuffin' I ever tasted!" Sage felt herself blush with delight.

"Thank you, Reb," she said.

"No, I mean it!" Reb continued, "It really is the best stuffin' I ever tasted . . . in my entire life!"

"Well, Sage has a way with . . . with sage!" Livie said. "Haven't you noticed that big barrel out by the back door, Reb?"

"Never come in by way of the back door," Reb said.

"Well, that barrel is just ready to bust apart it's so full of sage," Livie explained. "And let me tell you, all of us sitting around this table are mighty glad. Aren't we?" Sage felt her blush intensify as everyone nodded.

"Miss Sage Willows," Reb said. "I have half a mind to drag ya back to the ranch house with me. This is a fine meal!"

Sage blushed vermillion, jumping as she felt Scarlett kick her shin under the table. "I told you," the woman whispered. Sage kicked Scarlett back, afraid Reb would hear her.

Still, the knowledge he was pleased with her cooking, that she had found a way to get his attention, elated Sage. As much as she tried to argue otherwise, she was overjoyed at the attention from him.

✧

EUGENIA LOOKED FROM Sage to her nephew and back again. Normally Sage only made her cornbread and sage stuffing on very special occasions. Reverend Tippetts and Scarlett were no special occasion and neither was Mr. Winnery, and Eugenia smiled. Reb had caught her young friend's eye! No. It was more than that. He had captured Sage's attention and nothing had captured Sage's attention for a very long time.

Yet, she fretted. Reb's past, his pain . . . would it interfere more than she already worried it would? Still, Reb's delight, his genuine compliment about Sage's cooking, was rare. Not that he had been rude or behaved horrendously before. Not that he hadn't been a polite child. But his pain had hardened him, taken away his ability to accept people, to trust them. Though he was always kind, Eugenia knew many times it was forced and false. His compliment to Sage, however, was deeply sincere, and Eugenia smiled.

✧

AFTER SUPPER, ROSIE and Livie helped stack the dishes in the kitchen sink before everyone retired to the parlor. Sage never allowed herself, or anyone else, to hop up and do the dishes immediately after supper. She felt a meal should be enjoyed long after it had been eaten. Cleaning up could wait. And besides, parlor time with the widows and her other guests were just about the only true moments of happiness Sage had known in the past few years.

She sat on the sofa next to Scarlett and smiled as Reverend Tippetts told everyone about Winnery's bloated heifer. He was such a dear man and the kind of preacher who didn't own an air of self-righteous arrogance. She admired that about him, his humility, his ability to be true to God by being true to himself.

Sage glanced at Reb. He sat across the room in the big chair by the fireplace, and she was embarrassed when he caught her looking at him and winked at her. For Pete's sake! He was a shameless flirt. Either that, or he was far too casual with women. Sage looked away quickly and tried to concentrate on what Reverend Tippetts was saying.

"Well, Winnery and I both knew, if we didn't let the air out, then that heifer'd just up and die. Ain't that right, Reb?" Reverend Tippetts said. Reb nodded. "Me and Winnery—well, you ladies know this is our first try at raising our own beef. So I saw Reb in town and asked him what to do . . . and done it."

"The heifer's fine now," Winnery said.

Livie and Rosie looked at one another, perplexed expressions on both their faces. "Well, how did you get the air out?" Livie asked.

"Oh, for cryin' in the bucket," Mary grumbled.

"Oh, hush, Mary," Rosie said. "Not all of us were raised in the pig pen."

Sage smiled, glancing at Reb who smiled at her, indicating his own enjoyment of Mary and Livie's banter.

"Probably just stabbed it with your pocketknife. Right?" Eugenia said.

"Stabbed what with your pocketknife?" Livie asked.

"The heifer's belly," Reb answered.

"What?" Livie and Rosie exclaimed in unison, perplexed expressions replaced with horrified ones.

"It's the best way when it gets that bad," Eugenia explained. "You just shove your knife in their belly, give a twist so the wound don't seal up too fast, and that lets the air out."

Sage smiled as both Livie and Rosie began fanning themselves with their hands, feigning the need to faint from morbid revelation.

"I'll never eat beef again," Livie sighed.

"Me neither," Rosie said, nodding.

"Oh, for Pete's sake," Mary groaned with disgust.

"You'll just have to make fried chicken and bacon from now on, Sage," Rosie said. "I don't think I can eat beef again knowing what them cows go through."

"They slit their throats and butcher 'em up before the meat ever gets in yer stew, Rosie! And yer worried about Winnery's heifer getting poked with a pocket knife?" Mary asked. "And besides, I'm sure we could tell ya both a thing or two 'bout where yer fried chicken and bacon come from."

"Oh, I know where it all comes from, Mary, you old nag," Rosie said. "I just don't like to think about it. That's all."

Mary shook her head. "Ya know, Sage," she began, "we oughta get Reb to give us a cow when his herd gets here. Maybe these two ninnies need some toughenin' up."

Sage smiled. Oh, how she loved these people: the widows, the reverend and his wife, Winnery and—she paused in her thoughts as her eyes fell to Reb. No. She couldn't love Reb Mitchell. There was no time for it. She was too busy. And anyway, he couldn't possibly love her in return. He had plans, plans for reviving his aunt's ranch, for his herd, which would soon arrive from Santa Fe. Even if his plans did include a woman, Sage knew it wouldn't be a weathered, old spinster who ran a boarding-house.

She watched him closely for a moment, the rather alluring manner in which he lounged in the big parlor chair, the way he reached up and scratched the whiskers on his chin, how his eyes seemed to sparkle when he smiled or laughed.

"Oh!" Sage suddenly exclaimed. "Dessert! I forgot all about dessert!"

"Well, I'm glad ya remembered it," Reb said. "I love dessert."

"Me, too," Sage couldn't help saying as she smiled at him. Oh, he was delicious!

Chapter Three

"And I've got Mary's liniment here if ya wanna take it on back with ya, Sage," Mr. Getcher said. "It'll save her the trip in."

"Thank you," Sage said. "Her ankles have been givin' her fits these past few days."

Mr. Getcher chuckled. "And I bet ya been hearin' about it, too." Sage smiled and nodded. "She's a cantankerous old bird, that Mary Farthen," he said, still smiling. "But a body can't help but take to her."

Gareth Getcher owned the general store in town. He was a chubby man with dimples on his cheeks and very little gray hair left on his head. He had always reminded Sage of someone who should've owned a bakery in some big city somewhere. Ever smiling and friendly, Mr. Getcher was a dear soul and Sage was very fond of him.

"I hear Eugenia's nephew has everythin' ready out at the ranch," Mr. Getcher said. "Hear tell his herd is on its way up from Santa Fe."

"That's right," Sage confirmed.

Everywhere she went, people were talking about Eugenia Smarthing's nephew. It was almost irritating. Didn't folks have anything better to do?

Every conversation was, "Reb Mitchell," this and "Eugenia's nephew," that. He had literally become the talk of the town and, secretly, Sage resented it. She had come to feel very . . . well, possessive of Reb. He was Eugenia's nephew after all, and Sage had known him before anyone else. Since his arrival, everyone in the town had taken to Reb and Sage was jealous. The fact worried her, too. She had no right, no reason to feel the way she did where he was concerned. Still, she felt it and it troubled her, for Reb seemed to belong to everyone. Every woman he met fell in love with him, in one manner or another, and she feared the day would come when he would fall in love with one of them in return. The thought made her stomach ache.

Why, just that very morning, Sage had walked past Milly Michaels, Katie Bird and Dotty Benten standing outside the dress shop talking, talking about Reb Mitchell, of course. It had been Milly who stopped Sage and inquired about Reb's welfare.

"Have ya coaxed him out to the boardin' house for supper yet this week, Sage?" Milly asked. Milly Michaels was all of seventeen years old, but she tried to make people think she was older, more mature and wiser to life.

"His aunt had him out for supper last night, Milly," Sage said. "Along with Reverend and Mrs. Tippetts and Mr. Winnery. We all had a fine time." Although Sage was irritated with Milly's implication that Sage chased after Reb the way Milly did, Sage tried to appear indifferent.

"Oh, come on Sage," Milly said, unconvinced of Sage's lack of concern. "You're old, but you're not dead. Surely he's caught yer eye more than you let on."

The words echoed through Sage's mind like pieces of a shattered windowpane. Even now standing in the general store conversing with Mr. Getcher, the memory of Milly's words hurt.

"Reb says it's a fine herd he's bringin' up," Mr. Getcher said, pulling Sage's thoughts back to the moment at hand.

"Miss Eugenia seems to trust in it," she said.

"Well," Mr. Getcher continued, "He's a fine boy. A fine boy. He'll make some gal a good husband." Mr. Getcher winked at Sage and the sick feeling in her stomach thickened, for she knew it wouldn't be her, old Sage Willows, the town spinster.

Sage forced a smile and sighed. "Well, I best be gettin' back. If I'm not there when the ladies take to rummy, fists will be flyin' for certain."

Mr. Getcher chuckled. "Well, ya have a nice afternoon, Sage," he said. "And tell them ladies I send my regards."

"I will," Sage said, smiling at the man. He was a kind-hearted soul and Sage knew he rather liked Mary. She giggled at the thought of cranky old Mary and sweet-natured Mr. Getcher being fond of one another.

Sage stepped out of the general store and started toward the boarding-house. No sooner had her thoughts of romance between Mary and Mr. Getcher caused her to smile, than she felt anxiety rise in her when she heard Forest Simmons' angry voice behind her.

"Sage Willows!" he nearly shouted. "That mutt of yers done put my lady in the puppy way last month!"

Inhaling deeply, trying to find the strength to deal with yet another altercation with Mr. Simmons, Sage turned to face him.

"I'm sorry, Mr. Simmons," she told him. "I've . . . I've given him over to Reb Mitchell. What more do you want me to do?"

Mr. Simmons' eyes narrowed. "Well," he began, "If ya don't want to take care of my lady and her litter 'til them dadburned pups are weaned, then I'll just have to drown 'em."

Sage felt sick. She hated Forest Simmons, hated him for the mean old man he was, hated him for offering to marry her on several occasions. Forest Simmons had proposed to Sage three times. Each time he had told her he was willing to save her from spinsterhood if she would marry him and birth him a few boys. The thought always made Sage want to vomit, but she had kindly turned him down each time instead. Even if he hadn't been old and ugly, any man who would drown puppies made Sage's stomach churn.

"You know I can't see puppies drowned, Mr. Simmons," she said. "But . . . I . . ."

At that very moment, Bullet came bounding up to Sage, sitting at her feet and panting happily as he looked up at her. Sage felt a wave of respite wash over her, for if Bullet was nearby, then so was his owner.

"Hey there, Forest," Reb greeted, sauntering over from the blacksmith's shop across the way. Reb reached out and took Forest's hand, shaking it firmly. "I hear yer lady dog is expectin' a litter," he said. Sage wanted to burst into tears of relief at the sound of his voice. She looked to him and smiled when he quickly winked at her.

"Yep. She is, no thanks to yer mutt, here," Forest grumbled.

"Oh, he's a good dog, ain't ya, Bullet?" Reb said, patting his dog on the head. "And I was wonderin' if you'd be willin' to let me take that litter off yer hands once they're weaned." Sage's mouth gaped open slightly. She knew full well Reb had no use for a litter of pups. He already had Bullet.

"The whole litter?" Forest asked, disbelieving Reb's sincerity.

"Yep," Reb confirmed. "My saddle pal, Charlie Dugger, is headin' up here from Santa Fe with my cattle and they make up a purty big herd. I think havin' a few more dogs like Bullet around the ranch might come in handy. Charlie's wantin' a dog of his own, whether or not he stays on with me, and I just thought ya might be lookin' to give them pups away."

Forest looked at Sage. His eyes narrowed suspiciously. "Well, I don't know . . ." he said. Sage was furious at his antics and couldn't hold her tongue.

"I'm certain Mr. Simmons wouldn't mind handin' the litter over to you, Reb," she said, smiling sarcastically at the old man. "He was just now tellin' me how he planned on drownin' them once they were born."

Mr. Simmons' face tightened as he glared at Sage, but he spoke to Reb. "I just don't have the time to run around after a litter of pups. I told Sage here she'd have to take my lady and the pups in 'til they were weaned. I don't have the time for it."

"Drown 'em?" Reb exclaimed. "Hell! I mean . . . heck," he corrected, glancing to Sage. "I'll take yer lady and her pups 'til the litter is weaned. Better havin' 'em out at the ranch than cooped up at the boardin' house with the ladies."

"I s'pose," Forest mumbled. Sage was delighted in his obvious vexation. He had wanted to bully her around because he was just plain mean. But, like everyone else in town, Reb's charm won him over.

"Anyway," Reb said, lowering his voice and leaning closer to Forest. "Can ya just imagine Mary Farthen, Livie, and the rest of them ladies a chasin' around after a litter of pups?"

Sage's eyebrows rose in astonishment as she heard Forest Simmons chuckle, something akin to a smile spreading across his face.

"It would be a sight," Forest chuckled. With a heavy sigh, the old man finally agreed. "All righty, then. You can take my lady and her litter out to Buck's old ranch, just 'til the litter is weaned. As long as I don't have to bother with no rambunctious mess of dogs, ya can have the pups, I guess."

"Thank ya, Forest," Reb said, shaking the man's hand again. "I can't thank ya enough for doin' me such a favor."

Forest smiled proudly and Sage smiled, too, amazed at Reb's having won the old goat over.

"I'll bring her out in a week or two when she's closer to bustin'," Forest said.

"Oh, don't worry about that," Reb said. "I'll come in and get her when yer ready."

"Okey-dokey," Forest said. "Good day to ya, Miss Sage," the man said before turning, leaving and entering the general store.

Reb released a heavy sigh once the man was out of ear-shot and said, "Did I earn myself another pan of sage stuffin', Miss Willows?"

Sage smiled at him. How chivalrous he had been, coming to her rescue as he had!

"Oh, I think so," she answered. "I thought he was gonna eat me alive!"

Reb chuckled. "Ol' Forest might be old and ugly, but I don't think he has enough teeth left in his head to take to bein' a cannibal."

Sage covered her mouth with one hand, but not before a rather loud, unlady-like laugh escaped.

⁓

REB SMILED AS he watched Sage giggle. Her eyes seemed to light up with delight in a way he had never seen them light up before, and the fact caused some sort of long-absent warmth to seep into his veins.

He had been at the smithy's and just happened to glance across the way to the general store in time to see Sage come out with a basket full of goods in hand. He had also seen Forest Simmons approach her, seen the way the color drained from Sage's pretty face as the cranky old goat spoke to her. Further, he suspected what Forest was chewing her out about and knew he couldn't let Sage endure it any longer.

The last thing Rebel needed was a litter of rowdy pups tearing up his ranch house and outbuildings. But for some reason, Sage Willows brought out his protective nature, and now he found himself anticipating raising half a dozen pups. Still, he didn't put it past Forest to be serious about wanting to drown the litter and that was just plain ridiculous.

"Thank you, Reb," Sage said, once she had managed to stifle her delightful giggles. "Just let me know when you want to come by for supper and I'll make sure stuffin' is on the table for you."

"Good deal," he said. Unexpectedly then, Sage reached up, brushing at something on Reb's cheek. Reb was instantly unsettled by her touch. The soft, familiar scent of sage tickled his breath and he suspected she had been pinching sage leaves again. Further, an instant pleasure welled up in his chest at the feel of her fingers on his skin and he turned his face from her. The sensations her caressive touch had evoked in him had long been guarded, safely dormant somewhere deep within. She was dangerous, a threat to his resolve, and he hadn't been prepared to defend himself from such feelings. Most of the time he could flirt, tease, even do a little sparking with a girl here and there, without risking the slightest crack in his heart of stone. But Sage Willows was different. Reb had discovered the need to be well prepared defensively when in her presence and at that moment he hadn't been.

❦

SAGE LET HER HAND fall from Reb's cheek, her fingers going to her collar buttons and fiddling with them nervously.

"I'm sorry," she said. "You had . . . you had dirt on your face." She felt tears welling in her eyes. It had been a natural instinct that moved her hand to his cheek, but he was obviously not in need or want of her touch. Trying to distract herself from the desire to cry because of his obvious rejection, she reached down and patted Bullet's happy head.

"You . . . you just let your aunt know what day you'll be by for supper," Sage choked, brushing past Reb quickly. In that same moment, she noticed the clouds moving in from the west and she thanked the heavens for them. She knew she would sorely need them this day.

ଔ

REB SQUEEZED HIS eyes tightly shut for a moment, knowing he had offended her. But, he was self-protective, empty, with nothing to offer a woman. He knew her gesture had been merely that of one friend looking out for another, but he also recognized the warmth in his body when she had touched him, knew it sprang from desire, from the want of her continued touch. It would've been dangerous to allow her to continue touching him when his resistance was down. Yet, now he had slighted her, and that knowledge also caused him to feel.

"Come on, Bullet," he grumbled. "Let's get on home."

ଔ

SAGE SET THE basket of things she had purchased from the general store on the boardinghouse front porch. The rain hadn't arrived yet and she needed it so desperately. Careless of her well-being, as her impending tears often found her, Sage went to the barn and saddled Drifter.

She could feel the moisture heavy in her eyes, but the rain still had not come when she reached the creek bed. Quickly she tied Drifter's reins to a piñon tree and hurried over the hill to Ruthie's grave. As she knelt before the tiny gravestone, Sage felt the first blessed drops of rain on her cheeks and, with them, Sage's tears began to flow freely. The pain in her heart, caused by Reb's obvious disgust at her touch, stung unbearably sharp and harsh. She felt as if someone had actually plunged something into her bosom. She sobbed bitterly, cried out with the agony of loneliness and despair.

She loved him! She could no longer deceive herself, deny her heart, and the inward admission was excruciating. She kept seeing his face, the frown, which had instantly puckered his brow when she had touched him, kept envisioning the way his eyes narrowed with revulsion.

"Am I so revolting, Ruthie?" she sobbed quietly. "It . . . it was just a smudge . . . a little bit of dirt. I . . . I only wanted to . . ." But her words were lost, as tears and sobbing overwhelmed her again. The few soft drops of rain gave way to a heavier, colder downpour.

❧

REB HAD APPROACHED Ruth's grave from behind, for he had assumed he would find Sage there. When he had gone to the boardinghouse to offer some sort of awkward apology to her and found her basket sitting on the front porch, he had suspected she would go to Ruth. He did not expect, however, to see her kneeling on the ground before the tiny gravestone, drenched in tears as well as rain. Self-loathing overtook him at the sight. He turned Ned around and headed back to the boardinghouse. He would give Sage her privacy. He had stayed his distance and the noise of the rain would drown out any sound his retreat might make. As he rode back to the boardinghouse, his resolve was firm. He owed his aunt's friend an apology. No. He owed *his* friend an apology. Uncertain at that moment how to offer one to her, still he knew he must. He would wait for her to return, visit with his aunt and the other ladies, let Ned and Bullet keep company out in the barn, while he waited out the rain. Sage, a sweet, beautiful young woman, did not deserve to be ill-treated by the likes of Rebel Mitchell. He would simply have to be on his guard better when she was around. After all, it wasn't her fault Ivy Dalton had been born.

❧

"IT WAS A hard row to hoe," Reb's aunt told him. "Four little girls left orphaned. I say four little girls because Sage was only sixteen, a child herself, really." Reb nodded, agreeing with his aunt's opinion that Sage was very young to have had the responsibility of raising her sisters heaped on her shoulders. He thought of the girl now, kneeling before the tiny gravestone in the lonely pasture, crying in the rain. He clenched his jaw, angry with himself for adding to her misery.

"Rosie was livin' at Willows' when Matthew and Susan died, and I know she was a real help and strength to Sage," Eugenia continued. "Still, runnin' a boardinghouse and bein' a parent to those girls . . . well, Sage's life just got skipped over. Even when Clark Miller wanted to court Sage, Sage was too busy with Karoline and April's antics, and Clark turned his attention to Betty, the girl just two years under Sage. They got married . . . oh . . . about four years back and moved out to Texas. Then, April married a year or so later and, then, Karoline just this past year."

"Ain't real fair," Reb mumbled.

"Many things in life aren't fair," Eugenia said. "Are they now?" Reb looked away from his aunt, his teeth grinding with anger and resolve.

"So, anyway," Eugenia continued, "I think Sage has resigned herself to us, me, Rosie, Livie and Mary. And I think I would, too, if Forest Simmons was my only other choice."

Reb frowned. "Did that ol' goat really ask her to marry him?" The thought of Sage married to Forest Simmons made Reb's stomach churn.

Eugenia nodded. "Yes, he did," she told him. "Offered her a great life, too, told her he'd save her from bein' a spinster if she married him and had a couple of boys for him."

"Well, that just makes me plum sick," Reb growled.

"Which part, sweetie?" Eugenia asked. "Him callin' her a spinster straight to her face?"

Reb shook his head and growled with disgust. "No. The thought of her havin' to take to his bed."

ଔ

EUGENIA SMILED. REB was undone and she was delighted by it. Something had happened in town that day. Something other than what Reb had told her about Forest Simmons barking at Sage about his lady dog's impending litter. She hadn't quite been able to get out of him exactly what it was, but something had happened. She was convinced of it. Furthermore, whatever it was had completely rattled Reb and that is precisely what she wanted to see. Rebel Lee Mitchell needed some rattling.

She smiled and continued, "She refused his proposal, of course, and he got more and more hateful toward her every time she did."

"Well, ain't there plenty of young bucks around here?" Reb asked. He was irritated, nervous and angry. Eugenia smiled.

"Sure. Plenty of young does, too, boy. Or hadn't you noticed?" Eugenia asked.

Reb rolled his eyes and scratched his goatee. "Yeah, yeah, yeah. I noticed. They're like a pack of wolves a droolin' over a wounded baby." He shook his head. "Still, she ain't that much older than Milly Michaels and the rest of those honeycombs here 'bout. And she's a far sight better lookin'. A far sight!" he said.

Eugenia nodded. "Yes, she is," she agreed. "But she's resigned."

"To what?" Reb asked.

Eugenia chuckled at the silly man. "She's resigned herself to bein' alone. I think it's become easier for her to just sit around and laugh at us than to hope for somethin' more fulfillin' out of life." Reb nodded and Eugenia knew he understood all too well how Sage felt.

"So," Eugenia began, "what else happened in town today? I mean, it's rainin' like mad outside, I know. But, I get the feelin' you aren't just sittin' here waitin' for Rosie, Mary and Livie to get up from their nappin'."

Reb shook his head, shifted his weight uncomfortably in the parlor chair and nervously scratched his whiskery chin again.

"Oh, I . . . I done somethin' . . . somethin' wrong. I think, anyway," he mumbled. Eugenia raised a curious eyebrow.

"Like what?" she asked. Reb rubbed his hand across his face. It was obvious he was agitated.

"Well, when we was standin' out there in town, after ol' Forest had wandered off. Sage . . . she just reached up to rub somethin' off my cheek and I . . . I . . ." he stammered.

"You what?" Eugenia urged.

"I pulled away all kinda irritated like," he finally admitted.

"For cryin' in the bucket, boy—ya did not!" Mary exclaimed as she, Rosie and Livie stepped into the parlor. Reb rolled his eyes and shook his head. Still, a grin spread across his face quickly enough.

"You three are awful!" Eugenia scolded. "Don't you have a lick of sense in ya? I'm in here havin' a private conversation with my nephew— *my* nephew, mind you—and you three are eavesdropping like the devil's own!"

"Well, it's rainin'," Mary grumbled, somewhat humbly. "And ya know what goes on 'round here when it's rainin'."

"What goes on when it's rainin', Miss Mary," Reb chuckled. Eugenia could see his annoyance with the eavesdroppers had quickly disappeared. No doubt he was relieved at the interruption. After all, there wasn't any way he would feel pressured to reveal any more secrets to her now, not with three old nosey-bodies around.

"Sage-tears," Rose said quietly.

"What?" Reb asked.

"That's what we call the rain, Sage-tears," Livie explained.

"It's the only time Sage ever cries, when the rains come," Mary mumbled.

❒

SAGE WAS GRATEFUL for the fire in the parlor hearth, grateful Rosie knew her well enough to prepare one, that she knew Sage wouldn't be in until night had fallen or the rain had stopped. The rain had brought not only moisture, but cooler temperatures, and after being out in such weather for so many hours, Sage was chilled to the bone. It was always Rosie who left a fire for Sage, for she had known about Sage's rainy day tears for many more years than the others.

Sage had crept quietly into the house by way of the back door and now stood, dripping wet and shivering in front of the fire. Although her tears and sobbing served to aid Sage, the powerful release of emotion had left her tired and weak and cold. The warmth from the fire caused her trembling to increase as her body tried to regain its heat and strength.

Sage had taken the pins out of her hair long before returning to the house, and now she combed it with her fingers, drawing it over one shoulder so the fire's warmth could aid it in beginning to dry. Still, she shivered too violently for comfort. Having left her shoes and stockings just inside the back door, she began unfastening the buttons at the waist of her skirt. Letting the drenched fabric of her skirt and petticoats fall to the floor around her feet, she stepped away and began to work at the buttons on the back of her shirtwaist. Once her shirtwaist was removed, she stood before the fire in her camisole, corset and pantalets.

Already she was warmer, and when the soft blanket touched her shoulders, she smiled, grateful that Rosie had waited up for her. Rosie often waited up long hours into the night, waiting for Sage to return from one of her rainy excursions. Sometimes Sage would find the tub, sitting before the fireplace, hot water boiling on the stove. Rosie would help her pour the hot water into the tub and then leave her to her peace and a warming bath.

Smiling, Sage turned to thank Rosie for waiting up for her again this night. She gasped, however, horrified when she saw it was Reb who had placed the blanket around her shoulders and now stood before her, his eyes warm and dark in the firelight. Sage covered her trembling lips with one hand, and though she thought she had cried her eyes dry, she felt the excess moisture of threatening tears.

"I've been waitin' on ya," he said. His voice was quiet and deep, sweet like honey and butter. For a moment Sage was distracted by the fact that his shirt, un-tucked from his pants, hung open, revealing the flawlessly sculpted muscles of his chest and stomach. His hair was mussed, as if he had just awakened, and he ran his fingers through it slowly when he realized she was studying him. "You've been gone for hours," he added.

"I . . . I . . . I . . ." she stammered. The impropriety of the situation, coupled with the pure titillation of it, caused her mind to run empty.

"Ya lost track of time?" he asked. She could only nod, pulling the blanket tighter around her body. "I do that a lot," he mumbled, his eyes seeming to linger on the length of her hair. Sage was uncomfortable, painfully so, and she certainly wasn't used to appearing in front of any man with her hair down, regardless of her manner of dress.

"Why are you here?" she asked, rather more severely than she intended. Seeing him only brought her pain. She had spent the entire afternoon and evening purging her body of tears, driving heartache away, and now here it stood, handsome and alluring, before her.

"I . . . I wanted to apologize to ya," he said.

Sage turned from him, trying to concentrate on the fire in the hearth. "For what?" she asked. "I should be apoligizin' to you for saddlin' ya with a litter of pups, not to mention their daddy."

"I'm a hard man, Sage," he said, "and I don't trust women, especially ones any younger than Miss Mary Farthen." A soft warmth began to envelope Sage, and she couldn't discern if it began with the blanket Reb had draped over her shoulders or with his attempt at lightening her mood. She stiffened, however, when she felt his hands on her shoulders, coaxing her to turn and face him again. When she finally did, it was to find his eyes smoldering dark and enticing, his hair still delightfully mussed.

"But I know yer just tryin' to be my friend," he said. Sage glanced away, afraid he would see the tears in her eyes. Her heart was pounding so violently she feared it might beat itself to quitting altogether. His hand on her face as he cupped her chin, forcing her to look up at him, nearly melted her into a puddle at his feet.

"I'm . . . I'm just not used to bein' touched by pretty girls," he said, smiling down at her. Sage smiled, moved by his efforts to ease her mind. He dropped his hand from her chin and returned her smile.

"So," she ventured. "You're a hard man, who doesn't trust women, and you're a liar, too?"

"What?" he asked, obviously puzzled.

"Milly Michaels can't wait to get her hands on you and that alone tells me you've been touched by many a pretty girl," she told him. "And anyway, I don't quite fit in that 'pretty girl' corral anymore, now do I?"

Reb's eyes narrowed, his smile faded as he studied her for a moment before mumbling, "Yer right. Yer more the 'beautiful woman,' type," he said. Again Sage felt tears fill her eyes, and she turned her face from him quickly. How could he tease her so cruelly? Or was he teasing? The mad pounding of her heart caused her to think, perhaps, he was sincere, and that consideration caused her even more discomfort.

"Look here," he said. She obeyed and looked back at him to see him point to a smudge of mud on his cheek. "I smudged it up, just so ya could brush it off again."

Sage smiled. Sure enough! A dark and much larger mud smudge donned his cheek.

"Bullet wanted to go ahead and lick it off for me, but I told him I was savin' it as part of my apology to ya," Reb said smiling. Sage's heart softened, melted, warmed like butter in a hot skillet. As he took her hand, raising it and pressing it to his cheek, Sage felt her body begin to tremble with fascination.

"Will ya give me another chance at bein' yer friend, Sage Willows?" he whispered. Sage felt her breath increase to a rapid pace as he drew her fingers to his lips, placing a soft kiss on them. "One more chance?" he whispered again, rubbing the whiskers of his mustache across her tender fingertips. "And you've been pinchin' sage leaves again, haven't ya?" Sage smiled. It was true! On her way in through the back door, she had paused long enough to pinch a sage leaf from the plant in the barrel, savoring its fragrant aroma as she entered the house. Still, his touch, the feel of his lips, and the soft whiskers of his mustache on her fingertips were too enthralling, and she pulled her hand from his grasp, brushing the dried mud from his cheek quickly.

"Thank ya, Miss Sage," he said, smiling at her. "I'll sleep easier tonight knowin' yer home and safe . . . and not angry at me any more. Right?"

Sage smiled. "Do you still want that stuffin' I owe ya?" she asked, stepping back from him. His nearness was unendurable, for Sage wanted nothing more than to throw herself against his strong body and beg him to embrace her.

Reb smiled at her. "Yes, ma'am," he said empathically. "I need somethin' to keep me goin' while I'm raisin' all these dogs ya saddled me with."

Sage giggled. "You're the one who cut him loose," she reminded him.

He chuckled. "What was I supposed to do? Lie there on the porch all tangled up with ya? Folks woulda been talkin' for years." Sage's skin prickled with goose bumps, delighted by the memory of the first moments after she met Reb Mitchell. "I mighta had to make an honest woman of ya," he added. Instantly, Sage's smile left her face. She stepped back another step, further unsettled by his nearness and implications of intimacy.

"I'm just teasin' ya, Sage," he chuckled. Then, moving closer to her and lowering his voice, he asked, "Still, if it came down to it, who would ya rather have make an honest woman of ya? Old Forest Simmons . . . or me?" Sage felt her jaw go slack, her mouth gaping open in astonishment. Reb laughed, his smile brightening the dimly lit room.

"Oh, quit horsin' around, boy," came Mary's irritated voice from just beyond the parlor. "Just kiss her, dang it all!"

Reb turned on his heels, startled by Mary's sudden outburst. Sage was torn between the conflicting emotions of being mortified at Mary's eavesdropping and euphoria at the thought of Reb's actually following the older woman's order.

"Mary!" Sage scolded. "What are you doin'?"

Mary stepped into the parlor, carrying a glass of milk. She wore her usual sour expression and just about the rattiest old red nightgown Sage had ever seen.

"What am I doin'?" she exclaimed. "I ain't the one standing here half-neked in the parlor with a half-neked man," she grumbled. Reb chuckled, but Sage was embarrassed beyond any ability to speak further.

"Get on home with ya, Reb," Mary ordered. "If yer too ignorant to take advantage of this situation any further, then yer just a wastin' my time."

"Yes, ma'am," Reb said, still chuckling. Turning back to Sage, he said, "I need my stuffin' 'fore the week's out." He winked at her and left the parlor, retrieving his hat from the hat rack by the front door.

As he started to open the door, Mary grumbled, "Out the back, boy! People might see ya if ya go out the front there. Ya ain't got the sense God give a cricket."

Still chuckling, Reb tipped his hat and said, "Good night, then, Miss Sage . . . Miss Mary." He disappeared into the darkness of the kitchen and Sage heard the back door open and close quietly.

Sage sighed, uncomfortable under Mary's disapproving stare.

The old woman sipped her milk for a moment, studied Sage from head to toe and said, "Yer gonna have to pull yerself up by the bootstraps and go after that boy a little more vigorous, Sage." Sage's mouth gaped open in astonishment at Mary's forthright advice. "Oh, close yer mouth, girl," Mary said, smiling. "I know Rose and Livie ain't the only ones a dreamin' of Reb Mitchell's kisses." With that, she left Sage standing alone in the parlor, so warm from Reb's attentions she no longer needed the blanket he had placed about her shoulders.

Letting the blanket fall to the floor in a heap with her wet skirt and petticoats, Sage returned to combing her long hair with her fingers. She turned toward the fire, smiling. Reb cared enough for her, or at least for her feelings, to have waited until she came home so he could make things right between them. It had been over six hours since she had left her basket on the front porch, saddled Drifter, and ridden off into the isolation of the rain. He had waited six hours for her! Six hours! How Sage wished Milly Michaels could see her now, wished all the girls in town could've seen Reb waiting for her, draping the blanket around her shoulders and pressing a soft kiss to her fingers. She held her fingers to her lips, the very fingers Reb had kissed. However lightly he may have kissed them, still he had kissed them, and in kissing them he had kissed her, in a manner.

Sage sighed and, careless of leaving her wet clothes on the parlor floor, climbed the stairs to her bedroom. Any other night, sleep would be impossible after such euphoric moments as the ones spent with Reb in the parlor, but the heavy fatigue of expelling her heartache in the rain had weakened Sage, and she did fall asleep with the feel of Reb Mitchell's kiss on her fingertips.

Chapter Four

༄ ༃

The sun was barely peeking over the horizon and the scent of frying bacon filled the kitchen of Willows' Boarding House. Sage hummed a favorite melody, pausing to listen to the meadowlarks call for a moment before turning the eggs in the skillet. She couldn't seem to keep from smiling, for the events of the night before, the moments spent with Reb in the firelight of the parlor, kept floating through her mind. It seemed as though the pain of the day before was somewhere off in the distant past. All she could think of now was the fact Reb had waited for hours and hours to apologize to her.

She smiled as a robin suddenly alighted on the windowsill of the open window. "Did you smell the bacon, too?" she asked it. "I can't believe Miss Rose is still asleep. Bacon usually wakes her the moment it hits the skillet."

"I think Reb's herd is here!" Eugenia said, rushing into the kitchen and to the open window, causing the robin to take flight. "Listen, Sage." Sage paused and tried to hear something above the sizzle of bacon cooking.

"I don't hear anythin'," she said.

"Oh, come on!" Eugenia said, taking Sage's hand and pulling her toward the front door. Quickly, Eugenia opened the door and stepped out onto the porch and into the early morning sunshine. "Listen. Can you hear them?"

Sage closed her eyes and listened. A heavy, rumbling sound reached her ears. It grew less faint and she opened her eyes again, looking to the east and shading her face with one hand. In the distance, she could see a large cloud of dust, and then the herd appeared rising over a hill.

"It's them! It's Reb's herd!" Eugenia exclaimed. Sage smiled, for Eugenia's face was simply resplendent. No doubt the herd put her in mind of her husband and the wonderful life they'd spent together on their ranch.

"What's all the racket?" Mary grumbled, coming to stand next to Sage on the porch. Sage was glad the old woman had taken the time to bring a shawl with her, for she still wore the rattiest red nightgown Sage had ever seen.

"It's Reb's herd!" Eugenia told her. "Just comin' through town. Look there!"

Sage smiled as the whistles and cattle calls of the cowboys driving the herd became audible. She watched as the other residents in town stepped out onto their porches to see what the noise was. Soon the street was filled with cattle, kicking up dust and bawling their complaints as the cowboys drove them straight through the center of town.

"Good gravy!" Livie exclaimed, joining the others on the porch. She fanned the dust away from her face and coughed. "Sure are a lot of them."

"That there's a nice herd," Mary said.

"It sure is," Eugenia agreed, her face beaming. "I'm gettin' dressed and ridin' out to the ranch!" She turned and scurried back into the house.

Sage watched the cattle moving slowly past the boardinghouse and a certain amount of pride welled up in her, knowing this was Reb Mitchell's herd and the town was no doubt impressed with it. One of the cowboys, a faded bandana covering his nose and mouth, rode up to the boardinghouse and reined in his horse right in front of Sage and the others.

Tipping his hat, he pulled the bandana down around his neck and said, "Howdy, ladies. I'm lookin' fer Reb Mitchell and the Smarthin' ranch."

"Head straight the direction yer goin' for about 5 miles and ya'll run right into it, cowboy," Mary answered.

"Thank ya, ma'am," the handsome young man said.

"You Charlie Dugger?" Mary asked him.

"Yes, ma'am," the cowboy answered. He smiled, pulled the bandana up around his face again, and said, "Just hit town and already I'm a legend." The cowboy gave a sharp whistle and rode on. The herd continued to rumble through town and Sage's heart hammered with the excitement of it.

"Them boys will be hungry by the time they get that herd to the ranch," Mary said.

"Then we better get out there and get some breakfast goin'," Livie suggested. "Leave it to Rose to sleep through somethin' like this," she added, turning and going into the house.

Sage smiled at Mary. "I guess I can hold breakfast for you 'til y'all get back."

Mary rolled her eyes with irritation, shaking her head. "Sage Willows, yer as dumb as a door handle."

"What?" Sage asked, perplexed at why Mary would say such a thing.

"Yer goin' with us, silly girl." With that Mary turned and went into the house as well, leaving Sage excited at the prospect of seeing Reb again.

🙖

"I CAN'T FIND one hair pin in my bedroom!" Sage exclaimed, hurrying down the stairs to join the others.

"Well, we ain't got all day, girl," Mary grumbled. "Just braid it or somethin'. We gotta get out to Eugenia's place."

Eugenia smiled and hushed Rosie when she giggled. When she had awakened the night before to hear Reb and Sage talking in the parlor and caught Rosie and Livie eavesdropping from upstairs, the three had agreed to hide all of Sage's hairpins. It was high time the girl relaxed a bit.

"But I have to put my hair up and . . ." Sage began to argue.

"Oh, for crying in the bucket," Livie sighed. Going to Sage, she gathered her long hair in her hands and quickly wove it into a long, loose braid. "There now. You look fine, soft and approachable."

Sage frowned. "How do I usually look?" she asked.

Eugenia smiled and, taking Sage's hand, said, "Let's get goin'. That herd'll be there any minute."

"Let me drive, Eugenia," Mary said. "I can beat that herd to the ranch if ya let me drive the buggy."

"Oh, Eugenia, don't!" Livie exclaimed. "Mary's driving scares the daylights out of me!"

"Livie, you worry too much," Rosie said, taking her friend's hand and pulling her out the back door.

Eugenia looked to Sage who paused. "What's the matter, sweetie?" she asked.

"I can't possibly go," Sage said.

"Well, why ever not?" Eugenia asked, feigning ignorance. She knew how self-conscious Sage felt when her hair wasn't pulled back into a tight knot. She also knew how beautiful Sage's hair was, how it softened her appearance to have it down or folded into a soft braid.

"I . . . I . . ." Sage stammered.

"For pity's sake, Sage. We'll miss all the excitement," she said, taking Sage's hand and leading her out the door.

❦

"SLOW DOWN, MARY!" Livie hollered. "We want to get there alive," she said, one hand holding her weathered straw hat on her head, the other hanging onto the buggy for dear life.

"Whoopee!" Rosie shouted as Mary snapped the lines at Drifter's back, increasing his pace.

Sage giggled as she saw the rare expression of freedom and joy radiant on Mary's wrinkled face. Mary hid her emotions well most of the time, but this was one of the infrequent moments when she could not mask her delight.

Eugenia coughed as the dust kicked up by the herd filled her lungs. The dust irritated Sage's eyes, too, and she wiped at the moisture in them.

"Hurry up and pass them, Mary, before I choke to death," Livie whined.

As the buggy carrying the five women moved up alongside the herd, Charlie Dugger rode over to greet them.

"Hey there, ladies!" he shouted. "Ya racin' us to the ranch?"

"We're beatin' ya to the ranch, boy!" Mary shouted in return, snapping the lines again.

"Wooo Whooo!" Rosie hollered. "Fresh air and cowboys! Nothin' like it in the world!" Sage laughed, entirely amused by Rosie's antics.

Sage sighed, delighted in the knowledge she would see Reb again. The night before had been the stuff of dreams and, although she knew he would never see her as anything more than a friend, she also knew he cared about her. Hadn't he worried for hours over hurting her feelings? Hadn't he waited for her, apologized to her? Her heart swelled at the memory of his tender kiss on her fingers.

"We've got 'em now, gals!" Mary exclaimed as Drifter pulled ahead of the herd.

"Good!" Livie sighed with relief. "Now can we slow down, Mary?"

"Show some gumption, Livie," Mary chuckled. "We gotta get breakfast on 'fore they get there, ya ninny."

❧

REB SAT ON the front porch of the ranch house watching the sun rise higher in the sky. Yellow and pink had given way to bright blue as morning arrived and Reb had enjoyed watching the change. Bullet sat next to him, begging for another strip of jerky by tipping his head from one side to the other as he looked at his owner.

"Yer nothin' but a begger," Reb chuckled, placing a piece of jerky on the dog's nose. "Stay . . . stay . . ." he said. Bullet remained still, except for his tail, waiting for his master's permission to chomp down his treat. "There ya go, boy," Reb said. Bullet tossed the piece of dried meat in the air, catching it in his mouth and chewing it only thrice before swallowing.

Reb chuckled. "Yer a spoiled begger . . . that's what ya are," he told the dog. Sighing, he looked back toward the sky. He had hardly slept a wink since returning from the boardinghouse late the night before, his mind awhirl with confusing thoughts and emotions.

He had been disgusted with himself, slighting Sage the way he had done in town. Of course, he had finally confessed his behavior to his Aunt Eugenia, but even that hadn't made him feel any better. So, he had waited. He had waited for hours and hours, waited through suppertime, through sunset, until Sage had finally come home. Then, he had waited even longer, waited until she was half undressed before he had finally revealed his presence and begun to apologize to her. And he had made his peace with her . . . hadn't he?

Reb shook his head, uncertain about what to make of the moments spent with Sage in the parlor. Truth be told, he had almost taken her in his arms and had his fill of kissing her! That dangerous little rain-cryer was proving to be more of a distraction than he had thought, and it concerned him.

He thought of Ivy. Reb always thought of Ivy when he found himself in danger of thinking too much, feeling too much. Usually thinking of Ivy Dalton put a bad enough taste in his mouth that he steered clear of anything in a petticoat under the age of fifty. But he was fast learning Ivy's memory wasn't keeping him away from Sage as well as it should, and this concerned him.

Running his fingers through his hair, he looked at Bullet. "Yer a fine one to be smilin' up at me," he said. "If ya woulda had an Ivy Dalton of yer own, I wouldn't be havin' to mess with a litter of pups." Bullet began wagging his tail and panting, happy to have Reb's attention. Reb chuckled and scratched the dog's ears.

Suddenly, Bullet quit panting. His tail stopped wagging and his ears perked up as best the floppy things could. Reb frowned and followed the dog's line of vision, chuckling when he saw a black buggy come racing up over the hill, the petticoats of its five female occupants flying every which direction.

Amused by the delighted expression of Mary's face and the rather terrified expression on Livie's, Reb stood up, careless of the fact he wore only his blue jeans.

"Well, good mornin' to ya, ladies!" he called as Mary abruptly stopped the buggy, sending its passengers lurching forward.

"For cryin' out loud, Reb! Help me out of this confounded contraption!" Livie begged, panting as if she had run all the way to the ranch on her own two legs. Reb chuckled and walked to the buggy, offering Livie his hand.

"Not too fond of Miss Mary's drivin', are ya Miss Livie?" he said, helping her down from the buggy.

"She's tryin' to kill us all," Livie grumbled, putting her hand to her bosom dramatically. "Down, you fool dog!" Livie ordered as Bullet jumped up, putting his paws in the middle of her back. Reb laughed and offered his hand to his aunt.

"Mornin', Reb," Eugenia said, taking his hand and stepping out of the buggy. Eugenia reached down, patting the excited dog's head affectionately. "We saw your herd comin' through town and thought we'd come out and watch the fun."

"I thought I saw dust out yonder," Reb said.

"They're still 'bout two miles back," Mary said, stepping down from the buggy all by herself.

Reb smiled and Rosie gestured he should help her down, but instead of taking the hand he offered, she put her hands on his shoulders and waited for his hands to encircle her waist. Reb chuckled, easily lifting the flirtatious old gal down out of the buggy.

"Thank you, Reb," she said with a wink.

"Yer a shameless hussy, Rose Applewhite," Mary grumbled. Reb chuckled and offered his hand to the only other occupant in the buggy, Sage.

He noted how soft she looked in the morning light, how bright her eyes were and how pretty her hair was, braided and windblown instead of tied into a tight knot. Sage accepted Reb's hand, smiling at him as she stepped down from the buggy.

"Mornin', Sage," Reb said.

"Good mornin'," she replied. "Mary insisted we come out and have breakfast ready for your friends when they arrive." She glanced away from him and he noted the pink which rose to her cheeks suddenly. "Hey there, Bullet," Sage said as the dog sat panting at her feet. Reaching out, she scratched behind his ears.

"That's mighty nice of you, ladies," he said, turning to find four sets of feminine eyes looking him up and down.

"You've been working out in the sun without your shirt, I dare say, Reb," Livie said to him. It was only then he realized he didn't have a shirt on. They probably thought he was a perfect heathen, standing there before them in nothing but his blue jeans. He smiled, suddenly realizing the cause of Sage's blush.

"Yes, ma'am, Miss Livie," Reb chuckled. "Fergive me, though. I wasn't expectin' company."

"Nothin' to forgive, Reb," Rosie said with a wink. "Nothin' at all."

"Oh, for Pete's sake, Rosie," Mary grumbled. "He ain't a new puppy a wantin' his belly scratched. Reb, help us get this bacon and such in the house. We'll get breakfast a goin' while ya ride on out to meet up with yer herd."

"Sounds like a fine idea, Miss Mary," Reb said. Turning to Sage, he asked, "Did ya finally dry out last night?" He liked the way her blush deepened as he looked at her.

"Yes, thank you," she answered. His goatee tickled and he rubbed at it with one hand. It seemed to him his facial hair always tickled him when Sage Willows was about.

"You've got that fence up fine, Reb," Eugenia said. "You been workin' hard. I can tell."

Winking at Sage, he turned to his aunt. "Yep. It's been a heap a work. But I think all the weak fence is mended now. Still need to put somethin' up around that little gravestone out in Sage's pastures 'fore I open that gate, though."

"Quit flappin' yer gums, Eugenia," Mary ordered. "There's vittles to cook up."

Reb chuckled as his aunt rolled her eyes in irritation. "She's about as much fun as a toothache," Eugenia mumbled.

"I heard that, Eugenia Smarthin'," Mary growled, stomping up the porch and into the house.

"And she drives the buggy like a lunatic woman!" Livie whispered to Reb as she followed Mary into the house.

"I heard that, too, Livie Jonesburg," Mary called over her shoulder.

Eugenia raised herself on her toes and kissed Reb's cheek, patting it afterward. "You have fun with your herd, honey," she told him as she, too, went into the house.

Rosie winked at Reb on her way in, leaving Sage as the only one still outside. Reb looked at her to find her shading her eyes from the sun and looking in the direction of the far off, but very large, cloud of dust.

"They're gettin' close," he said. "Ya can hear 'em bawlin' if ya listen." Sage smiled at him and nodded, and before Reb had a chance to consider what he was saying, he said, "Ya can ride out with me if ya like."

What in tarnation am I doin'? he thought to himself. But it was too late.

"Really?" Sage asked him, her eyes lighting up like emeralds on fire.

"Sure," Reb said, still surprised at the offer he had made. "Ya can ride Ned. He's used to cowboyin'. I'll take the new geldin' I got last week. Come on. Ya can help saddle 'em up. Here, Bullet."

He had lost his ever-loving mind? As Reb headed for the barn, Sage and Bullet close at his heels, he smoothed his mustache nervously, trying to envision Ivy Dalton's lovely face. He couldn't, however, and it worried him. Ivy's memory was the only thing that could save him from making a fool of himself over a woman again. Now he had already stepped in it, up to his knees, by allowing his defenses to be broken by Miss Sage Willows. He would take her out to the cattle for now, and deal with what to do about the mess he was sinking into later.

Dang! She looked so pretty with her hair mussed up from the wind.

⋐⋙

SAGE FOLLOWED REB to the barn, often patting Bullet's happy head, her heart hammering wildly in her bosom. He had invited her to ride out to meet the herd with him! She couldn't believe he had done it! After all, he could've asked Mary or Rosie or even his Aunt Eugenia. Any one of them would've enjoyed the adventure, but he had asked her! Of course, the other ladies didn't really ride much anymore, but she wouldn't let that distract her from the fact he had asked her.

Sage completely forgot about the boardinghouse, her beloved widowed friends, and even fixing breakfast for the tired cowboys, her eyes falling to the back pockets of Reb's blue jeans as he walked. She smiled, noting their well-worn appearance. The top corners of each pocket had worn a little hole through his jeans and Sage wondered if he knew anybody could see straight through them to the white of his under-trousers. She bit her lip, trying to stifle an amused and delighted giggle.

"Ya might get a bit dusted up, Sage," he said to her as they entered the barn.

"That's all right. I plan on stayin' off to one side anyway," she told him.

They worked together, saddling Ned and the new gelding. Once the task was done, Reb took a weather-beaten old hat down from a hook in the barn and put it on his head.

"Here ya go," he said, taking a tattered bandana from the same shelf. He folded it into a triangle, moved to stand behind Sage, placing it over her nose and mouth before tying it at the back of her head. Standing before her once more, he tugged at the corner of the cloth, revealing her entire face again. "Just pull that up when the dust gets too much for ya, all right?"

"All right," Sage said, delighted with his attentions. He took another bandana down from the shelf, tying it around his own neck before helping Sage to mount Ned.

"Don't worry none about ol' Ned," Reb said stroking the horse's neck. "He's as calm as a Sunday breeze."

Reb mounted the new gelding and smiled at Sage. "Ya ready?" he asked. Sage nodded, amused that Reb still had not taken the time to put on a shirt. "Then, let's go!" He clicked his tongue and the gelding bolted out of the barn. Bullet shot out after them, barking with enthusiasm.

"Go on, Ned," Sage said, grateful for the older horse's slower start. Ned quickly broke into a gallop, however, obviously not wanting to be outdone by his new stable pal.

Sage loved the feel of the breeze on her face, the sun warming the top of her head, the fresh fragrance of sagebrush and piñon all around her. She laughed when Reb looked over his shoulder at her, smiling with excited anticipation. He slowed the gelding, waiting for her and Ned to catch up to him. Bullet's tongue hung from his mouth as he looked up to Reb for instruction.

"Just there, boy," Reb told the dog, and Bullet seemed please to trot along beside him. "It's a perfect day for bringin' in a herd, ain't it?" Reb asked. His smile was so broad and perfectly dazzling against the bronze of his sun-baked face and torso.

"Yes, it is," Sage agreed. Reb's enthusiasm was completely infectious, and Sage couldn't keep from smiling.

"So," he began as they rode slower. "Charlie brought 'em right through the middle of town, huh?"

"He did at that," She confirmed. Reb chuckled.

"Charlie Dugger never was one to be quiet about anythin'. He rode for the pony express when he was just a kid," Reb said, still smiling. "Everybody in town came out to see my herd?"

Sage nodded. "Everybody," she told him.

"Good," Reb said. "I worked hard buildin' up that herd." Sage was happy in Reb's obvious pride. He was a man who worked hard for what he had. He deserved to own a bit of satisfaction. Just then a large grasshopper landed on one of his broad shoulders and he flicked it away with his middle finger. Still smiling, he said, "I plum forgot to put a shirt on!" He winked at her, adding, "Hope ya don't mind too much." Sage shook her head, indicating she didn't mind at all.

Unexpectedly, he reached over and caught one of her hands in his as his stirrup tangled with her own for a moment. He drew her hand up to his face, brushing her fingertips across his mustache and smiling.

"You been pinchin' sage leaves again," he said. Dropping her hand, he clicked his tongue and sent the gelding into a gallop. "Come on, Bullet.

Woooo whoooo!" he whooped, taking his hat from his head and slapping the gelding's hindquarters. Sage laughed whole-heartedly, delighted with Reb's excitement.

"Go on, Ned," she said, loosening her hold on the reins. Ned seemed to draw pleasure from the freedom of the gallop, as did Sage. She felt happy, carefree, excited. Emotions, which had eluded her for so long, now traveled without restraint through every part of her being. Suddenly, the sun seemed to shine brighter, the wildflowers seemed more drenched in color, and Sage knew only elation.

When they reached the herd, Sage directed Ned to one far side of it. She had ridden plenty, but hadn't had much experience with herding cattle. Reb rode at a full gallop, reining in next to Charlie Dugger, and whistling loudly to Bullet to quiet his excited barking. The two men struck hands, and even over the rumble of the herd, Sage could hear the happy sounds of two friends greeting each other with joy and laughter.

Reb rode next to Charlie for a few minutes and then whistled, waving his arm in the air, gesturing to Sage to join them. The herd was enormous, more than just a little intimidating, but Sage knew Reb would look out for her. Brushing several wind-blown strands of hair from her face, she rode over to meet them.

Charlie Dugger pulled the bandana from his face and smiled at Sage as she approached.

"Dugger," Reb said above the rumble of the cattle. "This here's Miss Sage Willows. Sage, this here's my old saddle pal, Charlie Dugger."

Charlie Dugger touched the brim of his hat and smiled at Sage. "I seen this pretty young miss at the boardin' house when we was a comin' through town this mornin', Reb," he said. "Mornin', Miss Willows."

"Good mornin', Mr. Dugger," Sage said, blushing at his calling her pretty.

"Whatcha think of Reb's herd?" Charlie asked.

Sage smiled, nodding. "It's . . . it's big." Charlie and Reb both laughed.

"That it is, miss. That it is," Charlie said. "How much farther we got to go to the ranch?" he asked Reb.

"Less than a mile," Reb said. "Yer almost at the end of the trail, boy."

Charlie laughed and shook his head. "Good thing," he said. "My backside's been numb for two days."

A puff of dust suddenly filled Sage's nostrils and she coughed, elated when Reb reached over and adjusted her bandana around her face.

"Reb?" Charlie began, "think ya can double up somehow? Sammy's horse has been limpin' the last bit. He's been walkin' since town."

"Sure thing," Reb said. He held his hand out to Sage. "Climb on behind me," he said to her. "Sammy can take Ned," he told Charlie. Sage paused, however, unsettled at the thought of riding with Reb.

Reb wiggled his fingers and nodded at her. "Come on. I ain't gonna eat ya," he chuckled. He turned the gelding around, allowing Sage to ease over onto the horse's hindquarters behind him. Taking a deep breath, Sage removed her feet from the stirrups of her saddle and awkwardly mounted the gelding, Reb holding her arm tightly and helping her settle.

Handing Ned's reins to Charlie, he said, "Take ol' Ned back to Sammy and I'll ride on ahead of the herd. Meet ya at the ranch for breakfast."

"All righty," Charlie said, leading Ned toward the back of the herd.

"Hang on there, Sage," Reb chuckled, reaching behind him, taking hold of her hands and placing them around his waist to settle at his stomach. Reb nudged the horse with his stirrups, whistling to Bullet, and Sage tightened her embrace around him as they rode out in front of the herd.

"I love the smell of dust and cattle," Reb said, inhaling deeply.

"It's a good thing," Sage giggled. "'Cause we're covered in them both now."

Reb chuckled, patting her hands where they locked at his waist. "I'm gonna make Aunt Eugenia's ranch one of the best in the territory," he said. "You just wait and see."

"I don't doubt it one bit," Sage told him.

She loved the feel of Reb in her arms, the warmth of his skin, the movement of his muscles as he rode. She wanted so badly to lay her cheek against his back, tighten her embrace around him, and stay that way forever. She knew these were rare and precious moments spent with Reb. Fleeting ones. But she wouldn't let reality taint them. She looked up to the blue of the sky, the puffy white of the clouds floating overhead, and smiled. It was a moment she had only found in dreams. In fact, the moment itself was far more wonderful than even her dreams.

When the ranch house and barn were in sight, Bullet barked happily and raced up to the porch. Reb reined in before the barn and let Sage take his arm, helping her to dismount.

Bullet began barking as the herd approached. Soon Eugenia, Mary, Rosie and Livie were all out on the porch, shading their eyes from the sun and smiling as they watched the cowboys bring in the herd.

Reb rode out to help and, before long, the cattle in the herd were quenching their thirst in the creek beds behind the ranch house.

"There's the crick, boys," Reb hollered. "Get to it . . . 'cause I can smell the bacon fryin' already!" Sage laughed with delight as she watched the tired, dusty cowboys whoop and holler on their way to the creek. No doubt they were ready for a good washing off and a good meal.

The chuck wagon rolled toward the ranch slowly and Reb went out to greet its driver, an older man with a long white beard. Sage looked at the herd of cows, smiled at the smell of dust and manure and the sounds of the cowboys splashing in the creek behind the house. It was all so wonderful!

"Breakfast is 'bout ready, Reb," Mary called as Reb rode toward the barn, leading Sammy's lame horse behind him.

"Thank ya, Miss Mary," he called. "I'll be in shortly."

Sage smiled and followed him to the barn, intending to help him brush down the gelding and limping mare.

"Will she be all right?" she asked as Reb lifted the mare's foot to inspect it.

"Don't know," he said. "We'll just have to see." He let the mare's foot drop and sighed, smiling. "It's amazin', isn't it?" he asked, "how excited a man can get about a herd of cattle?"

Sage giggled. "And over a cloud of dust. You're filthy!" she told him.

Reb smiled and looked down at his chest.

"Yer purty roughed up, too, Miss Sage," he teased, nodding at her.

"Not as much as you are," she said, smiling. A thick coat of dust covered Reb from head to toe, and without any forethought, Sage moistened one index finger, reaching out and running it down the solid muscles of his chest. Holding the finger up for him to inspect she said, "See?" But Reb's smile had faded instantly, his eyes narrowing as he stared at her.

Abruptly, he reached out and caught her wrist in his hand as if to keep her from touching him again.

Slowly, he shook his head, whispering, "No, no, no."

Sage was horrified! How could she have been so forward, so indecent? Before he could reprimand her further, she opened her mouth to apologize, but the words never left her throat. In the next instant, Reb's grip on her wrist tightened, pushing her hand down and holding it at her back. His other hand rather roughly cupped her cheek, pulling her face to his as his mouth descended on her own in a firm, moist, very intimate kiss.

Sage stood stiff, frozen with astonishment. Not having experienced such moments in her life, she was surprised by Reb's unexpected attention and entirely awe-struck by the demanding, passionate nature of his kiss. The space inside her chest burned hot, uncomfortably so. Her fingers and toes were numb, her knees weak. Every inch of her body, even her hair, seemed to quiver with some euphoric tingling sensation!

Reb's hand, holding hers at her back, released her wrist, joining his other hand in cradling her face. The whiskers of his mustache and goatee, brushed the flesh around her mouth softly, and Sage's mind began to whirl in a mist of enchanted emotion. Her knees were weak. Reb's driven, delicious kiss bewitching her, she let her hands press gently against his chest. His mouth pressed even more firmly to hers for a lingering moment before he suddenly broke the seal of their lips, taking her hands in his and letting his thumbs caress her palms as he looked down at them.

Abruptly, he dropped her hands, turned and loosened the cinch of the lame horse's saddle.

"I better clean up a bit before I come in for breakfast," he mumbled. Sage stood still for a moment, struggling to steady her breathing and to find her balance. She felt dizzy, almost faint . . . the lingering affects of Reb's masterful kiss.

Finally, she managed to stammer, "I'll . . . I'll go check on things in the house." Quickly, she exited the barn, a trembling mess of conflicting emotion, and headed for the ranch house. Glancing up to the blue sky, she wished the puffy, white clouds setting so happily there would turn dark and ominous. She could feel the tears gathering in her eyes, tears of elation, tears of confusion, and tears of heartache.

What had happened in the barn? Reb had kissed her! But why? She had only touched him with one finger, only meant to tease him about the layer of dust clinging thick to his skin. She thought of his kiss again and stumbled, her feet still numb from his affectionate attention. And yet, something was wrong. With all that was right in the day, something was terribly wrong. Reb deeply regretted kissing her. She knew it. She wanted to run, to run all the way to Ruthie's pasture, throw herself on the ground and sob bitter tears of disappointment and confusion. But there would be no rain today.

"Bacon's all fried up, Sage," Livie said as Sage stumbled onto the porch.

"That's nice," Sage mumbled, brushing past her.

"You all right, honey?" Eugenia asked, sincere concern apparent on her face.

Sage forced a half-hearted smile. "Just not used to ridin' much anymore, I reckon," she said.

Ↄↄ

REB DRAPED HIS arms across the gelding's back, laying his head against the animal for a moment. What had he been thinking? One touch and his defenses had failed him. One slight caress from one of Sage's pretty fingers and his mind had emptied of any memory of Ivy Dalton.

He closed his eyes tightly and tried to recall the exact shape of Ivy's face, the perfect sunshine of her hair. All he could see was the lovely face of Sage Willows, her hair wind-blown and untidy, dust smudges on her nose and chin, the soft pink of joy on her cheeks. He stood straight, rubbing at the whiskers on his chin. What a kiss he had forced on her! Not some sweet, careful kiss like he had first given Ivy so long ago. No, he had really stepped in it, too tempted by the lure of her innocently parted lips, tasting her mouth without pause.

He looked down to the one clean streak of flesh on his chest, the place where her finger had traveled over it. Shaking his head, he swore angrily under his breath. It was time to reorder, restock his resistances. She wouldn't get to him again, wouldn't break through his emotional barricades.

Spitting in his hand, he rubbed at his chest, rinsing away the dust and vanquishing Sage's mark over his heart. Reb Mitchell had no heart. Not one made of flesh anyway. Still, as he walked to the creek to wash up with the others, he couldn't get Sage's face out of his mind, couldn't drive the sweet savor of her kiss from his lips. One touch was all it had taken. One.

Chapter Five

ଆ ଓଃ

"Saw some big cat tracks down by the crick there, Reb," Charlie Dugger said as he folded up another piece of bacon and popped it into his mouth.

"What?" Eugenia exclaimed.

Sage glanced at Reb. He nodded and breathed a heavy sigh. She quickly looked away, however, uncomfortable in his presence because of what had just happened in the barn.

"Yep. I saw 'em the other day, too," Reb admitted.

"Reb!" Eugenia said. "Why didn't you tell me?"

"He knew ya'd worry yerself to death," Mary answered. Eugenia looked to Mary, her mouth gaping open in astonishment.

"You knew?" Eugenia asked.

Mary nodded and said, "Gareth Getcher told me yesterday the Phillips found their dog all chewed up last week—figured it was a mountain lion by the tracks 'round its bloody carcass."

"Oh, for Pete's sake, Mary," Livie whined. "You've completely ruined my appetite."

"Ya done ate a half a pound a bacon on yer own while we was cookin' this mornin', Livie," Mary grumbled. "I 'spect ya'll live."

Eugenia covered Reb's hand with her own and said, "Is that why you looked so upset when you come up from the crick just now, boy? Are you worried about the cattle?"

Sage looked up to Reb, but immediately shifted her focus when his narrowed, angry-looking eyes met hers for a moment.

"Yep," Reb said. "Don't need a cat spookin' the herd."

"This here's the finest meal I've had in weeks, ladies," one of the cowboys said, smiling as he shoveled another bite of eggs into his mouth.

"Well, you boys look so nice and fresh after bathin' in the crick, we thought we'd fatten ya up some, too," Rosie told him.

A bevy of compliments followed as each hungry, and no doubt tired, cowboy said his thanks. Even the old chuck wagon driver seemed happy to eat something besides his own cooking.

Sage thought how tired they all must be, how sore their bodies were from being on the trail so long. Still, her mind was alive with confusion over what had happened between her and Reb in the barn. It had been fabulous! It had been heartbreaking, too. What had prompted Reb to act so strangely, so unpredictably? She thought of the feel of his mouth pressed to hers, the smell of his skin. She closed her eyes for a moment, trying to dispel the image of his handsome face, the way he had looked the moment before kissing her.

"You all right, Sage?" Eugenia was asking. Sage's eyes popped open and she forced a smile.

"I'm fine," she lied, noting the way Reb's eyes lingered on her suspiciously. "Just wishin' I had a fresh dress. This dust is chokin' me."

℘℔

EUGENIA STUDIED SAGE for a moment. Something was wrong. She looked to Reb. She sensed unrest in him, too. Had something happened during their ride out to meet the herd? She was certain it had.

"Well," she began, "we'll finish up breakfast for these hungry boys and get back to the boardin' house so you can freshin' up."

"Unless ya wanna run on down to the crick and . . ." Mary began.

"No, no," Sage interrupted. "I'll be fine."

🙰

MARY COULD BE so exasperating at times. Sage tried not to blush as she felt every pair of cowboy eyes in the room settle on her.

"We seen Ivy Dalton in town 'for we left, Reb," one of the cowboys said. Sage saw Charlie nudge the man with his elbow, frowning at him.

"Did ya now?" Reb mumbled.

"How is Ivy?" Eugenia asked. After glancing at Reb, who shrugged his shoulders in a gesture of indifference, it was Charlie who answered.

"Oh, she ain't changed much, Miss Eugenia. Not much at all," he said.

"Well, that doesn't surprise me one bit," Eugenia mumbled.

"You boys can take to the bunkhouse as soon as yer ready," Reb said, obviously uncomfortable with the conversation. Sage felt her heart begin to hammer with anxiety. At the mere mention of the name, Ivy Dalton, Reb had turned pale, angry, and he clearly wanted the subject hushed. "I'll check on the herd and meet ya out there later on to pay ya yer wages." He stood, ready to leave the table, but paused. "That was a hard trail, boys," he said. "I thank ya for yer help and hard work. Enjoy the rest of yer breakfast now, all right?"

The men all nodded and thanked him in return. He then simply left the room without another word.

"Seems to me the name Ivy Dalton don't set too well with Reb," Mary whispered to Sage. "Must be some history there, I reckon."

Sage glanced at Charlie Dugger. He smiled and nodded at her, a rather guilty expression on his handsome face. He had known darn well Reb didn't want to hear tell of Ivy Dalton and that fact drove Sage's curiosity to a peak.

"You stayin' on, Charlie?" Eugenia asked.

"Yes, ma'am," the man answered, running his fingers through his dark hair. "Plan on helpin' Reb out as long as he'll have me."

Eugenia smiled and said, "I'm sure he's plum tickled to have you."

"Hope so, ma'am," he said, smiling. Looking to Sage, he said, "Do ya run that boardin' house in town then, Miss Willows?" Sage smiled. He was a charming man, good-looking, too, not as handsome and not as charming, perhaps, as Reb, but sweet all the same. He looked somewhat older than the other cowboys, more mature, with a bit of gray at his temples.

"Yes, I do, Mr. Dugger," Sage answered. "It fell to me when my parents passed on some years back."

"Well, it's a nice lookin' place," Charlie said.

"It is," Sage said. "You'll have to come out for supper with us one night."

"I'd like that, Miss Willows," he said, smiling.

Sage smiled. She liked this Charlie Dugger. Furthermore, Reb seemed to like him, trust him, and he seemed to know an awful lot more than she did about their mutual acquaintance. Yes, it might be to her great advantage to befriend Charlie.

CR

REB SLAMMED A fist into a fencepost. Angrily unbuttoning his shirt—for he had managed to remember his manners and put a shirt on after returning from the creek—he breathed a heavy sigh and looked over the herd before him. How could such a wonderful morning have turned on him so quickly? He thought of how his spirit soared when he had first seen the herd, of how wonderful it was to see Sage smiling, her soft hair so wind-blown and free. He closed his eyes and remembered the feel of her face between his hands, the flavor of her kiss. She had been distressed by his kiss, he knew. She was inexperienced as well, uncertain of how to go about returning such a driven attack on her tender lips. It was further proof of his being completely damaged, worthless to anyone outside his family and tight circle of friends. He couldn't even offer a woman a decent kiss anymore.

He sighed again and patted Bullet's head as the dog settled at his feet. At least Charlie was with him now. Charlie would help him keep his head screwed on straight, help keep him from getting distracted by that delicious Sage Willows. He grimaced, guilt washing over him as he thought of Sage, hiding her own kind of heartache. Although he didn't fully understand what things in life now haunted her, he suspected it was pure disappointment, for the most part. She had sacrificed her own happiness to ensure that of her younger sisters. Those kinds of sacrifices scared a woman, left her lonely and hopeless, no matter how strong and independent she might appear.

Turning, he walked toward the creek. Well, he surely wasn't the man to fill her lonely heart. He thought again of Ivy, beautiful Ivy, Ivy and her heartbreaking ways. He would keep thinking of Ivy too, let Ivy's memory stop him from making another mistake with Sage like the one in the barn. "Ivy," he mumbled, as Bullet barked once, begging for attention. "Ivy," Reb whispered again. He frowned, disturbed by the fact that he could not clearly recall the young woman's face.

"WHAT'S ON YOUR mind, sweet pea?" Eugenia asked, sitting down across the table from Sage. Sage hadn't been herself since the day Reb's herd arrived over a week before. Although Eugenia was hoping her nephew would bring about a change in her young friend, further despair was not the change she had hoped for.

Sage shrugged her shoulders and said, "Just . . . just a little too hot today, I suppose." Eugenia's eyes narrowed as she looked at Sage.

"It is pretty warm today," Eugenia agreed. Sighing, she said, "I saw Charlie Dugger in at Mr. Getcher's today."

"Really?" Sage said.

"Yep. Seems him and Reb have the herd settled in. They did see an old mountain lion out in the east acreage yesterday," Eugenia said.

"Oh, no! Are they worried for the herd?" Sage asked.

"For the calves, mostly," Eugenia said. "Charlie says the cat looks old. Probably come down from the hills looking for easy prey. Bud Phillips had another dog go missing a few days back."

"Doesn't make me feel very safe," Sage mumbled.

"You might want to be careful goin' out to Ruth's grave 'til someone brings that cat down," Eugenia suggested. Then, taking a deep breath and mustering her courage, she said, "Boy, Reb sure got upset when that cowpoke mentioned Ivy Dalton the other day out at the ranch, didn't he?" Sage's eyes instantly lit up, her expression that of extreme curiosity.

"Yes," she said. "I . . . I had the feeling there was . . . well, some history there."

"Ooooh, yeah," Eugenia admitted, raising her eyebrows. "History would be the word for it." Eugenia looked at Sage. The girl was desperately interested.

"Well?" Sage urged impatiently. When Eugenia paused, Sage said, "Oh, come on, Miss Eugenia. You and Livie'll gossip 'til the cows come home usually. Are you tryin' to have me believe ya don't want to share what you know?" Eugenia smiled, delighted by Sage's excited interest.

"Well," Eugenia began, leaning forward across the table and lowering her voice, " by the time Ivy Dalton was sixteen, she was the prettiest girl for three counties. Beautiful blonde hair, porcelain skin, and the deepest brown eyes anybody ever saw." Sage glanced away, obviously disappointed in hearing of the girl's physical perfection. "Anyway," Eugenia continued, "she was plum gone on Reb for most of her life, and when she hit courtin' age, he finally set up and took notice of her." Eugenia shook her head. "That girl chased after Reb somethin' embarrassin'. A finer flirt you never did see, and Reb eventually fell prey to her charms, courted her for near to three years before proposin' to her, though. I always thought his waitin' so long was a bit suspicious on Reb's part, a mark of uncertainty. Do you know what I mean?" Sage nodded, but Eugenia could tell the story of Ivy Dalton was upsetting her. Still, if the girl were ever going to understand Rebel Lee Mitchell and his often unpredictable behavior, she had to have all the checkers on her board.

"Anyhow, Reb was pretty smitten. He really loved Ivy and so he asked her to marry him and she said she would," Eugenia explained. "But that Ivy—oh, she loved Reb—I don't doubt it for a moment. I think she loved him in a frightenin' manner, really. So much she thought he loved her just as frightenin', thought nothin' could ever change his mind about her." Eugenia paused, noting the way Sage shifted uncomfortably in her chair, an unhappy frown puckering her brow.

"Ivy figured if she could capture Reb Mitchell's heart, well then, it stood to reason she could catch any man she put her mind to," Eugenia said. "So she took to flirtin' with anything wearin' a pair of blue jeans under the age of fifty. But Reb wouldn't have it. He ain't like that. He's true, loyal and strong, and he told Ivy he wouldn't have her flirtin' around with every man in town the way she'd taken to doin'." Eugenia batted her eyelashes and raised her voice to a sickenly sweet tone. "Oh, Reb!" Eugenia said, imitating the girl. "You wouldn't want me to go through life wonderin' if I married the only man worthy of me, would you?"

"You're teasin' me, Miss Eugenia!" Sage exclaimed with disgust. Eugenia shook her head.

"Nope. That's what she told him," Eugenia said. "Well, Reb really loved Ivy, I believe, really loved her until that very moment. But Reb's pretty good about keepin' his wits about him and he told her, 'No,' he didn't want her goin' through life wonderin' if he was the only man worthy of her. He wanted her goin' through life already knowin' it. She lost everythin' that day, lost the best man in the world. Reb told her they were through. Took back the ring he'd bought for her, closed up his heart and went into the cattle business."

"And . . . and she just let him go? As easy as that?" Sage asked. Eugenia shook her head.

"Oh, no! She begged him, pleaded with him, told him she was sorry, that she was just tryin' to make sure he loved her. But Reb had wised up. I don't mean he isn't the kind to not forgive; he just isn't stupid. Ivy took up with a local cowpoke named Joe Stone, all the while beggin' Reb to take her back, tellin' him it was his fault she'd taken up with Joe, Reb's fault for breakin' her heart."

"But you . . . you don't think she really loved Reb?" Sage asked.

"Oh, I think she loved him all right . . . in a downright unhealthy manner. But she was bad through and through all the same," Eugenia explained. "And that's probably what hurt Reb the most, that he'd fallen for that kind of a woman. Bad thing is, I think he's convinced himself that all women are like Ivy, insincere, not to be trusted, incapable of lovin' him and nobody but."

ᙍ

I'D LOVE HIM and nobody but, Sage thought to herself. She was grateful for Eugenia's telling her about Ivy Dalton and Reb. The story seemed to explain so much, from his confusing behavior in the barn to his reasons for not falling prey to the flirting ways of Milly Michaels. She could understand his distrust after having his heart betrayed and broken. Her own heart ached for him, for although she hadn't shared the same kind of experience, she understood heartache and she loathed Ivy Dalton.

"Well, I'm glad he finally saw her for what she was," Sage said. "He had a narrow escape. Imagine bein' saddled with that kind of a woman for your entire life."

"True," Eugenia agreed. "But I worry it ruined him for any other woman, all the same."

Sage sighed and thought of the blissful moments she had spent in Reb's arms in the barn. Reb Mitchell was the finest man she had ever known. He was kind, caring, strong, handsome, intelligent and funny, and although her heart ached for his pain, she was glad Reb hadn't married Ivy Dalton. If he had, she would have never known so many breathless moments in his presence. Still, it would take a unique woman to heal his heart, and Sage regretted not being unique enough to do it herself.

"Oh, someone will come along someday, Miss Eugenia," Sage sighed wistfully. "Some pretty young girl with a fresh innocent heart."

"Well," Eugenia said, placing one of her hands in Sage's, "you're a pretty, young girl with a . . ." Sage pulled her hand away from Eugenia's and stood up from the table.

"I'm none of those things, Miss Eugenia," Sage told her. "And I'm not blind either. You'd like nothin' more than to see Reb save me from bein' the town spinster . . . but . . ."

"Oh, nonsense, Sage!" Eugenia argued, rising from the table herself. "Spinster, my fanny, girl! You're all of twenty-three years old!" Sage shook her head, which was beginning to pound.

"Let's don't discuss it anymore, please, Miss Eugenia," Sage said. "I . . . I need to take a walk before I start supper. Reverend Tippetts and the others will be here earlier tonight. Rosie invited them all for cards."

"Um . . . Sage?" Eugenia began. Sage turned and looked at her. The older woman wore a guilty, timid expression.

"Yes?" Sage urged, nervous to hear what she had to say. Surely she realized Sage didn't want to talk about Reb Mitchell and Ivy Dalton anymore.

"I . . . I plum forgot to tell you," Eugenia stammered. "I invited Reb and Charlie out for supper tonight, too. You always fix us so much when Scarlett and the reverend are out and I didn't think you'd mind. Do you?"

Sage felt her innards begin to tremble. Of course she minded! She needed more time, not for preparing supper, but for preparing herself to face Reb again. Still, she forced a smile.

"Of course I don't mind, Miss Eugenia," she lied. "But . . . I really do need some fresh air."

"Thank you, Sage," Eugenia said. "I just worry about them boys eatin' nothin' but hard tack and jerky all the time. It isn't healthy."

"I know," Sage agreed. "It's fine. I'll be back shortly." She left by way of the back door, pausing to pinch a few leaves of sage from one of the plants in the barrel.

🕉

DRIFTER SEEMED TO enjoy the hot, dry air of summer as much as Sage did. Still, he was thirsty when they finally reached the creek bed. Sage tied his reins to a nearby piñon, still pinching the sage leaves between her fingers and inhaling their fragrance as she strolled toward Ruthie's grave. As she walked up over the hill, she gasped. She saw Reb. He was putting the finishing touches on a new fence surrounding Ruthie's gravesite.

Sage wondered how long he had been there, working to protect Ruthie from the destruction which might be caused by grazing cattle. It was obvious Reb had taken great care in constructing the fence, for it had nine posts in its square and the wire was pulled taught and straight. It wasn't a tall fence, by any means. It wasn't much higher than Reb's waist. Sage realized her breathing had stopped. She hoped he wouldn't turn and see her before she had a chance to escape down the backside of the hill. However, her hopes were vanquished as Reb's gelding stomped the ground, causing the man to look up see of her.

"Sage," he called out, waving to her with one hand, indicating she should join him. "What do ya think?"

Sage swallowed hard and forced herself to walk toward him. The last time she had seen him was the morning the herd had arrived at the ranch, before he left the breakfast table after squelching the conversation about Ivy Dalton. He had been angry then, but seemed happy enough now.

"I wanted to make sure ya didn't feel she was bein' smothered by this new fence," he said as she approached. "So I kept it open and a ways away from the other little fence. Think it's all right?"

Sage forced a smile and nodded. "It's perfect," said. "Thank you . . . for goin' to all the trouble."

Reb smiled and said, "Ain't no trouble. Yer doin' me a favor by lettin' me run my herd out here. Remember? Look here," he said, slipping between two posts sunk close together with no wire strung between them. "No gate to mess with. Ya just slip right though these two. I sunk 'em far enough apart so a person can get through easy, but a cow can't get more than a head in." Sage smiled and followed him between the two posts. "I was worried this new fence might make ya feel too closed in. What do ya think?" It was the third time he had asked her for her opinion.

"I think it's perfect," she said.

He breathed a sigh of relief. "I'm mighty glad to hear that. Been workin' on it all day," he said.

"Thank you," Sage said.

Reb nodded and smiled, but a moment later his eyes narrowed and his smile faded. "I . . . I was hopin' it would turn out good enough that maybe you'd forgive me for the other day," he said. Sage looked away from him, feeling a blush instantly rise to her cheeks. "I was just . . . just so glad to see the herd come in and I . . ."

"It's fine, Reb," Sage interrupted, turning toward the gate leading to Ruthie's grave. The kiss in the barn had been the stuff of dreams, and she knew if Reb were to apologize to her, the memory would be tainted. She wanted to pretend he had wanted to kiss her, enjoyed kissing her, might kiss her again one day. If he told her it was a mistake, told her it would never happen again, then . . .

"But it ain't fine, Sage," he said, interrupting her thoughts and catching her hand in his. She looked up to him, afraid she might not be able to hold back her tears were his apology to be a long one. "We've come to be good friends, Sage . . . and I don't want ya thinkin' . . ."

"I'm not thinkin' anythin'," she lied, turning from him. He held tight to her hand, however.

"Yes, ya are!" he argued. "Yer thinkin' I'm disrespectful of ya somehow. But I ain't. I just . . . I just lost my head for a minute. I was so dang happy to see the herd finally come in. And I don't want ya to think I'm gonna take to slobberin' on ya all the time the same way Bullet does."

Sage looked at him. He seemed so concerned, so desperate she forgive him. Yet, she was saddened. She liked the idea of his "slobbering" all over her, if what had happened in the barn was his definition of it. He had done exactly what she had feared he would. He was apologizing for the kiss.

"Are ya gonna forgive me?" he asked. Sage forced a smile.

"There's nothin' to forgive," she told him. He smiled, seeming relieved. He nodded, squeezing her hand for reassurance.

"Thank ya, Sage," he said, still holding her hand. "But there is one more thing," he added. He looked down at her hand, taking the sage leaves from her fingers and waving them under his nose before stuffing them in his shirt pocket.

"What's that?" she asked. In truth, she simply wanted the conversation to end. She wished the rain would come and give her its permission to cry.

"Well," he began, raising her hand to his face and rubbing her fingertips over his mustache as he sniffed their sage fragrance. "I done a right terrible job of kissin' ya, too."

Startled by his words, Sage pulled her hand from his grasp and turned toward Ruthie's grave. Whatever was he talking about? His kissing her had been the most wonderful moment of her life. How could he possibly think otherwise? Furthermore, the sound of his voice even uttering the word "kissin'" caused her skin to tingle.

"I hope ya'll forgive me for that, too," he said. "And that ya'll give me a chance at doin' a better job of it someday."

Sage felt her mouth drop open in astonishment as she whirled around to face him. Her heart was pounding madly and she could feel her palms begin to perspire.

"What?" she whispered.

Reb chuckled and said, "Oh, quit lookin' like yer gonna drop dead. I'm just funnin' with ya."

"Hey, there!" Charlie Dugger called, reining in next to the fence at that very moment. "Howdy, Miss Sage," he greeted. "Fence looks good, Reb."

Reb winked at Sage as he said, "Yep. It come out fine."

"I'm lookin' forward to supper tonight, Miss Sage," Charlie told her. He dismounted and squeezed between the fence posts to join them.

"I'm . . . I'm lookin' forward to havin' you, Mr. Dugger," Sage stammered. She was still rattled from her conversation with Reb.

"Call me, Charlie," he told her, taking one of her hands in his, raising it to his lips, and kissing the back tenderly. Sage smiled, delighted by his gesture.

"Well, ain't we just all propered up today?" Reb chuckled.

"Don't mind him, Miss Sage," Charlie said, linking her arm through his. "He spends too much time wallerin' with the hogs to have a stitch of manners left in him."

"What time ya want us in for supper, Sage?" Reb asked.

"Well," she began, distracted by the way Charlie kept smiling at her. "The others will be over about five tonight. There's a mad game of rummy planned."

"I'll follow ya home right now, if ya want, Miss Sage," Charlie flirted. Sage giggled. He was a charming man.

"Can't afford to have ya do that, Charlie," Reb said. "I already got Bullet, thanks to Sage here. Don't think I can handle another one of her mutts."

"Oh! That reminds me," Charlie said. "Ol' Bullet was barkin' to the moon earlier this mornin'. I took a look out by the crick, but didn't find nothin'."

Reb scowled and nodded. "That ol' cat's just a waitin' for a calf to wander close enough," Reb mumbled. "I think we need to hunt him down in the next couple of days. I don't want to lose any stock." Reb looked to Sage a worried frown puckering his brow. "You be careful comin' out here alone, Sage."

"Of course, I will," she said. "I'm always careful."

"No ya ain't," Reb argued. "I've seen ya out here more'n once when I coulda walked up behind ya and ya never woulda known I was there 'til it was too late."

"Too late for what?" Sage asked. She was irritated two-fold by the fact he had been near when she was visiting Ruthie and hadn't shown himself, and by the fact he was implying she couldn't take care of herself.

"Ya saw me comin' in the barn, Sage. I didn't sneak up on ya or nothin'," he said, lowering his voice. "And look what happened there." Sage felt herself blush and glanced away from him, dropping her arm from Charlie's.

"I can take care of myself," she said.

"I don't know what happened in the barn, Miss Sage," Charlie said. "But Reb's right. That ol' cat's hungry and desperate. Ya be careful, now." Sage smiled at Charlie, pleased by his concern.

"I always am, Charlie," she said. "Supper's at six tonight, unless you want a round of rummy with the ladies at five."

Charlie chuckled, "Oh, I don't think so, Miss Sage! I heard tell of them ladies and their card games. I'd stand a better chance 'gainst that ol' mountain lion."

"We'll leave ya to yer pasture, Sage," Reb said, rather gruffly. "Hope the fence will do."

"Six this evein' then, Miss Sage," Charlie said, touching the brim of his hat as he slipped between the posts. Sage smiled at him and nodded in return. Charlie mounted his horse and said, "See ya back at the house, Reb." He rode off, leaving Sage feeling quite cheerful.

"Those ladies need a little schoolin'," Reb said. "One of these days

I'll just have to show them a thing or two 'bout playin' cards." He seemed irritated. Sage guessed he had simply spent too much time in her company. He gathered his tools together and stuffed them in his saddle-bags. He mounted his horse and touched the brim of his hat. "Lookin' forward to supper, Sage," he said. He turned and rode away without another word.

Sage frowned. Reb's manner had changed so quickly from that of friendly flirtation to irritation. For a moment, she wondered if perhaps Charlie's attention to her had caused his sudden change in mood, but she shook her head, knowing it was impossible.

"You're sproutin' weeds faster than I can keep up," she said to Ruthie as she knelt down and began weeding. Still, as hard as she tried to concentrate on weeding, Sage's thoughts kept returning to the conversation she was having with Reb before Charlie arrived. She smiled, a delightful shiver traveling up her spine as she thought of how he had teased her about kissing her again. Oh, she well knew he was merely teasing her, trying to soften the discomfort between them. Still, the very idea thrilled her. In truth, even though he had been teasing, it gave her hope, hope that perhaps he would kiss her again someday.

❧

"CHARLIE!" REB CALLED. Charlie looked over his shoulder, reining in as he waited for Reb to catch up with him. "What ya doin' flirtin' with Sage that way, boy?"

Charlie laughed. "Me? Oh, I was just seein' how far gone ya are on her already."

Reb chuckled, shook his head and said, "Yer dreamin' things, my friend. Sage Willows is just a friend of my aunt's."

"Don't be tryin' to pull my leg, Reb. I know ya better than yer own mama knows ya," Charlie said.

"I still got too much Ivy wrapped around my head, Charlie. And ya know it," Reb reminded his friend.

"Maybe," Charlie admitted. "But it's not yer head I'm thinkin' of. It's yer heart."

Reb chuckled again. "I ain't got no heart, Charlie. Just a cold piece of a stone where a heart should be."

Charlie nodded, saying, "And my left arm here? Ain't really there neither." He chuckled. "What happened in the barn that she didn't see comin', Reb?" Reb smiled and shook his head, glad to have his friend back with him.

"The touch of Sage, Charlie," he said. "Just the touch of Sage."

Chapter Six

ಳಿ ೞ

"**N**ow, for Pete's Sake, Rose," Mary grumbled. "Don't be showin' yer bloomers to Reverend Tippetts and Winnery if a miracle should happen and ya win a hand or two this evenin'."

"Oh, Mary," Livie said. "Rosie only shows her bloomers to us. You know that."

"Well," Mary said, placing the deck of cards in the middle of the parlor table. "It don't hurt none to remind her now and then."

"First of all, Mary," Rose began, "I'll show my bloomer ruffles to anybody I darn well choose." Sage smiled as she saw Mary's eyes narrow, her jaw tight with determination. "And second, Scarlett Tippetts herself was a dance hall girl before . . ."

"Before she married the reverend. I know, I know," Mary interrupted. "But ya don't see Scarlett aflashin' her bloomers."

"How do you know she don't, Mary?" Rose asked. "Are you with her every livin' minute of the day?"

"Settle down, ladies," Eugenia giggled. "Everyone will be here shortly and we don't want you two bickerin' when they arrive."

Rose smiled and said, "All right, Eugenia. I won't let Mary get under my skin." However, she threw her skirt up over her back and wiggled her behind in Mary's direction. "Wearin' my pink bloomers tonight, Mary," she said. "The ones with the red ruffles."

"Oh, for cryin' in the bucket," Mary grumbled. Still, Sage could see the gruff old woman fighting a smile.

"I'm startin' to smell those pies, Sage," Livie said. "Mmmmm! Like the perfume of heaven."

"They do smell delicious," Sage agreed. Peach cobbler was Sage's favorite. The peach trees in the orchard were heavy with ripe, delicious fruit, and she couldn't resist making a couple of cobblers as an after-supper treat for her guests. Secretly, she hoped Reb would be as impressed with her peach cobbler as he was with her sage stuffing.

After returning from Ruthie's pasture, Sage had worked extra hard on her supper preparations. Tuesdays were always special, but with Reb and Charlie in the guest mix now, she wanted to serve an excellent meal, not just a good one. She had made sage stuffing, fried up a heap of chicken parts, snapped fresh green beans from the garden, sliced up a few ripe tomatoes, and baked up some potatoes, all slathered in butter and rosemary. The peach cobblers, still baking in the oven, would top off the evening perfectly.

A knock on the front door signaled the arrival of Reverend Tippetts and his counterparts, and soon the evening was light with laughter and friendship.

"The smell of them cobblers turns my mouth to waterin' somethin' fierce, Miss Sage," Reverend Tippetts said as he waited for Livie to deal the cards.

"I hope they taste as good as they smell," Sage said.

"Oh, I'm sure they'll taste even better," the reverend chuckled. As Livie finished dealing the cards, he said, "Why don't you ladies give ol' Winnery a chance at winnin' this hand. He ain't quite the rummy player . . . not like he is at poker anyway."

"Mr. Winnery?" Eugenia asked. "Do you want us to cheat for you?"

"No, ma'am," the tall man mumbled. "I'll get to winnin' soon enough."

Sage drew a card and discarded another.

"Don't let them fool you, Mr. Winnery," she said. "They only cheat for themselves."

"Sage!" Livie gasped. "How can you accuse us of cheating with the reverend sitting right here?"

"Oh, the reverend cheats well enough to take care of himself, Livie," Scarlett said, winking in her husband's direction.

"Reverend Tippetts!" Rose exclaimed. "Is that true?" Reverend Tippetts shook his head and chuckled.

"Not in the company of ladies, Miss Applewhite," he said.

"We dusted off at the back door," Reb said as he and Charlie entered the parlor. "Hope ya don't mind us just showin' ourselves in, Sage." Sage's hands began to tremble slightly at his sudden appearance.

"Oh, no. Of course not," she managed.

"We heard all the laughin' and goin's on and didn't want to break up yer game," Charlie said. "Charlie Dugger," he added, offering his hand to Reverend Tippetts.

Reverend Tippetts shook Charlie's hand and said, "Nice to meet ya, Charlie. This here's my wife, Scarlett, and my ol' saddle pal, Winnery."

"Ma'am. Mr. Winnery," Charlie said, nodding to the others.

"Is that peach pie I smell, Sage?" Reb asked, going to his aunt and affectionately kissing the top of her head. Sage couldn't help but smile. She loved the way he doted on his aunt.

"Peach cobbler, actually," Sage answered.

"Even better! I told ya we was in for a treat, Charlie," Reb told his friend. "Ain't nothin' like supper at the boardin' house." Sage's insides fluttered, pleased at his compliment and enchanted by his handsome smile. He walked over to Sage's chair, leaned over until his face was very near her ear and asked, "Any stuffin' beforehand?"

"Maybe," Sage giggled. His breath on her cheek caused the hair on the back of her neck to tingle and she sighed, for it seemed all was well between them once again. Thinking of his kissing her in the barn still caused her heart to hammer, but at least he no longer seemed angry.

"You boys want to join the game?" Reverend Tippetts asked.

"No thank ya, reverend," Reb said. "At least, not me. I think I'll just sit down and watch the goin's on for now."

"Me, too," Charlie agreed, sighing and revealing his fatigued state. "I'm tuckered out from the day.

"You boys been workin' hard gettin' that herd all settled in and such?" Winnery asked.

"Yes, sir," Reb answered.

"And now we got that ol' cat to worry about," Charlie added.

"Gareth Getcher told me just this afternoon that he's missin' a couple of cats," Scarlett said.

"Ain't natural for a man to have more'n one cat anyhow," Mary mumbled

"Mary!" Rose exclaimed.

"Cats are for old ladies and little girls," Mary added.

"Don't pay her any mind, Scarlett," Livie said. "She's just mad because she's lost two hands in a row." Scarlett smiled, obviously amused.

✑

"MMMM!" EUGENIA SIGHED. "Them cobblers are smellin' delicious!"

"My cobblers!" Sage exclaimed, leaping to her feet. "I've burnt them for certain," she said, rushing toward the kitchen. Eugenia smiled, delighted that Reb's arrival had distracted Sage so completely.

"Go on in and give her a hand, will you, Reb?" she said, patting Reb's knee affectionately. "She'll be in a tizzy all night long if those cobblers burn."

"Well, we don't want Sage in a tizzy, now do we?" he chuckled, rising from his seat on the sofa and striding toward the kitchen.

✑

"NEED SOME HELP?" Reb asked as he entered the room. Sage had just opened the oven door to see the cobblers were, indeed, finished baking.

They weren't over-baked, but another moment in the heat of the oven would find the top crusts too brown.

"Quick!" Sage said, snapping her fingers at him as she realized she had taken her apron off when the first supper guests had arrived. "Hand me somethin' to take them out with. Should be a towel hangin' somewhere or an apron." Almost immediately Reb handed her a wad of white cloth, and Sage quickly took the first cobbler from the oven, setting it on the stovetop. Then she removed the others. "Thank you," she told him as she went to the table and set the cobbler on a wooden cooling rack. Returning to retrieve the other cobbler from the stovetop, she added, "One more minute and they'd have been ruined. Completely ruined!"

Sighing, as she studied the perfectly golden crusts of the cobblers, she wiped her hands on the cloth Reb had handed her. "Now, for a little butter and sugar and . . ." But her words caught in her throat as she turned to see Reb standing before her completely bare from the waist up. Gasping, she held up the cloth she had used to retrieve the cobblers from the oven, blocking her view of him. Oh, she had seen Reb Mitchell without his shirt plenty of times, even been kissed by him in the barn when he was in a similar state of undress. But in the kitchen of her own home, with the Reverend Tippetts in the very next room—it was indecent!

"Let's just skip the butter," Reb said. Then, dropping his voice, he leaned forward, pulled the top of the cloth down and, smiling at her, said, ". . . and head straight for the sugar."

Sage could not stop the crimson blush rising to her cheeks as she stammered, "Where . . . where on earth is your shirt, Reb Mitchell?"

Reb chuckled, pulling the cloth from her hands. "Ya said to hand ya somethin' to get the cobblers out with."

"I meant a towel, an apron or the like," Sage explained, putting a trembling hand to her throat and trying not to stare at his muscular chest and arms. Somehow, his standing in her kitchen in such a state unsettled her far more than it did when he was out at the ranch house working.

"Well, I don't know where ya keep yer towels and aprons, and you were in such an all-fired-up hurry, I just grabbed the first thing that come to mind," he explained.

"Well . . . well, for pity's sake, put your shirt back on before someone comes in here and sees ya like this," Sage ordered, unable to meet his gaze.

However, when Reb chuckled, she glanced up at him to find an all-too-amused grin on his handsome face as he said, "Did ya get it all sticky with peach cobbler juice?"

"For cryin' in the bucket, Reb!" Sage exclaimed in a whisper as she hurried to the window and pulled the curtains closed. "You can't run around the boardinghouse half . . ." Again Sage's scolding words were silenced as she turned to see Reb had advanced on her. He now stood directly in front of her, so close she could feel the warmth of his breath in her hair. Trying to calm her quickened breathing, trying to still the mad rhythm in her heart, she took two steps sideways intending to step around him. But it was apparent he was enjoying her discomfort far too much and he simply matched her steps, even going so far as to take another step toward her. A mere inch of emptiness spanned the space between his body and her own, and Sage's entire being began to tremble. Visions of the kiss he had given her in his barn began to fill her mind and her entire being began to burn warm at the memory.

"What . . . what're you doin', Reb?" she asked him, though still unable to look up and meet his gaze.

"Oh . . . I'm like that ol' mountain lion. I'm just stalkin' my prey, that's all," he mumbled.

Sage's body was trembling so violently she was certain Reb could see it. Rebel Mitchell was far too improper. To say such things to her! And in her very own kitchen! Whatever was he thinking, anyway? Hadn't they just that very day made their peace about the kiss in the barn? Had he already forgotten his regret at having kissed her then?

"You are a terrible tease, Reb Mitchell," she said, finding the courage to look up into his face. "Now . . . now finish putting your shirt on before someone walks in here and thinks . . ."

"I'll put my shirt on when I'm darn good and ready, Miss Willows," he said in a whisper. As he reached back to tuck the shirt in the waist of his trousers, Sage made a quick attempt to step around him. But Reb was quicker and took hold of her arm, pinning her gently against the wall.

Sage's breath quickened, she felt dizzy and weak as he whispered, "Now . . . what were ya sayin' about sugar?" Reb's hands slid caressively up and over her shoulders to her neck until he held her face between their strength. Sage was surprised at the excess moisture gathering in her mouth, as if anticipating the taste of a sweet summer peach. Her cheeks burned pleasantly under his palms, his touch sending her flesh into ripples of tingling goose bumps. Reb's eyes locked with her own, and Sage held her breath as his head began to descend toward hers, slowly. Panic was rising in her. Oh, how she had dreamed of another moment like this! As before, the moment was far more intense than her dreams and she feared she might not be able to remain conscious were Reb to actually kiss her again.

Sage reached to her side, pulling a peach from its place in the basket on the cupboard shelf. A moment before Reb's lips would have met her own, she pressed the peach to his lips and choked, "Peach?" Reb smiled, obviously amused by her nervous attempt to stall him.

"All right," he chuckled, taking a bite out of the juicy piece of fruit. But, this gave her only a moment of reprieve. Once he had swallowed the bite of peach, he pushed the peach aside, his lips finding hers in a tender, lingering kiss. Sage's hand slowly dropped to her side, the peach falling to the floor.

It seemed to Sage that Reb was being more careful with her this time, easing her into a deeper kiss rather than simply beginning with the driven sort of kiss he had given her in the barn. She realized he was teaching her as well, leading her into returning his kiss in a way she wasn't able to in the barn. The kiss in the barn had been far too unexpected for Sage to have returned it properly, even if she had owned more experience, which she did not. This manner of kissing, however, was different. Although it quickly mounted to the same temperature, the same driven fierceness, it had begun differently.

All manner of bright colors seemed to explode in Sage's mind and she found it difficult to breath, for the delightful flutter in her bosom increased as Reb's kiss grew in intensity. His hands found her waist, pulling her body flush with his own, and Sage had no choice but to let her hands rest at his shoulders. The smooth warmth of his skin beneath her palms both relaxed and impassioned her, and Sage let herself return the man's masterful kiss. Encouraged by her response, Reb's mouth began to work an affectionate spell about her, coaxing her into a deeper involvement—moist, heated kisses, laced with the flavor of summer peaches. Sage reveled in the scent of his face, the feel of his whiskery mustache and goatee on the sensitive flesh around her mouth, in every detail of kissing him. Reb's kiss was flawless and Sage was astonished at how perfectly their mouths melted together, as if this hadn't been merely their second kiss, but one of many familiar kisses shared before.

Suddenly, Sage felt a sharp pain in the vicinity of her heart. She knew Reb was only playing with her, teasing and toying with her to unsettle her. As much as she longed to stay in his arms, drink more deeply of his perfect kisses, Sage knew the only way to endure the life which stretched out before her was to face it. Dreams of Reb Mitchell were nothing but make-believe and she must keep her feet firmly on the ground. After all, she had a boardinghouse to run, and supper to serve to guests.

Reb drew away from her, breaking the seal of their kiss as Sage stiffened in his arms and pushed at his shoulders.

"I'm . . . I'm late gettin' supper on," she said as she smoothed her skirts and pushed past him. Reb caught her hand and she looked at him, trying to withhold the tears begging to escape her eyes.

"Sage, don't be angry at me now . . ." he said.

"I'm not," she told him. "I understand." Reb's brow puckered in a frown.

"Ya understand what, Sage?" he asked.

"Cowboys," she flatly responded.

Reb's frown deepened. "What do ya think ya understand about cowboys?"

Sage took the butter down from the cupboard shelf and scooped a bit out with the butter knife, letting it melt on one of the cobblers. "Oh, you know how cowboys get. They go too long on the trail without flirtin' and sparkin' and their blood just gets to boilin' like Saturday night stew. You said it yourself, that first day you arrived, 'Ain't nothin' wrong with a little sparkin.' Milly Michaels' daddy would tan your hide if you took to returnin' all the attention she slathers on you, and Katie Bird's would expect you to propose marriage before he'd even let you get close to lookin' at her. So I figure that leaves me, the safe girl, to spark with . . . not havin' a daddy to worry about. And everyone knows no one's ever even considered . . ."

"I appreciate yer regardin' me so highly, Miss Willows. Not to mention yerself," he growled as he angrily pulled his shirt on. Instantly, Sage regretted her accusation, the words she spoke in trying to protect her heart.

"I . . . I didn't mean . . . I just meant I understand and I won't expect . . . I don't hold you to . . ." she stammered.

His angry expression, coupled with his index finger pointed in her face, ceased any apology she was trying to offer.

"Ya need to quit thinkin' ya know so much, missy," he growled. "Especially where I'm concerned. 'Cause when it comes to me . . . ya don't know nothin'."

"Oh, don't I?" Sage asked. Reb's eyes narrowed.

"I don't doubt ya've heard tell of Ivy Dalton . . . and I don't fault Aunt Eugenia for tellin' the tale to ya," he growled. "I ain't even gonna deny that I purty much stay clear of women 'cause of her. And maybe I do take to teasin' ya too much, but it's cause I like ya, Sage. And I like to think we're good friends." He stepped closer to her again, lowering his voice as he added, "And don't tell me ya didn't enjoy that kissin' just now as much as I did." Sage felt her cheeks turn vermilion and glanced away for a moment. "Everybody needs a good kiss now and then, Sage, and unless ya haul off and slap me right here, well, ya can bet I'll do it again. I warned ya today, out in Ruthie's pasture, that I had a mind to kiss ya again."

"I . . . I thought you were only teasin' me," Sage whispered.

"Oh, I wasn't teasin' then, sugar," he mumbled as he looked down at her. "But . . . go on ahead and slap me," he said. "Slap me now . . . hard as ya can across the face . . . and I'll walk away and never touch ya again. I promise."

Sage looked down to the floor, catching sight of the peach lying there.

Instantly, her body began to shiver with pleasure, residual delight at having been kissed by Reb again.

"I . . . I couldn't slap you and ya know it," she mumbled. She fought the tears gathering in her eyes. "But . . . but I still know that you tease me because I'm safe."

"Ain't no woman on the earth that's safe, Sage Willows," he grumbled. He shook his head, sighing heavily before chuckling, "'Specially ones named after plants." He smiled and took her hand in his. "Ya gonna forgive me . . . again?" he asked. He smiled. "There's just somethin' about ya that winds me up—puts the devil in me—and I can't help but try to make ya blush."

Sage smiled at last, although rather wistfully. He was too wonderful not to forgive, too wonderful not to hope for another kiss. Even if he was just teasing her, at least he counted her his friend, and that was something to be cherished.

"I do understand," she said. "My daddy was that way with my mama." When he raised a suspicious eyebrow, Sage babbled on, "I mean . . . I mean . . . not that you . . . not that I . . . I know you don't . . ."

"I know what ya mean, Sage," he chuckled. "Ya see? That's just what I'm sayin'. I like to rattle ya. And ya rattle easier than them other ladies in the parlor." Sage's heart fell to her stomach with a thud. He was comparing her to the widows now. Had she become his sparking target simply because she was younger than the rest of the residents of the boardinghouse?

"I better get back in there," he said. "'Fore my Aunt Eugenia decides I'm in here ruinin' yer good name." Taking her hands in his, he raised them to his lips, kissing the back of each one tenderly.

Once he was gone, Sage released a heavy breath and blinked back her tears. Pulling one kitchen curtain aside, she glanced out the window into the night sky. She was disappointed to see the stars in the heavens, wishing instead for clouds and rain. Oh, how he had toyed with her emotions! Without even realizing it, he had taken her to the very zenith of joy one moment, only to drop her into the depths of misery the next.

Sage's mind told her she should be flattered, glad and content with the fact Reb liked her enough to tease her, kiss her and be honest with her. But her heart longed for him to be hers, to want her and love her the way she did him. Oh, and how she did love him! How she wanted to belong to him, be the cause of his happiness, feel safe in his arms every moment. But, as with everything in her life, it seemed she would have to settle for less than a dream, less than the love many people found together.

Sage had reconciled herself to her life as the lonely proprietress of a boardinghouse before and she could do it again. At least this time, she would have the memory of Reb's kisses to keep her company in the lonesome years to come. She would hold to those blessed moments in his arms, be glad for them, and try not to pine away after what she couldn't have from him. Truth be told, as miserable as she was knowing Reb would never belong to her, she was happier for having the small part of him she did.

Reb sat in the parlor, listening to the friendly banter of the card players. Yet, his mind couldn't let go of his behavior in the kitchen. What was the matter with him? Hadn't he just that morning asked Sage to forgive him for what happened in the barn? Hadn't he had to explain to her why it happened? In truth, he hadn't really explained to her why he had kissed her in the barn. Oh, he had come up with some ridiculous excuse—being happy over his herd finally arriving—and in her innocence, Sage seemed to accept his sad rationalization. But now . . . this incident in the kitchen! What had he been thinking? The fact was, he had not been thinking. He had walked into the kitchen to offer his help and hadn't been able to resist teasing her.

He adored the way her face turned cherry-red when he teased and flirted with her. He savored the taste of her kiss, the way her body fit so perfectly against his own. Again, he had offered some pitiful reason for his behavior, tried to wiggle his way out of telling her the truth. The truth was, she was getting under his skin and not the way a tick buried its head in either. She was entirely upsetting his plans to stay clear of a woman with the ability to claim his heart. Sage Willows was really getting to him, making him forget the way Ivy had crushed his ability to trust and to love.

"Ya all right, Reb?" Charlie asked. Reb nodded and pulled his thoughts back to the moment.

"Yep," he said. "Just thinkin' on that mountain lion and the herd," he lied.

"Well, don't worry about it," Charlie said, yawning. "Soon as we're through with supper, I'm headin' back to the ranch and get me a short rest. You been up the past two nights. I'll keep an eye out tonight." Reb just nodded, his thoughts still with Sage.

"Anyone for supper?" Sage asked, stepping into the parlor. She glanced at Reb when everyone stood up and started toward the dining room. He quickly winked at her and was relieved when she bestowed a forgiving smile on him. He wished her hair was folded in a long, loose braid the way it had been the day the herd came in. Still, it would've made her all the more tempting and that was the last thing he needed—Sage to be any more tempting than she already was.

Chapter Seven

*T*wo weeks later, Forest Simmons' lady dog finally bore her litter and Reb was in town to pick up the dogs he had promised to look after. He had stopped by the boardinghouse and it being Tuesday night, Reverend Tippetts, Scarlett and Winnery were at The Willows', too. The residents of the boardinghouse and their guests sat in the parlor after supper, visiting the way they always did.

Sage couldn't keep from staring at Reb. Every time she looked at him, her stomach filled with butterflies and she couldn't help but remember the kisses she had shared with him. She let her eyes linger on his mouth as he spoke, unable to think about anything except the feel, the taste of his kiss! The fabulous knowledge that Reb's mouth, the same mouth that spoke and smiled and laughed here in the parlor with friends and family, that same mouth had been pressed to her own in a delicious exchange. Sage bit the inside of her cheek in an effort to keep from smiling, tried to swallow the excess moisture that flooded her mouth as she thought of his kiss.

Yes, her heart ached with the knowledge he would never be hers, but it soared at the same time with owning the attention she received from him. It was just as people always said, it was better to have known him for a time, than to never have known him at all.

Reb looked over and caught Sage looking at him. He winked at her before telling his aunt, "Oh, now don't go tellin' that story, Auntie. There won't be a woman left in the world that'll want me kissin' her now." Sage blushed slightly under his gaze and turned her attention to Eugenia who had begun to tell a story about Reb in his youth.

"Well, Reb was maybe . . . oh, how old were you, boy?" Eugenia asked.

"'Bout three, I reckon," Reb admitted, slouching down further in his chair. Sage smiled, excited to hear the story. Apparently, it wasn't one Reb was comfortable with and that fact made it all the more interesting.

"Yep. He was about two or three and cute as a button. Buck and I had given him a kitten from one of our litters, and Reb just doted on the cat something terrible. Anyway, he'd named the cat Calico, and eventually she had herself her own litter. Reb was just as kind and as carin' as a child could be. He set her up in the barn with a basket and a blanket so she could keep her kittens warm after they come," Eugenia explained. "Well, one day, Buck and I was out visitin', and all of a sudden, Bridie notices Reb ain't nowhere to be found. All of us were in a panic, of course, 'cause Reb was forever gettin' into trouble in some way or the other, and we just knew he was up to no good somewhere. Well, we're all lookin' high and low for the boy, and when we found him . . ." Eugenia had to pause, for she had suddenly begun to laugh and was having trouble catching her breath.

"It ain't that funny, Auntie," Reb mumbled, shaking his head and chuckling.

"We found him . . . we found him . . ." Eugenia said, as she tried to keep from laughing and to catch her breath. Everyone else in the room began to catch her laughter, and Sage giggled at the sight of the older woman so knotted up with mirth.

"Oh, for cryin' in the bucket, Eugenia," Mary grumbled. "Get on with the story. We ain't got all night."

Eugenia inhaled a deep breath. "We found him out in the barn, helpin' Calico cleanin' up her kittens . . ."

"Oh, how sweet," Scarlett said. "Reb, if that isn't the cutest thing I ever heard."

"Unfortunately, Mrs. Tippetts," Reb began, "ya ain't heard it all."

Eugenia wiped the tears from her eyes and continued, "Oh, he was helpin' that fool cat clean up her kittens, all right . . . lickin' them over with his own tongue!"

"Oh, good gravy," Mary mumbled as even she broke into laughter. "Is that true, boy?" Reb nodded and Sage laughed out loud at the thought of an innocent, caring little boy helping his mother cat clean up her litter.

"I'm afraid so," Reb admitted, though he obviously wasn't as amused at the story as everyone else was. "I come into the barn and seen ol' Calico a cleanin' up her kittens," he began, "and I remember thinkin to myself, *Poor ol' cat . . . tryin' to clean all them kittens with just her one little tongue. I* mean, she had eight kittens in that litter and I knew how sore her tongue must be from lickin' 'em all. So, I picked one up and started into helpin' lick 'em clean." Reb chuckled at the memory. Everyone was overcome with laughter, even Mary and Mr. Winnery.

When Eugenia finally caught her breath, she said, "Buck and I nearly dropped down and died right then and there!" She paused to laugh for another moment before continuing, "There he was . . . our little Reb . . . a tiny kitten in each hand . . . just a lickin' the little things clean like it was nobody's business!"

Mary was still laughing, too, although not quite as heartily as perhaps everyone else. Then, she added, "It's a wonder ya didn't get sick, boy."

"Oh, but I did, Miss Mary," Reb said. "Not with any disease or the like, but them cat hairs just kept pilin' up in my mouth. I swear my stomach still rolls around at the thought."

Livie was fanning herself with one hand, torn between humor and horror as she said, "Oh, Reb! That's just . . . that's just awful!"

Reb shook his head and said, "I told ya, Auntie . . . not a woman anywhere will have me now. Ya've spoiled my reputation with that story."

"I'll still have you, Reb," Rosie flirted, promptly sitting down on the young man's lap.

"Will ya, Miss Rosie?" Reb chuckled.

"Rose Applewhite!" Mary scolded. "Now ya leave that boy be."

Sage laughed, too, although a tremor of jealousy traveled through her as she watched Rose harmlessly flirt with Reb. She wished she could be so forward and flirtatious with him, plop right in his lap as Rosie had done and smother him with kisses.

Reverend Tippetts wiped the moisture from his eyes and said, "Boy, that's the funniest thing I done heard in a long time! In a long time!"

Reb smiled, bouncing Rose on one knee, sending her into schoolgirl giggles.

"I'm glad ya found it amusin', reverend," Reb said.

"Rose Applewhite!" Mary scolded again. "Ya shameless flirt! Get down off that boy's knee! For pity's sake, woman. The Reverend Tippetts is sittin' right here!"

"Oh, you're just jealous, Mary," Livie said, going to sit on Reb's other knee.

"Hush, Mary!" Rosie said. "We're just reassurin' Reb that he's still attractive . . . even if he did spend his young years playin' at bein' a mama cat."

"Why thank ya, Miss Rosie, Miss Livie," Reb chuckled as the laughter continued. Reb bounced the two women on his knees and they giggled like silly little girls. Sage smiled. She loved the way Reb teased her friends. He brought happiness and a fresh sort of joy to their lives, the way no one else ever had or ever could.

"Anyone for more cobbler?" Sage asked. It was getting near to eight and she knew how Scarlett liked to turn in early.

"After a story like that," Livie began, "I don't think I could eat another bite of anything! Even peach cobbler, Sage." Sage nodded and smiled.

"And we better be gettin' on home, too, Whipper," Scarlett said with a sigh, "though I do so hate to see the evenin' end."

"Me, too, darlin'. Me, too," the reverend agreed. "Now, don't ya go helping Forest Simmons' lady dog too awful much in cleanin' up her pups there, Reb," the man chuckled.

"Oh, I won't, reverend. I won't," Reb said.

❦

ONCE REVEREND TIPPETTS, Scarlett and Winnery had left, Sage sat down on the parlor sofa and sighed contentedly. She smiled as she looked to Reb, who had been talked into playing a few hands of rummy with her lady friends.

"Now, Reb," Mary began, "I'm assumin' ya know how to deal correctly."

"Yes, ma'am, I do," he said, grinning.

Mary nodded and said, "Good. Don't need another shifty dealer like Livie here."

"I deal fine, Mary, and you know it," Livie defended herself.

"Come on, Sage," Eugenia said. "Play a game or two with us." Sage smiled and shook her head.

"I really should do up the dishes and . . ." she began.

"Nonsense!" Rose exclaimed. "The dishes can wait. You've been workin' all day and it's high time you had some fun. Now come on. Deal her in Reb."

"Oh, I don't know . . ." Sage began to argue.

"Oh, come on, Sage," Reb said, winking at her. "I'll make it interestin'." Sage frowned.

"What do ya mean by that?" Mary asked. Reb raised his eyebrows and shrugged his shoulders.

"You'll see," he said. "Charlie's got his eye on the herd for a while yet. I got some time to spare." He looked to Sage, a rather daring expression on his face. "Ya ain't chicken, are ya, Sage?" Sage smiled at him. How could she possibly refuse?

"Deal me in," she said. Reb chuckled and dealt a hand to Sage.

❦

AN HOUR LATER, the residents of Willows' Boarding House and their handsome guest still sat in the parlor playing cards. Sage was having a wonderful time. Reb made the game far more exciting just by his teasing manner and inability to win.

"I have to say it, Reb," Mary finally said. "Yer terrible at rummy."
Reb chuckled and nodded.

"Don't I know it," he said. "But, it's just 'cause there ain't anythin'
at stake here."

"What do ya mean, boy?" Mary argued. "Winnin' or losin'. Them
ain't stakes enough for ya?"

"Course not," Reb said. "You ladies need to hop it up a bit here, make
it worth fightin' for."

"You mean . . . like gamblin', Reb?" Rose asked.

"Exactly," Reb confirmed. "Ain't no reason for me to want to win
'cause, if I do win, what's my prize? Miss Mary grumblin' at me and Miss
Livie pattin' my hand? Nope, we need to set some serious stakes."

For some reason, Sage began to tremble inwardly. Some sort of excited
warning was whispering to her, even though she had no idea why.

"In case ya ain't noticed it, Reb," Mary began, "we're all widows here,
and I, for one, don't want to gamble away my means of survival."

"Oh no, Miss Mary," Reb told her. "I'd never let ya do that and ya
know it. I was thinkin' more along the lines of . . . well, Miss Sage has
been wantin' the boardin' house whitewashed, right?"

"Yes," Sage timidly admitted.

"And Miss Rosie, yer always teasin' me 'bout wantin' a little sparkin'
time on the front porch swing," he added. Sage's eyebrows raised in
astonishment. Surely he didn't intend to bet such things as whitewashing
an entire boardinghouse or sparking with a woman more than twice his
age?

"You've got our attention, Reb," Rose giggled.

"Now, hold on, ladies," Sage said. "I don't think we should . . ."

"Oh, hush up, Sage," Mary grumbled. "Let the boy talk." Sage's
mouth dropped open in wonder. Even Mary was falling prey to Reb's
cunning ways. Reb smiled and winked at Sage.

"Well, I say we set up some stakes, individual ones, and I play each
of you ladies in turn. If I win, each of ya antis up to whatever I want. If
you win, I pay up to each of you," he said.

"Reb!" Sage exclaimed. "You can't possibly be serious. You'd be willing to bet whitewashin' the entire outside of the boardin' house on one hand of cards?"

"Nope," he said. "Two out of three hands."

Rosie clapped her hands together with excitement. "I'm in! I'm definitely in!"

"Me, too! Me, too!" Livie giggled. Sage looked at them, stunned into silence.

"Sounds interestin', boy," Mary mused. "Count me in."

"Miss Mary!" Sage exclaimed.

"And I certainly have stakes to offer," Eugenia said. "What about you, Sage? Wouldn't you like to have a fresh spread of whitewash on the boardin' house?"

"Well, yes . . . but . . . but what if I lose?" Sage asked.

"Then I win whatever stakes I set down on ya," Reb told her. His smile was intriguingly naughty.

"I'm first!" Rose said. "What do you want if I lose, Reb?" she asked. Reb scratched the whiskers on his chin, his eyes narrowing as he contemplated.

"I want me a back rub," Reb said. "A good, hard backrub, half an hour maybe. My back's been awful sore of late."

"It's a bet for that," Rose said. "And as far as my winnin's?" Reb shrugged his shoulders.

"Name it, Miss Rosie," he said. Again Sage's mouth dropped open. He was insane! Didn't he know these women well enough to realize he would probably lose every hand? Furthermore, didn't he realize what kind of winnings they would want?

"I want some waltzin'," Rose said. "And a long, lickery good-night kiss!"

"Rose Applewhite!" Mary exclaimed, a moment before the same words could escape Sage's mouth.

Rose shrugged her shoulders and said, "It's what I want. I haven't had me a night of dancin' and a kiss from a good-lookin' man in a long time."

"Done," Reb said, chuckling and without pause. Sage looked at him, her eyes widening in awe. Could he possibly be serious? "How 'bout you, Miss Livie?" he asked.

"You first, Reb. If you please." Livie told him. Still the sudden blush which rose to her cheeks told Sage Livie's stakes might be as high as Rose's.

"Okey-dokey," Reb began. He leaned back in his chair for a moment and studied Livie. "I got some mendin' needs doin'," he said. "Shirts, blue jeans and such. If I win, ya do my mendin'."

"Done," Livie said. "And now for my terms." She paused and studied Reb for a moment. "If I win, I get a buggy ride with you, an entire afternoon of sunshine and fresh air. Maybe a picnic, too."

"Done," Reb chuckled. No doubt he was relieved by Livie's stipulations after having heard Rose's.

"I want me a day of ridin' out with yer herd, Reb," Mary said. "I don't want no one worryin' about me fallin' off a horse and gettin' hurt—just want me a day of ridin' out at the ranch. Ya have to promise not to nag me about bein' careful. If I fall off and break my neck . . . too bad. Just haul me off to the cemetery and cover me with dirt. But I'm sick to death of not ridin' just 'cause everyone thinks I'm too old." A sliver of painful compassion pricked Sage's heart. In her one request, Mary had revealed so much hidden desire and pain. It was very touching.

"Ya have my word, Miss Mary," Reb agreed. Sage could see, by the warmth which suddenly enveloped his expression that compassion, had washed over him as well.

"And yer stakes, boy?" Mary asked. Reb seemed to consider the situation for a moment, before a sly smile spread across his face.

"If I win, Miss Mary, ya have to sit on the porch swing with me for a whole hour, at high noon, a holdin' my hand, no matter who walks by," he said, finally.

"What in tarnation?" Mary exclaimed. Sage smiled, for she could see how completely Reb understood Mary. Mary was in the game for the thrill of winning and nothing more, but Reb had just made it more interesting.

"Take it or leave it, Miss Mary," he said. "You win and ya get yer day of herdin' cattle. I win and I get . . ."

"My reputation in the mud," Mary mumbled. Reb shrugged his shoulders.

"I understand if yer afraid to . . ." he began.

"I ain't afraid of nothin'," Mary interrupted. "And that includes men and dyin'. Done, Reb Mitchell. Done."

"I'm ready, Reb," Eugenia said, then.

"What do ya want, Auntie?" Reb chuckled.

"No, no. You go first," Eugenia instructed.

"All righty then," Reb said. "Let's see." He looked at his aunt and seemed pensive. "I win and I get myself supper every night for a week . . . meanin' you come out to the ranch and stay a week with me." Sage smiled at his tender-hearted, understanding offer. She knew how badly Eugenia missed the ranch, how she had tried not to smother Reb by visiting too often. Eugenia's eyes filled with tears and she smiled.

"Done, my darlin'. Done," she told him. Reb smiled, reached out and squeezed his aunt's hand with his own.

"And?" he asked, waiting for her stakes to be set.

"I win," Eugenia began, "and you promise to stay on and run the ranch as long as I want ya to." Sage looked to Reb. Would he agree? Oh, certainly he'd brought his herd up from Santa Fe, but that didn't assure his staying.

"Done," he said, quietly. Sage's heart swelled as she watched the nephew smile adoringly at his beloved aunt.

It was all so sweet, somewhat surreal and inappropriate, but sweet all the same. Sage could not believe how willing Reb was to please the little grey-haired ladies.

"Sage?" he said, unexpectedly turning to her then.

"What?" she gasped. In all the excitement, she had completely forgotten that her turn to place stakes would arrive at some point, too.

"Do ya want me to whitewash the boardin' house?" Reb asked. "Or do ya have a better idea?"

"Oh, Reb," she said. "I couldn't ask you to do that. It's a terrible big job." Reb shrugged.

"It's a big chance yer taken," he said. "Ya haven't heard my stakes yet." Sage began to tremble nervously again.

"What . . . what are your stakes?" she asked.

"Nope," he said. "You go first."

"I don't know about this," Sage said, her hands wringing in her lap.

"Oh, come on, Sage!" Mary grumbled. "It's all in fun."

"Yes, Sage. Don't lose your courage now," Livie added.

Sage looked to Reb, his delicious smile bright and warm. She thought of the other stakes he had set down: a rubbing for his sore back, mending, staying on at the ranch. Even his stakes for Mary weren't too shocking.

"Very well," she said at last. "I win and you whitewash the boardin' house."

"Shake my hand on it?" he asked, offering his hand to her. Sage put her hand in his tentatively, thrilled as he clasped it tightly. "Done," he said.

"And your own terms, Reb?" Rose inquired.

"Oh, nothin' too terrible," he said, picking up the deck of cards on the table and shuffling them. "Just an evenin' of havin' my way with her."

"What?" Sage exclaimed, jumping up from her chair, her heart pounding madly.

"Ya already shook on it, Sage, so sit down and wait yer turn to play," Reb chuckled.

"I did not agree to . . ." Sage began.

"Oh, simmer down, girl," Mary said. "He ain't serious."

"Oh, but I am serious, Miss Mary," Reb said.

"Reb Mitchell," Eugenia scolded, giggling at the same time.

"Oh, I don't mean nothin' so scandalous as you ladies are thinkin' up," he sighed. "Just some friendly conversation, a little hand-holdin', a might good bit of sparkin' . . . and whatever else comes to mind."

"Reb," Sage stammered. "You . . . you can't possibly be serious." As madly as her heart beat with excitement, her body likewise trembled with anxiety. She wanted him to be sincere, but at the same time, she hoped he was just teasing.

"Quit sittin' the fence, Sage," Mary said. "She's in, Reb. Who ya playin' first?"

"Might as well be you, Miss Mary," Reb said. "And since I know how strongly ya feel about dealin', I'll let you deal the first hand."

"Reb, I . . ." Sage began.

"Quiet there, Sage," he said, holding a hand up to her to indicate she should be silent. "I gotta pay attention here."

CR

TWO HOURS LATER, Mary Farthen had won herself a day out herding Reb's herd, Livie Jonesburg had managed to become responsible for Reb's mending, and his aunt had won the right to have Reb stay on at the ranch as long as she wished. Sage had nearly wrung her hands raw with each game of rummy lost or won. Only Rose stood between Sage and her turn to recklessly gamble with Reb.

Reb had won the first hand of rummy with Rose, Rose had won the second, and now the pile of cards in the center of the table was getting smaller as the discard pile grew.

All at once, Rose laid down her hand of cards, leapt up from her chair and hollered, "Rummy!" Dancing around the room she sang, "Rummy, rummy, rummy!" swishing her skirts this way and that.

"For the love of Pete, Rose," Mary grumbled. "Remember to keep them bloomers to yerself. No sense in damagin' poor Reb any further this evenin'."

Sage sat with her mouth gaping open, entirely stunned at Rose's victory. Waltzing and a kiss—that had been the stakes she had laid down—and now she had won the hand! Reb chuckled and shook his head.

"Well, Miss Rose," he said. "Ya got a date in mind for our night of waltzin'?" At least he had proven trustworthy, willing to pay what he had gambled away.

"Waltzin' and a kiss," Rose reminded him. Waltzing over to where Reb sat, defeated, but looking as amused as anyone else, Rose plopped down on his lap. "This Friday night, Reb. Meet me here, at the boardin' house at six sharp." Reb chuckled again.

"All right, Miss Rosie," he said, pinching her cheek adoringly. "Six on Friday night."

Rose jumped to her feet once more, singing, "Rummy, rummy, rummy," as she took another turn around the room

"Well, it's gettin' late," Sage sighed. "We best be gettin' everyone off to bed here pretty quick." Sage stood, and headed toward the kitchen.

"Hold on there!" Reb exclaimed. "Don't ya go boltin' off like a frightened little filly. Everyone else made good on their bets." Sage smiled at him and shook her head.

"Oh, Reb," she laughed. "I know it's all just in fun. Quit teasin'." It was Mary who stepped in front of Sage, blocking her escape.

"Now, Sage, ya made a bet with the young man and we can't let ya duck it," Mary told her. "Besides," she continued, "what're ya afraid of? Yer just about the best rummy player in town."

Sage looked to Reb. He winked at her, smiling triumphantly.

"Ya owe me two outa three hands, Sage," he said. "I got witnesses."

"Oh, go on, Sage!" Livie said. "Don't you think a night in Reb's arms would be worth losing for?"

"Livie Jonesburg!" Mary scolded.

"Oh, you know what I mean, Mary," Livie said. "Quit playin' the Reverend Mother to us all."

"Besides, Sage," Reb said. "What if ya beat me? Ya've been talkin' about wantin' the boardin' house whitewashed since the day I arrived." In truth, Sage could think of nothing more wonderful than losing to Reb. Spending an evening with him, secluded and alone, with the prospect of his kissing her again, was more dreamy than anything. Still, she couldn't lose to him, for she feared it would be obvious that she wanted to.

At last, she inhaled deeply and said, "Very well, Mr. Mitchell. Prepare to spend a day or two workin' for me, instead of runnin' your herd."

"Well, we'll see about that. Won't we?" he said, handing the deck of cards to her.

଄

SAGE'S HANDS TREMBLED as she held her cards. One card. That's all she needed. Just one more three to finish her set and she would win! Reb had won the first hand they'd played, Sage the second. Now Sage sat, holding everything she needed to beat him, save one silly three.

"I swear, Sage," Rose said. "You've gone pale as a ghost."

"Hush, Rose," Mary scolded. "Ya'll break her concentration."

"Go on, Miss Rose," Reb chuckled. "Break her concentration." Timidly Sage drew a card, a four of hearts. She tossed the card to the discard pile and waited. Reb smiled, his eyes lighting up with triumph as he took the four of hearts from the top of the discard pile, placing it in his hand.

"Rummy," he said, chuckling. "Rummy, rummy, rummy! Ain't that right, Miss Rose?" Sage sat, mouth gaping open in astonishment. She had lost! She had actually lost! Reb looked at her, obviously and utterly amused by her stunned silence.

"Well, Sage," he began, "I got me a previous engagement on Friday . . . so why don't we just say . . . I'll drop in Saturday and collect my winnin's."

"Now . . . now, Reb," Sage stammered, a nervous smile, a pleading expression washing over her face. "Why . . . why don't I just fix you up a nice supper on Saturday. Let's say chicken, some mashed potatoes, some of my special sage gravy. You're . . . you're always tellin' me how much you like the flavor of my sage . . ."

"Oh, I like the flavor of sage, all right," Reb interrupted, smiling at her as he smoothed his mustache with the side of an index finger. He moistened his lips and winked at her. "Yes, ma'am! I do love to savor the taste of sage! And I plan on gettin' my fill of it Saturday night. But supper won't be necessary, Sage."

Sage felt her cheeks run vermillion as the other ladies in the room giggled. Even Mary giggled, and Sage sighed when Eugenia winked at her.

ᚙ

IT WAS VERY late when Reb set out for the ranch. Once he was gone, the older ladies of Willows' Boarding House retired quickly, giggles and whispers about their sinful card playing with Reb buzzing about in their wake. Sage lay in bed for hours, struggling for sleep, struggling to calm herself about the prospect of having to pay her debt. She'd lost in gambling. In fact, it was the first time in her life she had gambled, and the outcome proved the vice was wicked.

Still, she couldn't help but smile, a thrill running through her, as she thought of spending time alone with Reb, of his collecting his winnings. Saturday night couldn't come fast enough!

Chapter Eight

✂ ✃

"It fits!" Rose exclaimed, clapping her tiny hands. "It fits perfectly! I knew it would! Oh, Sage! To see you there . . . that dress . . . it takes me back. It truly takes me back."

"It should take you back, Rose Applewhite," Mary grumbled. "Back to jail for showin' so much skin. Sakes alive, Sage. Ya look like ya done stepped straight out of the town saloon!" Mary exclaimed, though her tight smile displayed approval.

"Miss Rosie!" Sage exclaimed as she looked at her reflection in the standing mirror. "I can't believe you used to . . . I can't believe you talked me into puttin' this on! It's hardly proper." Still, Sage couldn't help but grin as she studied her reflection. Her hair was piled high on her head in a profusion of curls with several ringlets cascading over her shoulders. Her shoulders, in fact, were nearly bare except for the ruffled, lacy, capped sleeves of the dress's bodice. The purple and crimson satin dress barely covered her knees in the front, tapering down at the sides to hang nearly to her ankles in the back. It was the most ruffled thing Sage had ever seen, embellished beautifully with long black ribbons and a profusion of black lace. Still, scandalous or not, as she studied herself in the oval standing mirror, hair piled high, black stockings, and dancing boots laced tightly, Sage could not help but be delighted.

"It's . . . it's . . . it's ridiculous," Sage giggled. "I look like a . . ."

"Like a princess!" Livie exclaimed.

"More like a hussy," Mary grumbled.

"Wonderful, isn't it?" Rose sighed.

❧

EUGENIA SMILED AND chuckled to herself. She could not believe the change in Sage! With her hair so soft, curled, and loosely piled, with the bright colors of the dress . . . all of it combined to entirely transform the girl. It was obvious from Sage's countenance that it had been a very long time since she was pleased with her appearance. Eugenia's innards thrilled with delighted anticipation. Oh, she was indeed anxious about the little plot she and her dear friends had hatched. Still, it was for Sage's own good. And Reb's. Sage would get over any residual anger she might feel once Reb had "had his way with her," as he put it.

❧

"YOU'RE BEAUTIFUL, SAGE," Eugenia sighed. "If only Reb could see you now."

Sage laughed and shook her head. "If Reb could see me now . . . or any other man for that matter . . . I think I'd drop dead in my tracks." Still Sage giggled again as she looked in the mirror.

"Now," Rosie said, taking Sage's hand. "Upon the table with you, Sage. Let's work on your high kick."

"Oh, no you don't, Miss Rosie," Sage said, shaking her head. "You talked me into puttin' this silly costume on, but you're not gonna push me any further than that."

"Oh, please, Sage!" Livie whined. "Just do a little dancing for us. I mean . . . Rose has nice bloomers, but I've never seen a real dancehall girl dance before. Just a little . . . just for me?"

Sage smiled and shook her head. How could she refuse her friends. The little imps were too delightful, to happy and full of life. She admired them for the lives they had lived, for the hardships they had endured, and for the joy and mischief which still bubbled in them. And besides, though it was late Friday afternoon, Reb wasn't due to meet with Miss Rose for two hours yet, and certainly no one else was expected at The Willows'.

"Well . . . well all right," Sage agreed. "But only if you promise to draw all the drapes in the dinin' room. The kitchen table won't hold my weight."

Rose squealed with delight, as did Livie and Eugenia. Mary simply chuckled, her wrinkled face softening into a broad smile.

"Good gravy!" Sage laughed. "You all act like you're five years old."

"I just want to see my dress dance again," Rosie said, leading Sage to the dining room. "And it wouldn't hurt ya to liven up a bit, Sage. You spend entirely too much time bein' serious."

"Draw them tight," Sage instructed, as Eugenia and Mary drew the dining room drapes to ensure privacy. "I swear . . . if anyone catches me doin' this . . ."

"Oh, just hush up, Sage, and enjoy the fun," Mary said. Sage glanced to Mary for a moment, astonished at the woman's demand.

"Up on the table now, Sage," Rose instructed. "Now, you've seen me do this before." Rose began prancing about and clapping her hands. Sage shook her head and stepped up onto a chair and then onto the table.

"Oh, this is silly," she giggled.

"A little silliness eases the heart by a mile," Eugenia added.

"And besides . . . you look beautiful!" Live sighed, dreamily clasping her hands at her bosom.

"There's a yellow rose in Texas, I'm going home to see!" Rose began to sing. "Daa la la laa la la laaa . . ." she continued, increasing the tempo as the other ladies began to clap in unison with her. "Come on now, Sage!" Rosie exclaimed. "Kick up your heels a bit! And swish your skirts . . . like this!" Rosie took hold of the front of her dress, hiking it up to her knees and swishing it this way and that in time with the clapping. Sage shook her head, smiled and imitated her friend. "Now . . . add some prancin'. Just like a pony! That's it!" Rosie giggled. "Perfect!"

"Daa la la laa la la laaa . . . la la la laa la laaa!" Rosie sang as the others continued to clap.

"Yer a natural, Sage," Mary laughed, her face beaming with delight. "I guess ya shoulda taken up life as a dancehall girl 'stead of a boardin' house marm."

Sage giggled and continued to dance on the table. She was careful, not wanting to scratch up the table's surface, but the dress, the stockings, the dancing, all of it did free her somehow. Somehow, dressed as she was, her hair done up so fancy and feminine, somehow she felt liberated, enlightened, as if she could be happy always.

Sage smiled, pleased at the perfectly mirth-filled expressions of her friends. Even if the situation hadn't been as fun as it was proving to be, all of it would be worth the now resplendent joy on each woman's beloved face.

Turning her back to the ladies then, Sage wiggled her hind end the way she'd seen Miss Rosie do so many times after winning a hand of rummy. Each woman erupted into giggles and laughter and Sage laughed, too. Sage laughed whole-heartedly until she turned around to see Reb, standing in the back of the room, a broad smile on his face, his eyebrows raised in an expression of astonishment.

Instantly, Sage ceased in her dance, gasping, as her hand flew to her mouth. She felt the hot crimson of the deepest sort of blush rise to her cheeks and cover her entire body.

Seeing Sage's horrified expression, the widows of Willows' Boarding House ceased their clapping and turned to follow Sage's gaze.

"Well, hello there, Reb!" Rosie greeted. "Sage was just entertainin' us a bit this afternoon." Sage was frozen with embarrassment, mortified at being found in such a state by Reb Mitchell! "Doesn't she make a perfect dancehall girl?"

Reb's smile broadened as he nodded and said, "Ain't seen nothin' the like of it 'cept in my imagination."

"Don't stop now, Sage," Mary urged. "Ya got a real audience. Might as well give him an eyeful."

But Sage knew Reb had already had an eyeful, and she was close to tears because of it.

"I take it then, Miss Sage," Reb said as he strode toward the table, "that Miss Rosie forgot to tell ya somethin'."

As he walked toward her, Sage instinctively put out a hand in a gesture he should come no closer. "Stay . . . stay right there, Reb," she stammered. "I . . . I . . ."

"I plum forgot, Sage," Rosie said, looking at her friend. The old woman's eyes twinkled with deep mischief. "I . . . I can't go with Reb this afternoon. Remember? Reb was due to make good on his bet with me and give me an evenin' of waltzin' and kissin'. But I . . . I made other plans, so I told him you and I wouldn't mind switchin'. I'll go with Reb tomorrow and . . . and you can go with him now."

"That should work out just fine, Sage," Livie said. Sage noticed Livie's eyes also twinkled naughtily. "Then you can help me with my baking tomorrow while Rose is gone."

Sage shook her head, horrified, as Reb stepped up to stand just before her. He began at the tip of her boot, his eyes traveling up the length of her as he chuckled.

"Ya definitely weren't expectin' to see me, were ya?" he said. Oh, he was handsome! Sage held her breath for a moment, temporarily stunned by both his good looks and her compromising situation.

"You haven't got anythin' planned, Sage, I'm sure," Eugenia said. "So why don't you just run up and change and have a nice time with Reb tonight."

"I . . . I . . ." Sage stammered. She gasped as Reb reached out and took hold of one of her ankles. Quickly, he reached up, grasping her wrist, and placed her over his shoulder.

"Oh, don't ya bother with changin', Sage," Reb said, as he turned, Sage thrown over his shoulder like a sack of flour. "I'm more'n happy to take ya just the way ya are. This is sure to be the best night of my life!" Again he laughed as he carried Sage toward the back door.

"Put me down!" Sage exclaimed, beating on Reb's back with her fists and attempting to kick her legs in an effort to escape. "I can't be seen like this!" But Reb locked one powerful arm at her knees and continued to make for the door.

"Oh, but ya have been seen, Sage Willows," Reb chuckled. "So what's the use of changin' yer clothes now?"

Sage looked up to where her four supposed friends stood watching her being carried away. They donned the playful smiles of imps, even Mary, and Sage knew she'd been tricked.

"How could you?" she cried, tears welling in her eyes. "How . . . how could you all do this to . . ."

"Life shouldn't be all tatters and tears, Sage. Ya need to have some fun," Mary told her as the old women's expression changed to that of earnestness. "And ya have it now, ya hear?"

"Oh, she'll have fun all right, Miss Mary," Reb said, kicking open the back door. "I promise ya that."

Reb closed the door behind them as he stepped out of the house. Craning her neck, Sage watched as he strode toward his wagon.

"Please, Reb!" Sage pleaded. "If anybody sees me . . ."

"No one will see ya, Sage," he told her. "Just me." Then she heard him laugh, felt the deep rumble of his chuckle as he said, "I ain't never had my way with a dancehall gal before. Should be mighty interestin'."

"Reb! Please!" she pleaded, but he lifted her off his strong shoulder, setting her down none too easily in the wagon bed. Instantly Sage tried to stand, intent on escape. But, Reb took hold of her arm and pulled her to him. Her face was only a few inches away from his, and she could sense the scent of him, all leather and horsehair, bacon and saddle oil.

"I swear yer comin' with me now, Sage. One way or the other," he said in a low, somewhat provocative voice. His eyes sizzled with mischief. "I'll hogtie ya if I have to."

"But . . . but I can't be seen like . . ." Sage began.

"Nobody's gonna see ya, Sage. Ain't nobody along the way to the ranch," he told her. "Nobody but me. I'm takin' ya home for supper . . . which I'm cookin' up my very own self," he proudly added. "The hands are all out with the cattle. Even Charlie . . . and there'll be nobody to see ya but me." Sage tried to climb out of the wagon, but Reb's strong arms stopped her. "I *will* tie ya up, Sage," he repeated. "I ain't missin' this chance for the world." He smiled and winked at her and asked, "So, what'll it be? Ya wanna ride in the wagon nice and easy? Or do ya want me to tie ya up first?"

The tone of his voice, the smoldering warmth of his eyes combined to mesmerize her, and Sage was momentarily bewitched into silence. Slowly the embarrassment and fear began to leave her, replaced by an enchanting thrill and delighted anticipation.

"I . . . I'll go easy," she managed to answer. For in truth, she wanted nothing more than to go with him, to be with him, to capture his attention as it appeared she had. Sage had the odd sensation she would be grateful to the widows for their trickery one day.

Reb smiled and nodded. "Good," he said. "Now hunker down in the wagon 'til we're a ways out of town. Then ya can hop up on the seat with me."

Sage nodded and sat down in the wagon. Clasping her hands together, she tried to calm their nervous trembling. Reb jumped up on the wagon seat and slapped the lines at the horses' backs.

"When ya lost that last hand of rummy the other night," he said to her over his shoulder as the wagon lurched forward, "well . . . I knew I'd been lucky. Don't think I realized just how lucky, 'til I walked into yer dinin' room just now though."

Sage shook her head, amazed at her gullibility where the widows were concerned, feeling guilty about how delighted she had been when she had first seen her reflection in the mirror while wearing Rose's dress. Heaven had a way of making people pay for mistakes, and Sage was certain she would surely pay for letting her guard down. Yes, she was sure she would pay for enjoying a moment of liberation and happiness. But looking at Reb, her heart fluttering once more at the sight of him, she wondered if paying for a mistake might be rather delightsome this time.

"Reb . . . you . . . you won't mention this . . . to anyone, will ya?" she ventured, still certain she wanted her silly situation to be kept to Reb's knowledge and only his.

He glanced over his shoulder, smiled at her and said, "I ain't the kind of man to share my winnin's, Sage. Yer secret life as a dancehall girl is perfectly safe with me."

Sage couldn't help but smile. His teasing manner was so charming. Still, she closed her eyes as she thought on her reflection in the mirror only a short time before. She was scandalously clad! She drew her knees up to rest her chin on them, folding her arms against her black-stockinged calves. She tugged at the loose and ruffled capped sleeves, endeavoring to affix them somehow to her shoulders. How utterly shocking she must appear! She thought of unpinning her hair, of pulling it back into a knot or at least a braid, but the damage had been done. Reb had seen her already. What good could come of the ridiculous notion of changing her hair? There was nothing to be done. She would muster the courage to pretend she was dressed in her usual day dress, to imagine she wasn't any different in appearance than she normally was.

Sage sat silently, her emotions tossed back and forth between humiliation and delighted anticipation, waiting until the team had drawn the wagon out of town and to a more secluded venue. She blushed when she heard Reb chuckle to himself

"Them ladies are down right naughty," he said. "Don't think I don't have sympathy for ya, Sage," he added, "but with their mischief makin' things so good for me, how can I do anythin' but thank 'em?"

CR

REB SHOOK HIS head, still astonished at the situation. By rights, Sage ought to turn the widows out into the street for such a trick. But who couldn't love them all the more for their mischief? And Reb was glad for it! He'd never forget the way his pulse had quickened, how good his smile felt as it spread across his face when he'd walked into The Willows' and seen Sage dancing on the table. He had always suspected she had it in her, a free side, a fun side, a side to her she kept hidden. And she was beautiful! Not merely because she'd been dressed all in lace and ribbons, pretty legs showing all the way up to her knees . . . no! It was the sense of unguarded freedom about her, the sense of rebellion and the moment of casting caution to the wind.

True enough, he'd wanted to pull her off the table, take her in his arms and truly make good on collecting his winnings. But it was the carefree, happy expression on her face that attracted him most in those first moments. Oh, certainly the site of her bloomers had been an additional benefit, but in truth, it was the joy of her countenance he would always remember.

Still, Reb knew he would have to be careful. Sage was a tempting little pie crust and he'd savored the taste of her before. Furthermore, even though he had several times explained to her that he was only teasing about 'having his way with her,' he would have to be careful. He'd have to watch himself, restrain passion if it threatened to spark between them. Rather, *when* it threatened to spark between them. And it would, for Reb already knew there would be no way he would let Sage escape without tasting her kiss again.

ଔ

SAGE FELT HERSELF blush as Reb laughed out loud once more. "Hop up on the seat with me, girl," he demanded. "Ain't nothin' but cattle and coyotes to see ya now."

Sage did as she was told, amazed at how spirited she was feeling. Settling into the seat next to Reb, she marveled at how one dress could so entirely change her disposition. The bareness of her arm brushed Reb's shirt sleeve and instantly her skin prickled with the delightful sensation of a million goose bumps breaking over her.

"Now do tell me, Miss Sage Willows, proprietress of Willows' Boarding House, how ever did those old women get ya into that getup?"

Sage blushed and shook her head. She smiled, capable of seeing the humor of it all. She thought back on the hours prior to Reb finding her dressed like a dancehall girl, prancing about on her own dining room table. She could clearly see the plot then, the four old widows' mischievous scheme taking form.

She sighed heavily and said, "They thought I needed some . . . some teasin', I suppose. They do get tired of everyday life and are lonely at times." Sage felt a pang of compassion pinch her heart at the thought of her dear old friends and the lovers they had each buried in the earth. "Miss Rosie said she'd been rummagin' around in some old trunks and found this dress, that it looked to fit me perfectly. Then somehow, they all coaxed me into puttin' it on."

"And that's why I oughta be callin' ya Gullible Gerty from now on?" Reb teased.

"It sure seems that way," Sage said, trying to adjust one of her sleeves in an effort to cover her shoulder.

"Well, don't go bein' too awful hard on yerself, Sage," he said. "I seem to be as easy to fool as the next cowpoke. Remember, I got me a waltzin' date set with Miss Rose myself."

"Waltzin' and a kiss!" Sage reminded him, giggling. Reb had been as easily tricked as she had, for she knew there was no doubt Miss Rose Applewhite would give Rebel Lee Mitchell an evening he'd not soon forget.

"Oh, yes," Reb said, smiling. "That kissin' part is what has me a bit rattled. What kind of a kiss, do you suppose, she's gonna have in mind?"

Sage giggled, surprised that the notion of Reb's kissing Miss Rose didn't upset her somehow.

"Let's see," Sage said, smiling at Reb. "As I remember, she said she wanted, 'a long, lickery good-night kiss.' Isn't that the way she said it, Reb?"

Reb chuckled and shook his head, saying, "I believe that is exactly what she said."

"Maybe this'll teach you about the evils of gamblin'," Sage told him. "After all, Reverend Tippetts is always preachin' on the evils of it."

"Reverend Tippetts ain't never seen you dressed up like a dancehall girl," Reb said, winking at Sage.

Sage smiled, flattered and delighted. The knowledge that Reb found her attractive, dressed as she was, had begun to sink in, and it made her more comfortable about the entire affair.

"Reverend Tippetts has never had to kiss Miss Rosie, either," Sage reminded him. "She won't let you get away without it, Reb," she added, "Miss Rosie will have her kiss." Sage laughed. Reaching out, she placed a hand on Reb's cheek for a moment, needing to touch him, wanting to assure herself he was real and not just a dream. Touching him was too stimulating to her senses. The manner in which her palm seemed to tingle unnerved her greatly.

Dropping her hand quickly, she added, "And she'll have it right on the mouth."

It seemed her touch had rattled Reb, somehow, as well. The amused smile on his face, only a moment before, dissolved instantly, a slight frown puckering his brow. Immediately, Sage began to scold herself for such a brazen act. She was reminded of the last time she had touched him in such a casual, yet somewhat affectionate manner. The day his herd had arrived, when she'd touched him in the barn, simply wiped at the thick layer of dust on his chest, he'd been instantly angry. And yet, he'd been instantly something else as well, for he'd kissed her in that next moment . . . kissed her as Sage could never have imagined being kissed.

"Well then," Reb rather growled. Sage held onto the wagon seat as Reb abruptly reined the team to a stop. "I ain't gonna let ya get away without it neither. The way I figure it, if losin' a bet is gonna cost me, then it's gonna cost you, too."

Sage's heart began to hammer as she watched Reb climb down from the wagon. He held his hand up to her, gesturing she should take it. "Come on down then," he said.

"Why?" Sage asked, tentatively placing her hand in his and climbing down from the wagon.

"I said I'd have my way with ya, didn't I, Sage Willows?" he asked, placing his hands at Sage's waist and pushing her back against the wagon.

"But . . . but you were only teasin'," she reminded him. "Only teasin' me. Remember?"

He smiled and chuckled, but only for a moment, before his expression went serious once more as he said, "I wasn't teasin'."

Instantly, his mouth took hers in a deep and driven kiss that threatened to draw her breath so completely from her lungs as to find her fainting. The fiery flames of instantaneous passion seared within her bosom! His hands at her waist, his mouth melded with hers, the feel of his mustache and goatee against the tender flesh of her face . . . all of it blended instantly, bearing Sage away in dreams of owning him, of belonging to him completely. She fancied his body was trembling, sensed he yet restrained himself. For several moments, his kiss was so determined it was nearly painful. Bound fast in the power of his arms, Sage wondered at her ribs being crushed to dust. Sage imagined her fingers, hands, and feet were numb. Her knees threatened to weaken and give way beneath her.

She gasped as his mouth left hers for a moment, his breathing heavy and labored as he pressed his lips to the hollow of her throat, and Sage allowed her hands to travel to the back of his neck, losing her fingers in his hair. This simple gesture seemed to encourage Reb even further, and Sage gasped as he took her face between his powerful hands. The smoldering flame in his eyes, his labored breathing, told her he was struggling to restrain an even greater passion.

"Here and now," he said, his voice low, alluring, thick, and warm like maple syrup. "Let's you and me decide what kind of a kiss I'm gonna give Miss Rose tomorrow night. Do ya think I should kiss her sweet . . . like this?" Reb asked as he kissed Sage's cheek. His thumb caressively traveled over her lips. "Or sweeter even . . . like this?" Sage could not withhold the soft sigh of pleasure which escaped her as Reb placed a soft, lingering kiss on her tender lips. "Maybe I should tease her a bit," he whispered. He kissed her neck, lightly, slow, three times in succession. "Ya know what I mean? See if she truly wants me to kiss her," he added.

"She does," Sage whispered as he again took her face in his powerful hands and gazed down at her.

"Does she?" he asked, a grin of intrigued mischief spreading across his handsome face.

"Yes," Sage breathed. Oh, how desperately she thirsted for his kiss! Her mouth watered at the anticipation of it, and she knew she must have his mouth to hers again.

Again Reb caressed her lips with one thumb as he asked. "But which kiss do ya think she wants? Which kiss do *you* want, Sage?" He kissed her cheek lightly. "This one?" He kissed her lips softly. "This one?" He pressed his lips to the sensitive flesh of her neck asking, "This one?" He looked at her then, his eyes narrowing, his thumb traveling over her lips.

Sage could endure his taunting no longer. Reaching up, she took his face in her hands, pulling his head toward hers, as she said, "This one," a moment before taking his mouth with hers. She kissed him deeply, letting the flavor of his mouth wash over her like a warm summer rain. He returned her kiss ardently, acceptingly. She heard a low moan rumble in his throat a moment before he took the reins himself, binding her in his arms, pulling her body flush with his own as he endeavored to consume her with passion.

Once he broke from her for an instant, long enough to whisper, "This is my favorite kiss, too. Good choice, Miss Willows."

Reb kissed her again, deeply, firmly, passionately until Sage thought she might never again draw sufficient breath. She felt her inhibitions melting away, felt courage, confidence, and a sort of liberation filling her body and mind. Perhaps Rebel Mitchell was obtainable! Perhaps she could win him, own him, marry him, bear his children! All thoughts of the boardinghouse and of the widows' dependency on her fled. Only thoughts of at last being cared for herself, protected and loved, filled her mind. In her dreams, born in those moments, she could well imagine a life with Reb, a life filled with passion, joy, cattle ranching and babies all her own. Visions of sleeping in his arms, warm and secure, wafted through her mind, visions of smiling, laughing and caring for Reb and their children. Visions Sage had so long been afraid to let run freely in her soul burst forth, filling her with hope and happiness.

"This ain't exactly safe for ya, I don't think," Reb mumbled, suddenly breaking the seal of their lips and shaking his head. Sage was flushed, overly warm and breathless.

"I'm . . . I'm perfectly fine," she said, uncertain as to his meaning. How could being held in the strength of his arms, lost in the blissful sensation of his kiss prove harmful to her? She watched as he stepped back from her, removed his hat and ran his fingers through his hair.

"Maybe yer fine right now . . . but any more of this . . . and I might be too tempted to make good on collectin' my winnin's by downright and truly havin' my way with ya," he told her.

"Oh, I'm not worried," Sage said, smiling at him as he motioned for her to climb back up onto the wagon seat. "You would never . . ."

"Never say never, sugar," he chuckled. "Never say never." He helped her back up onto the wagon, running his fingers through his hair once more before returning his hat to his head. He climbed up to sit next to her, exhaled a deep breath and slapped the lines. "The baked beef waitin' for us at the ranch is gonna seem mighty dull after what I just tasted," he said, smiling at her with a wink. "After all, yer the first dancehall girl I ever kissed," he said, chuckling as she blushed.

Sage smiled, wanting nothing more than to take Reb's arm, rest her head on his shoulder and revel in the lingering sensation of their affection- ate exchanges. Yet, all at once, her doubts, her reserve, and the reality of who she truly was renewed afresh. In the quiet space of only a few moments, Sage, the momentary dancehall girl, was old Sage Willows once again . . . old Sage Willows the proper, spinsterly proprietress of Willows' Boarding House.

Sage frowned. Why couldn't the joy, the zenith of what had just transpired between her and Reb linger a while? Why did she immediately lose courage and confidence once he had released her? Sage glanced to Reb, and even though he smiled and winked at her, Sage struggled, struggled to believe his affections were administered with sincerity.

Their conversation was light-hearted as they rode toward the ranch. The splendor of the early evening spoke of ease and light-heartedness. Yet, even with the brilliant fire of the Indian paintbrush growing in bunches along the trail, the scent of the wild sage and the happy sight of furry critters scurrying here and there through the beautiful high-plains grasses, even with the warmth of the burning sun, Sage could not recapture the ecstasy of the moments spent kissing Reb.

Reb seemed at ease, smiling, discussing the silly widows and their intricately hatched plots. He discussed the ranch with Sage, his concerns for the herd and the mountain lion he knew was in the area. He told her of the new hands he had hired, of Milly Michaels' shameless flirting with Charlie Dugger, chuckling at his friend's discomfort.

Sage likewise spoke of the widows, told him of her sisters and their families, inquired as to the well-being of Bullet, Mr. Simmons' lady dog and the puppies. Yet, there seemed no real depth to their conversation. Sage wondered, if perhaps, she expected too much. Perhaps, light-hearted stories and concerns were the best kind. Perhaps, it was good she and Reb were casually cheerful.

Soon the ranch was in view and Reb helped Sage down from the wagon before leading the team toward the big barn.

"I'll have 'em unhitched in a jiffy and then we'll sit down to supper," he told her with a wink. "Ya can run on in the house if you'd like . . . or the pups are in the old barn by the corral."

Sage nodded and smiled. She loved puppies! To her, the tummies of little puppies were one of he sweetest scents on earth. She smiled, quickly glancing about to ensure none of Reb's hands were likely to see her in such a state of attire. As she neared the dilapidated old barn, the sudden angry barking of adult dogs caused her to startle. Sage hastened her step when she heard a dog yelp and the frightened squeaking of puppies. Had a fox gotten in the old barn? The noises coming from the direction of it were those of fear.

"Bullet?" she called. "Bullet?"

Suddenly, Sage gasped as a large mountain lion stepped out of the barn, a dead puppy trapped in its powerful jaw. The predator was rather gaunt and otherwise weathered in appearance.

"Reb?" Sage squeaked as the mountain lion instantly dropped the dead puppy. The indescribable, scratchy cry of the mountain lion's warning sent waves of terror through Sage's body. It was obvious the cat was old, but it was also perfectly clear it was still capable of killing a human being. "Reb? Reb! Rebel!" Sage screamed as the cat took two stalking steps toward her. There was no other choice but to turn and run!

Sage heard the mountain lion's hoarsely purred threat again, but did not pause to look back. It was not until she felt fiery claws tearing the flesh on her back, felt the enormous cat's teeth plunge deep into her shoulder, felt her body hit the ground hard . . . it was then she knew she would die.

Chapter Nine

"Sage!" Rebel shouted running toward her. He had known instantly—when he heard her cry out for him—he had known at once it was the mountain lion. The cat released its hold on Sage as Reb ran toward it. He didn't fear the cat—Sage was in danger. He tried to focus on the threat and on distracting the beast from Sage. He tried not to panic at the knowledge that Sage lay bloodied on the ground. The beast lunged at Reb, and he managed to pull the knife from his boot, but not before the massive claws of the animal shredded the front of his shirt, tearing into his flesh.

SAGE TRIED TO scream as she watched Reb wrestle with the enormous mountain lion. She tried to sit up, but the pain at her back and shoulder, coupled with the shock of being attacked, weakened her. She could only watch in horror! The cat's jaws snapped at Reb's throat. Somehow he managed to avoid them.

The animal's claws tore through his pants at one thigh, and Sage screamed, "Rebel!" as blood spilled down his leg. She knew he could not fight the cat for long, and she screamed again, certain she was about to see him killed. Somehow, Reb managed to hook two fingers into the animal's nostrils. He scrambled to turn the beast and wrenched its head back as he swiftly and fatally drew his knife across its throat. Blood spewed from the big cat's neck as Reb released it, letting the vanquished creature drop to the dirt.

Sage let her head fall to the ground again, the excruciating pain at her shoulder and back draining any remaining strength from her. The tears spilling from her eyes blurred her vision, tears born, not of her own pain, but of the sight of the blood staining the front of Reb's shirt and pants.

"Rebel," she breathed as he collapsed to his knees beside her. "Reb, we . . . we . . . have to get you to town . . . to . . . to Doc Roberts."

CR

"I'M . . . I'M FINE, sugar," he told her, afraid to touch her for fear of causing her greater pain. "I'm . . . I'm fine . . . but we need to get ya into the house . . . get . . . get this cleaned up here."

"No, no," Sage panted, trying to raise herself from the ground. "You'll . . . you'll get infection if we don't get to Doc Roberts' place and . . ."

"It's no good," Reb told her, tentatively touching her undamaged shoulder. He panted with the residual exertion of fighting the cat. "He ain't there. I saw his boy this mornin' and he told me Doc Roberts is up at his daughter's place 'til the end of the month. We'll . . . I'll have to take care of this myself. Then we'll figure on gettin' ya back to the boardin' house. I'd . . . I'd take ya now, but we'd better . . . we'd better get these wounds cleaned before we do anythin' else. Ya . . . ya might bleed to death before we got to town anyway."

Reb's body shook uncontrollably, but not from his own pain. He trembled with fear—fear born of concern for Sage's well-being, for her life! The torn flesh at her back, the deep wounds of the mountain lion's claws, soaked the fabric of her dress with blood. The puncture wounds at her shoulder bled. He closed his eyes for a moment, thanking heaven the beast had not had time or the strength to tear her flesh any further. Still, she was in danger, in danger from loss of blood and from infection.

With Doc Roberts away, Reb was certain it was best to tend to Sage's wounds immediately, rather than try for town. Further, he wasn't certain, because of his own injuries, that he could get Sage safely back to the boardinghouse. Already he felt weak and light-headed. What good would it do to try for town if he passed out, leaving them both prey to the buzzards and coyotes? Frantically, he gathered her in his arms, grimacing with his own pain as he carried her to the house. She felt heavy and he was further reminded of his weakened condition.

"Rebel," Sage gasped, her hand going to the torn flesh of his torso. "Oh, Reb!" she breathed a moment before she lost consciousness.

Once inside, he laid her on her stomach on the kitchen floor, and with still trembling hands, set a pot of water to boil.

"Oh, God," He breathed the prayer. "Settle me down here enough to do this, please." Retrieving the knife from his boot, he wiped the bloody thing on his pant leg and began to cut away the back of Sage's dress. His eyes filled with moisture, and he drew in a deep breath as he gazed at the torn flesh. The sight of her soft skin, so smooth, so pristinely fair, only accentuated the bloody wounds which now marred it. Reb closed his eyes for a moment, inhaling deeply several times. It would do Sage no good if he were not able to remain strong and settled.

His hands trembled violently, and he felt the sting of excess moisture in his eyes, wincing as he opened them and again looked at the soft, tender and torn flesh of Sage's back. Four long lacerations traveled several inches from her right shoulder blade downward. Though Rebel knew a younger, stronger cat would have done much greater damage, it sickened and terrified him to see Sage's tender body so wounded.

Quickly he went to the wash basin and retrieved a brick of soap. He filled the basin with fresh, cool water, retrieved a bottle of whiskey from the basin cabinet, and set them on the floor next to Sage. As he scrambled to find a needle and thread in his aunt's old sewing table, he was startled as he heard Sage moan.

"Don't wake up yet, girl," he mumbled as he retrieved the pot of hot water from the stove and dropped to his knees next to her. "Not yet."

Tearing what remained of his tattered shirt from his body, he dipped it in the hot water, then carefully cleaned the area around Sage's wounds. He lathered the soap and ran it over the wounds at her back and shoulder.

Dipping his fingertips into the hot water, he soaped them up. Drawing in a deep breath, he inserted his smallest finger into one of the bite wounds at Sage's shoulder. He repeated this action several times on each wound, finally rinsing all the wounds with whiskey. He poured the whiskey over the claw lacerations on his own back and across the wounds at his chest and on his leg, only as an afterthought.

Reb found it difficult to thread the needle for his hands shook fiercely from the strain of handling Sage's tender, torn flesh so roughly. His eyes again blurred with restrained tears. Finally, he was able to thread the needle.

With tremulous hands, he began to carefully stitch the wounds on Sage's back as best as his rough sewing skills would allow. Each time he inserted the needle into her tender, torn flesh, he whispered, "Keep breathin', sugar . . . but don't wake up yet." He tried to be careful, to make his stitches small and as close together as his shaky hands would allow. With his forearm, he wiped at the nervous perspiration on his forehead and wiped at the tears in his eyes with the back of his hand.

It seemed he had spent an eternity stitching her delicate flesh. When he at last finished, he winced and let a tear escape one eye as he looked at the young woman's mutilated flesh. The attack most likely would leave her scarred quite brutally. Her tender, soft, beautiful back would forever bear the mark of Reb's lack of a physician's skill. Still, it was her life which mattered, and Reb patched the bite marks as best he could with a couple of rough stitches as well. Again he thanked the heavens that he had arrived before the old cat had mustered the strength to completely tear the flesh from Sage's shoulder.

Pouring more whisky over his torso, he threaded the needle once more and went to work on himself. The pain of stitching his own wounds paled in comparison to the pain he had known in stitching Sage's. Again he thought of how near she'd come to death, hoping she would not yet come near to it because of his lack of skill and knowledge.

As he stitched his injuries, Reb glanced at Sage every few moments, ensuring she still breathed . . . still lived. He found he could hardly look at her without tears filling his eyes. He found himself wanting to plunge the needle deep into his own flesh, causing himself more pain for her sake.

"We shoulda tracked it," he growled to himself. "Me and Dugger shoulda tracked that thing until we'd killed it."

It was his fault. All of it! Sage's wounds, the danger she was in because of them. He'd been too busy with running the ranch, playing cards with old women, and daydreaming of Sage to track that cat, to keep the very object of his daydreams safe. He shook his head, remembering the thoughts he had been having only an hour before, thoughts of making Sage his own, of kissing her every day the way he had when he had stopped the wagon on the way to the ranch. He thought of how she'd looked in those moments, so wildly free and happy. Closing his eyes, he could remember the way she had smiled at him, the taste of her kiss and he knew—he knew he did not deserve her. He did not deserve Sage Willows. What had he been thinking by pursuing her even in the very least? How could he have thought he might be the man to make her life full and happy? If such a thing as nearly getting mauled to death, torn to shreds by a mountain lion could happen to her while in his care, what other atrocities would his existence rain upon her?

❧

SAGE OPENED HER eyes, grimacing and gasping at the pain her regained consciousness shot throughout her body. It felt as if searing flames were burning into her back and shoulder. Intense throbbing sensations emanated from both sources of injury and caused an ache in her head to keep time with them. She squeezed the tears from her eyes, blinking to clear her vision. The sight which met her only caused her to wish oblivion would find her once more. Reb sat cross-legged on the floor next to her, a needle and thread in hand. He ran his fingers over the roughly stitched wounds at his chest, wounds from which blood still oozed. Then, stretching out his left leg, he tore open his pant leg, pouring whisky onto the wound at his thigh and grimacing as he pinched one of the lacerations together and began to stitch.

"You . . . you need a doctor," Sage breathed. Reb glanced to her, frowning, and she fancied there was excess moisture in his eyes. No doubt the fact he was sewing his own wounds caused an incredible insult to his already horrific injuries.

"I'll be fine," he mumbled, returning his attention to stitching his leg. "But . . . but we need to get ya home. Dugger and the others oughta be ridin' in any minute and they can take ya back. Aunt Eugenia and the others will do better for ya than I have." Sage felt a tear travel over the bridge of her nose as Reb dropped the needle he'd been using and reached out to put a hand on her arm. "Let's get ya to my bed where you'll be more comfortable. This hard ol' floor won't do nothin' to ease yer . . ."

"No," Sage told him as she stared at the needle and thread dangling from his half-stitched wound. "Please . . . please don't make me move yet. Just . . . just let me lie here awhile until I feel a bit better." He looked pale and she knew she must recover enough to help him mend his injuries. "If . . . if you'll just give me a minute, I can help you, I can help you to . . ."

"Shh," he said, brushing a strand of hair from her cheek. "I'm just about finished. It'll be fine. Maybe not the best stitchin' job in town . . . but I'll be fine." His frown deepened and again Sage saw moisture gathering in his eyes. "I . . . I did the best I could on ya. It . . . it ain't a pretty job . . . but it's the best I knew how." Sage closed her eyes, several more tears escaping them. How long had she been unconscious? Long enough for Reb to tend to her before caring for himself.

He forced a smile that told her he wasn't certain either one of them was out of danger yet. Then he took hold of the needle and thread still dangling from one of the lacerations on his leg, and with trembling hands, began to stitch once more.

"Reb!" Charlie hollered as he and three other men burst through the door and into the kitchen. "Ya all right, Reb? We seen the cat out there and . . ." Charlie was struck silent, his eyes widening as he looked first from Reb to Sage and back again. "Miss Sage!" he exclaimed.

"You boys get the wagon hitched back up," Reb ordered, pointing at the other hands. "We gotta get Miss Willows back to town."

"Yes, sir," one of the men said, motioning to the others to follow him.

"Looks like we need to be gettin' both of ya back to town, Reb," Charlie said, shaking his head. "I ain't never seen such a mess a blood!"

"I'll be fine," Reb said. "But Sage is hurt bad. We need to get her back so them old ladies can look her over . . . make sure I done things right. She's hurt worse than me."

"Um . . . Reb . . . I don't think ya've quite got a handle on yer condition here," Charlie said, walking over to Reb and bending down to further inspect the wounds on his chest.

Sage winced as Reb suddenly reached up, taking hold of the front of Charlie's shirt and growling, "I said . . . get her back to town and I'll be fine!"

"Reb!" Sage exclaimed as Reb began to sway back and forth.

"I think . . . I think we best take Miss Sage back to town," Charlie said, reaching out to steady his friend. "But I ain't too all fired certain you'd make the trip all right, Reb."

"Fine. Fine," Reb mumbled. "Just . . . just get the girl . . ."

Sage gasped, wracked with her own bodily pain and that of her fevered mind, as Reb completely collapsed in a bloody, unconscious heap on the floor. Sage tried to raise herself, tried to move toward him, to reassure herself he still lived. But the pain of her injuries was too great and she felt her head hit the floor hard as she, too, succumbed to the reprieve of darkness.

∞

EUGENIA SMARTHING SPENT more than four days out at the ranch tending to Reb. His wounds were far more severe than Sage's. When Eugenia had arrived at the ranch to find Reb unconscious, still bleeding and so terribly injured, the first thing she had to do was to attend to his awkward attempt to mend himself. She cleaned his wounds, stitched him properly and waited. He had been taken with a terrible fever over the next several days, but somehow survived and was healing slowly. Or so Mary, Rose and Livie assured Sage daily.

"Eugenia says that boy is strong as an ox. Even the pain of her wiping out his wounds with lye didn't keep him unconscious. He kept wakin' up and growling at her when she was workin' on him," Mary told Sage for the umpteenth time as she herself lay still weak and uncomfortable in healing from her own injuries. "He done a right good job on you, though . . . thank the Lord," Mary added, helping Sage to sit up in bed, fluffing the pillows at her back. "No sign of infection. Ya've even got some pink back in yer cheeks this mornin'." Mary smiled and brushed a strand of hair from Sage's forehead.

"Maybe I'll come down to the kitchen for supper tonight," Sage said. She smiled gratefully at Mary. The widows had been so wonderful, so helpful and nurturing since the mountain lion attack, cooking for themselves and waiting on Sage hand and foot. In truth, Sage enjoyed being cared for. It was the first time in years and years she could remember someone caring for her, instead of doing all the caring.

Still, her anxieties over Reb were nearly overwhelming! No matter how often Rose, Livie and Mary reassured her of Reb's increasing good health, it took every bit of her strength to keep from bursting into tears at the mere thought of him, at the visions which leapt to her mind each time she closed her eyes, the visions of the mountain lion attacking him, tearing him.

Charlie had been out to see Sage several times. He further assured her of Reb's healing. Likewise, he told her he and the other hands had the ranch well in hand. Still, Sage sensed something distressing, something she couldn't quite put her finger on. Charlie told Sage Reb blamed himself for the attack. Reb knew he should have hunted the cat down long before, instead of letting it roam about, an easy threat to cattle and anything else made of meat.

A constant nagging, insecure, frightened feeling had settled deep within Sage's being. No matter how hard she tried to concentrate on the glorious, impassioned moments she had shared with Reb on the way to the ranch that day, it was always darkened by some ominous, foreboding feeling. A sort of sickening sensation whispered to her that the course she'd been set on with Reb before the attack was irrevocably altered.

"Rose has chicken and dumplin's and all the fixin's set up for supper tonight," Mary said, taking one of Sage's hands between her own and patting it lovingly. "Tonight would be a good night to trot down for supper."

Sage forced a smile and said, "I'll come down, Miss Mary, but I doubt I'll be trottin'."

Mary laughed and shook her head, amused. "Now that's our Sage!" The old woman seemed to study Sage for a moment, her smile fading slightly, her eyes narrowing. "Ya know, I was attacked by a mountain lion once, myself."

"What?" Sage asked, astonished. Mary nodded and looked upward as the memory seemed to wash over her.

"I was twelve," she began, "and Mama and I were out castratin' pigs." Sage bit her lip, stifling the urge to giggle. Mary's face was suddenly so solemn, but as usual, her manner of starting a story was rather surprising. "It was awful hot that day," Mary continued, "and I was mighty irritated at havin' to help with the castratin'. Course, it had to be done. Them males is much easier to handle once they've been castrated. They feed out better most times, too," Mary explained. Sage nodded, still biting her lip, still trying not to giggle. "Anyhow," Mary began again, "Mama and me was about our business and, all of a sudden, this big ol' cat just comes out a nowhere! I mean, they're rare in Oklahoma as it is, but here it come . . . right at me! Mama seen it comin' and hollered for Pa, but he was too far away, and before I knew it, I was standin' face to face with the biggest ol' cat I ever did see!"

Sage frowned, listening intently, trying to imagine a young Mary, facing down a mountain lion. For a moment, she could see the scene in her mind's eye and realized, knowing Mary as she did, it was not an unexpected story.

"It sorta hissed at me once," Mary continued, "showin' its teeth. I was so scared, I couldn't move. I was still holdin' that pig down when that ol' cat swiped at me with one of its front paws. For a second, the pain was so bad I thought that the thing had tore my arm clean off! Mama pulled me back, snatched up the pig I'd been holdin', took hold of its hind legs and threw it off to one side. The ol' cat musta liked the smell of the pig's blood more'n mine, 'cause it went after the pig and left me be. My daddy come a runnin' up 'bout then, leveled his ol' Brown Bess and blew a hole in that ol' cat's head the size of Texas!" Sage could only shake her head, once again awed to silence by one of Mary Farthen's tender childhood stories. Sometimes Sage wondered how Mary lived long enough to get married and raise a family.

"Look here," Mary said, reaching around to unbutton her dress. Sage watched, astonished as Mary proceeded to slip her left shoulder and arm out of her dress. "See them scars?" the old woman asked. "That's where that ol' cat got me." Sage frowned, her own wounds suddenly throbbing anew, as she looked at the four long scars on Mary's upper arm. "They healed up just fine. See?" Sage nodded, but was speechless, horrified at the sight of the thick, purple scars. She knew the injuries on her back, the scars they would undoubtedly leave, would be at least as brutal and unsightly as Mary's were.

"Course, my . . . my mama didn't stitch mine nearly as neat as Reb stitched yers," Mary stammered, becoming suddenly aware of what Sage must be thinking. "I swear yers already look better than mine do."

"M . . . Mary?" Sage whispered then. "You . . . you know I haven't had the gumption to . . . to look at my . . . my back yet."

Mary smiled and uncharacteristically cupped Sage's cheek with an affectionate hand as she said, "Them wounds'll heal just fine, Sage."

"Are . . . are you certain?" Sage asked.

"Positively certain," Mary said with an affirming nod.

"And . . . and . . . what about Reb's?" Sage asked.

"Reb's a man!" Mary exclaimed, raising her eyebrows in a gesture of superior knowledge. "Men're s'posed to be a bit banged up. Makes 'em more . . . more manly."

In truth, Sage was just as worried about Reb's emotional scars as she was about his physical ones. The widows and even Charlie had told her very little about his frame of mind, just that he blamed himself for the attack. Sage knew the man she had fallen in love with well enough to know it would permanently damage him. She thought of the woman who had scarred his heart, of Ivy Dalton and the mark she had left on Rebel Mitchell. Heartbreak and anger were the brands she'd left on his soul. Sage did not even want to imagine what kind of mark regret and guilt would leave.

"I . . . I'm worried for him," Sage stammered.

"Well, we'll just get him out here to see ya as soon as we can. Might be easier to take you to him though. He's had a rougher time of it than

you. Either way, once he sees you're just fine he can quit frettin' over it."
Mary put her arm back in her dress sleeve. "He's over the fever now.
Maybe we can haul ya out there tomorrow."

෬

HOWEVER, AS SAGE lay in bed that night, gazing out her open window
to the summer stars, the feeling of foreboding returned. Was there
something the widows weren't telling her? She was badly hurt, yes, but
fit enough to travel. Why hadn't they taken her to see Reb? Why had they
kept telling her to wait, wait until his fever was over, wait until he was
better mended? It seemed too intentional, as if everyone was trying to
keep her from finding out something. Was he wounded far worse than
they told her? Or, had he been so angry over the attack, over being
wounded because of her, he'd decided her friendship and her kisses
weren't worth the trouble.

Chapter Ten

"*H*e doesn't want to see me, Ruthie," Sage said. She tugged at a small weed invading Ruthie's space of serenity. "Oh, they won't tell me that. Even Mary won't tell me that, but I know it's true. I was . . . I was foolish to even imagine he could ever . . ." Sage let her words trail off into silence once more.

Fighting the tears begging for release, Sage reached out and caressed the soft petals of one of the beautiful red roses growing around Ruthie's tombstone. The velvet of the petals usually served to soothe Sage, but this day it did nothing to cheer her.

"At least your roses are bloomin' beautiful this year," she said. "But a little more rain would help." She closed her eyes, trying to dispel the vision of Reb, that always lingered in her mind. "A little rain would be a blessed thing just now."

Sage held her breath, swallowed hard, choked back her tears. She wouldn't cry. Not on such a sunny day. She wouldn't cry even for the pain and doubt in her heart.

Reb did not want to see her. No matter what the widows said, she knew it was true. Reb was strong. Mountain lion attack or not, he was too strong, too determined, to stay away if he'd really wanted to see her, if he really cared for her.

At first, she'd been willing to ride out to see him, just as Mary had suggested. But when the widows had exchanged glances of uncertainty, she knew something was wrong. To her it was inappropriate anyway, chasing after him like a saloon tramp. Still, she would've done it if she'd had the courage. Yet doubt was thick as soup in her now.

Her mind concocted a million different reasons for the change she sensed in Reb. Perhaps, he'd realized he didn't want to lead Sage into believing he cared for her. Or, worse, perhaps his nearly getting killed by a mountain lion had turned his heart back toward the woman he had loved once before. Perhaps, he was reconsidering staying on at Eugenia's ranch, considering returning to that Ivy Dalton.

"He can't leave, Ruthie," Sage said out loud at the thought. "He bet Eugenia and he lost. He promised to stay as long as she wants him to." Sage breathed a heavy sigh, however. She knew nothing, nobody could hold Reb Mitchell if he didn't want to be held. Raising her face to the sky, she closed her eyes, wishing once more for a few dark clouds, the hope of release.

Looking about her, she saw three black cows slowly making their way toward the little fenced area. They were slow, carefree-looking creatures, with Reb's brand on their hindquarters. Sage envied them a moment, envied their careless meandering.

She looked back to Ruthie's tombstone and sighed once more.

"Oh, Ruthie, as odd as it sounds, sometimes I feel as if . . . as if you're my only true friend. I can talk to you and you always have time to listen to me, to hear my silly ramblin's and worries." Sage frowned. "I wonder so often what you looked like. Was your hair light or dark? What dress did your mama put you in to lay you to rest? Did you have a favorite doll? Is it with you now?"

Covering her mouth quickly with one hand, Sage held her breath to stop her tears. "I love him, Ruthie. I love him so much!" she whispered. "Why can't he love me? I don't even care that no other man ever has! I just want Reb to love me!"

For the first time in nearly nine years, Sage cried without waiting for the rain. Suddenly, the aching in her heart, her desperate need to see Reb, to be held by him, to have him smile at her, was overwhelming. She collapsed in a heap of harsh sobbing and endless tears, careless of the flowers and sage growing over the little grave, careless of the three cows who stood watching her, jaws shifting from side to side as they chewed mouthfuls of sweet pasture grass. For the first time in nearly nine years, Sage could not keep the pain in her heart, the aching in her soul, silent and hidden. She wanted to cry out for Reb, scream his name, run all the way to the Smarthing ranch and beg him to love her. Instead, she simply sobbed, her tears of heartbreak moistening little Ruthie States' soil blanket.

શ

"THIS IS PURE nonsense, Reb," Eugenia scolded as she angrily folded a blanket and set it on the foot of the bed. "This . . . none of it was your fault. It wasn't Sage's fault either."

"Of course it wasn't her fault," Reb grumbled.

"Then you saddle up and ride back to the boardin' house with me to see her," Eugenia demanded. "You're gonna break that girl's heart, Reb . . . if you haven't already."

"I ain't gonna break her heart," Reb said. "She's probably glad to be rid of me. What kind of a man would let her get tore up like that?" Eugenia sighed and shook her head as Reb rubbed at his temples with one hand. "I shoulda hunted that cat down, Aunt Eugenia," he said. "I swear . . . I think my heart 'bout stopped when I seen it take her down. I see it every time I close my eyes . . . see that cat at her . . . see her bleedin' all over the kitchen floor."

Eugenia frowned, her own heart aching for Reb's pain. She did not miss the way his hands had begun to tremble as he spoke of the cat attacking Sage. She knew he hadn't feared a moment for his own life, but the sight of the cat nearly killing Sage had shaken him up something awful. Somehow he'd convinced himself it was his fault. He'd convinced himself Sage wouldn't want to have anything to do with a man who would've allowed such a thing to happen to her.

"I . . . I put her in terrible danger just because I couldn't keep my wits about me," he continued. "You seen her that day, Auntie! She was so beautiful, so free somehow," he said. "It's a wonder I made it all the way back here without throwin' her down in the grass and . . ."

"She was happier than I've ever seen her since I've known her, Reb," Eugenia interrupted. "And . . . and it's because she's in love with you." There! She'd said it. Come hellfire or angels, she'd said it!

But Reb shook his head, held up a hand in gesture she shouldn't say it again.

"Now you know as well as I do, Aunt Eugenia, I ain't got nothin' to give a woman in that regard," he said.

"Oh, horse manure and goose drizzle!" Eugenia exclaimed. "If you aren't the dumbest post on the fence, Rebel Lee Mitchell, then I don't know who is." Reb straightened up, looked at Eugenia with an astonished expression. And well he should, for she was sick and tired of his whining. "Not once, Reb," she began, "not once did I ever see you look at Ivy Dalton the way you look at Sage Willows! Not once! So don't tell me you don't love her, Reb! Don't try to tell me you don't!"

"I never said I didn't!" Reb exclaimed. "I said I ain't got nothin' to give her. I never said I didn't want her. But I'm damaged, Aunt Eugenia! I don't trust myself to be able to hold onto her heart. I don't trust myself to hold her at all! And she sure as hell shouldn't trust me! That cat nearly killed her and it was my fault! Do ya really think she's gonna want me now? Do ya think she's gonna trust me after that? If I can't even keep her safe from harm, what makes ya think she's gonna trust me in any other regard? And if ya can't trust a person, ya can't love 'em. Believe me, if I know anythin', then I know that."

"That's nonsense, Reb!" Eugenia told him. "That mess with Ivy Dalton was a completely different bowl of beans, boy! And you know it! You trusted Ivy with your heart and she stomped on it. She broke your trust, sure enough, she did! But I think it was your pride and your trust in yourself that got most damaged, Reb. Oh, your heart recovered all right. But your faith in yourself didn't and you're afraid, afraid Sage will love you the way Ivy did, because you're good to look at, handsome, and all the other girls want you. But you know darn well, that isn't Sage. Sage would no more hold you responsible for what happened with that cat than you would her!" Eugenia shook her head, wagging a scolding index finger at Reb and adding, "This is pure nonsense you've talked into your own head, Reb. I was willin' to give you some time, due to that awful fever you took to and your wounds bein' so bad. But you've had your time, and now, you get on your horse and you ride out to the boardin' house to see Sage. Don't you dare leave her to wonder what you're thinkin'. Don't you dare leave her talkin' to that poor little dead girl out in the pasture and cryin' her eyes out over you."

"Ain't been no rain," Reb mumbled. "She ain't been cryin', especially over me."

"You ride out to the boardin' house, Reb," Eugenia told him. "Maybe not today. Maybe not tomorrow. But you do it. I think you know Sage is in love with you. But fear, or somethin' else I don't know about, is tryin' to convince you otherwise. Beat it down, Reb. If not for your own happiness . . . for hers."

☙

REB WATCHED HIs Aunt Eugenia ride away in the buggy. Reaching down at his side, he scratched Bullet behind the ears, wincing at the pain caused when the dog landed its clumsy paws on the wounds at his thigh. Reb wondered for a moment if Bullet had been at the ranch house that day instead of out with Charlie and the herd—would the cat have been in the barn?

He turned around and headed back into the house. As always, his stomach rolled at the site of the dark brownish-red stain on the kitchen floor. Charlie assured Reb over and over it was Reb's own blood that Eugenia hadn't been able to scrub away, that Sage's wounds were less severe, bled less. But to Reb's eyes, it was Sage's pain he saw each time he looked at the floor, each time he looked at himself in the mirror.

He closed his eyes and thought of the moment he'd walked into the boardinghouse to see Sage all gussied up in one of Miss Rose's old dancing dresses. Sage's smile had been mesmerizing! He'd never seen her so unguarded, so happy. He'd been sure then and there he would have her for his own. One way or the other, he'd decided to own her. He envisioned stopping the wagon in the pasture on the way to the ranch, remembered how breathtaking it had felt to hold her in his arms, sighed at the memory of the way she'd succumbed to him and to her own desires.

He winced, remembering the way she'd stepped forward, taken his face in her soft hands, kissing him hard on the mouth. Even now, with Bullet licking his hand, the wounds at his chest and leg still aching, even now it was the thrill that had traveled through him when she'd kissed him that dominated his senses.

He wanted her in his arms! He wanted her in his house! He wanted her in his bed! He wanted her in his life!

Opening his eyes, Reb turned and beat his fist against the wall. He beat it hard against the sturdy wood planking until his knuckles and fingers ached as badly as his other wounds.

Eugenia was right. Why was he comparing anything having to do with Sage Willows to anything having to do with Ivy Dalton? Surely Sage knew he hadn't meant for the cat to attack her that day. He was a coward not to face her. Yet something in him whispered to him, asked him, did his fear truly originate with the fact Sage might not trust him? Or did it begin with the idea she might lose interest in him the way Ivy had?

Either way, Reb knew that to avoid facing her would surely mean the end of any chance he had at winning her heart. Therefore, the question remained, would he follow fear and cowardice, or could he conquer fear, find bravery and perhaps win Sage? If he did, could he keep her or would she tire of him? Which was worse, to never try, or to try and risk rejection? Surely it was worth whatever pain he might endure to own her, even for a time. Wasn't it?

☃

ONE WEEK PASSED and then another, and still Sage had not seen Reb. She'd tried to give up hope. Each day as she visited Ruthie, nearly sobbing herself sick, Sage tried to rid herself of any hope he would come to her. So many times she'd saddled Drifter, determined to ride out to the ranch, seek him out, ask him why he had abandoned any interest he may have had in her. Each time, however, she ended up talking to Ruthie, instead, fearful of what Reb might answer.

Sage's poor, troubled mind imagined many reasons for Reb's avoidance of her. Again, she mulled the possible reasons around and around in her mind, adding new possibilities to the already long list. The wounds at her back, for instance. Perhaps the scars left by the mountain lions attack were too gruesome. Perhaps, she mused, he simply did not want to be reminded of their ugliness. Still, she knew such shallow considerations were not in him.

And so, she reviewed the other reasons already plaguing her mind. Perhaps, he'd simply had a change of heart, found her too weak, too uninteresting to pursue any more. Perhaps, and it was her worst fear, perhaps he really had changed his mind about the infamous Ivy Dalton. In her most secret places of worry, Ivy Dalton and her one-time hold over Reb's heart and mind, was Sage's greatest fear.

Still, whether because of the repulsive scars, simple disinterest, or a love of the past, whichever the reason, with each passing day it became more clear, Reb was not going to return to her. Her eyes longed to gaze at him; her mind longed to hear his voice. Her body and soul ached to be held in his arms and her mouth watered for want of his kiss. Yet, Sage knew and she tried to accept that she would have to return to life without him.

The life Sage had known before Reb Mitchell stretched out before her, tedious, uneventful and dreary. Oh, certainly she loved the widows. Certainly the sun shone bright. But, it would never be enough again. It hadn't been, anyway, but it certainly wouldn't be enough now. Yet she tried to go on. What else was there to do, but go on?

One day, having rubbed down Drifter after a ride to Ruthie's pasture, Sage smiled as she saw Charlie Dugger walking toward her. Her thoughts were hopeless and grim, yes, but she saw no reason to pour her anxiety over anyone else. So, as she walked toward the boardinghouse, she smiled as she saw Charlie approaching. It was Tuesday, after all, and the Reverend Tippetts, Scarlett and Winnery were coming for supper. Of course, she knew Reb wouldn't be there, but for a brief moment, when she saw Charlie smile and touch the brim of his hat, her heart leapt. Perhaps he would come! Perhaps Eugenia had somehow convinced Reb to join Charlie and come to supper.

Yet, as Charlie approached, Sage felt the now familiar pang of heartache in her bosom. Reb would not come. Perhaps never again. And if he did, it would not be for her sake. He'd always come for his aunt's sake in the first place. She realized that now.

"Hey, there, Miss Sage," Charlie greeted.

"Hello, Charlie," Sage said, forcing a friendly smile, hoping her eyes were no longer red from her sobbing and tears in Ruthie's pasture.

"Um . . . I . . . um . . . I was wonderin' if I might have a word with ya," Charlie said.

"Of course," Sage said. The last thing she wanted to do was talk with Reb's best friend. She always felt as if Charlie were going to tell her something final about Reb, as if he would be the one to confirm that Reb had no interest in her. Yet, he was a kind man and her friend as well. He'd visited her often after the mountain lion attack and was always very kind and polite.

Charlie inhaled a deep breath. Taking Sage by the hand he led her to the side of the boardinghouse.

"Ya . . . ya have to come out to the ranch, Miss Sage," Charlie blurted. "Ya just have to come out there and straighten Reb out."

For a moment, as always, Sage thought, *Yes! I'll go! I'll go to him!* But she shook her head.

"Charlie," she began, "Please. If he doesn't want me . . . I mean . . . if he doesn't want to see me, then I can't . . . ."

"But he does, Miss Sage!" Charlie exclaimed. "He does! He's just . . . he's just feelin' like he failed ya. He's blamin' himself for the big cat, you gettin' hurt like ya did. He . . . he can't get past it, Miss Sage."

Sage leaned back against the boardinghouse wall. She shook her head and held onto her tears. Oh, how she wished it were that simple. How she wished all she had to do was convince Reb the cat's attack wasn't his fault. Maybe there was hope in that . . . if that was all it was. But Sage knew there was more. She felt it.

"He didn't fail me, Charlie," she whispered. "You know he didn't. He's just . . . he's just a kind man . . . who . . . who flirted with me a little. He's just been thinkin' better of . . . of spendin' so much time with me and . . . ."

"Miss Sage," Charlie repeated, taking both her hands in his as he pleaded with her. "Surely ya know him better than that. He . . . he's blamin' himself so hard for what happened to ya, for the damage that cat done ya. That's all. That's all it is. It ain't nothin' else."

∞

REB'S EYES NARROWED as he watched Charlie take Sage's hands in his own. The man had been his friend for years! Years! But this was too much! How could Charlie pursue Sage, knowing how Reb felt about her? He'd beat the life out of Charlie, that's what he'd do!

Then Reb remembered he had never really confessed his feelings for Sage to Charlie. For all Charlie Dugger knew, Reb Mitchell was through with women. Hadn't Reb told Charlie so himself? And on many, many occasions?

Still, he doubted it was all Charlie's fault anyway. Reb knew how *he* felt in Sage's presence, and it stood to reason, any other man would be as captivated by her as he was. Still, for the first time in a long time, Ivy's face was brilliant and clear in his mind.

Two weeks. It had taken him two weeks to find the courage to seek out Sage and ask her forgiveness. Two weeks and she'd already moved away from him and toward another man. He grimaced, squeezed his eyes tightly shut. It couldn't be true. He could still taste the delicious flavor of her kiss, still sense the feel of her body in his arms. He could see the way her eyes lit up when he entered a room, the blush painting her cheeks whenever he flirted with her.

Turning from the scene before him, he dug deep into his soul, into his heart. He had to know. He had to know if she could forgive him for the mountain lion attack. She wasn't like Ivy Dalton. He was certain of it. Sage would not toy with him, then quickly tire of him like he was a new puppy. She loved him, he was sure of it. Nearly sure of it, anyway. Hoped it was true at least.

He'd walk for a few minutes, gather his thoughts. He knew Charlie and he knew Sage. There was no dalliance between them. He knew it. He had to know it. He had to! He'd fought his fear, wrestled with cowardice and ridden all the way to town. He'd almost turned back several times, it was true. Even now, his hands trembled at the thought of facing her. Still, she lived, she breathed, she smiled. Surely she would forgive him.

He knew he wasn't worthy of her, knew Charlie Dugger probably was. Yet he wanted her. He had to face her. He had to try and win her trust once more.

Yep. He'd walk for a while, tell himself Charlie was only being kind, inquiring about her well-being or some such nonsense. He'd walk a while and then he'd face her. Surely, she was only being kind to Charlie. That's it. They were just friends talking.

He'd walk a while.

❨

"JUST RIDE OUT to the ranch and see him, Miss Sage," Charlie pleaded. "Seein' ya will make all the difference in the way he's feelin' both body and mind."

"Charlie," Sage said. "What'll he think of me? If I go chasin' out there after him, he'll think I'm . . ."

"He'll think ya care enough about him to do it. He'll think ya forgive him for lettin' the cat get to ya," Charlie interrupted. "Surely, ya know how much he cares for ya, Miss Sage."

Every ounce of Sage's being wanted to believe Charlie, wanted to believe Reb cared for her. She closed her eyes, remembering the mischievous expression on his face the night he'd cornered her in the kitchen, shared peach-flavored kisses with her. She envisioned the alluring fire in his eyes when he'd stopped the wagon in the middle of the pasture on the way to the ranch, teasing her about, "having his way," with her.

"I know yer afraid, Miss Sage," Charlie said, smiling at her. "Reb can be a frightenin' man." Sage smiled and Charlie chuckled. "But ya gotta come out to the ranch and let him know ya don't blame him for what happened."

Sage smiled at Charlie. Perhaps she could find the courage to go to Reb. Certainly, propriety dictated he should come to her, that a women never went chasing after a man. Yet, if what Charlie said was true? Could Rebel Lee Mitchell really be afraid of facing her?

"Let me . . . let me have some time to gather a little courage, Charlie," Sage said. "I'll try."

Charlie smiled and nodded. "I know it's hard, Miss Sage. Reb can be a mighty difficult man to read at times, but I believe ya know what he's thinkin' where you're concerned. He needs ya, Miss Sage. More'n even he knows."

Sage smiled at Charlie again. He was a kind man and a good friend. She did feel more hopeful in talking with him. Maybe, just maybe, she could find the courage to face Reb. Maybe he really did think she blamed him for what happened, no matter how ridiculous a notion it was.

"I've got to get in and get some supper on for the ladies and our guests," Sage told him. "I'll . . . I'll see you out at the ranch tomorrow . . . maybe."

"Good deal," Charlie said, smiling at Sage with approval. "I'll be lookin' for ya then." He tipped his hat and added, "Bye now."

"Bye," Sage said, smiling as she watched him walk away. Maybe Charlie was right. Maybe it wasn't her weakness that had kept Reb away. Maybe he hadn't changed his mind about her. Maybe he really was feeling some sort of misplaced guilt over what had happened to them. Sage sighed, allowing hope to flicker in her bosom once more.

She paused at the barrel full of herbs by the boardinghouse back door, pinching off a sprig of sage and drawing it to her nose. At the anticipation of seeing Reb again, Sage felt light-hearted, excited and tingly. She closed her eyes and pictured his face, his eyes, his kiss.

Sighing, she pushed open the back door and entered the boarding-house. Her hope was renewed. The widows had been telling her all along she needed to relieve the fever in Reb's mind. Still, somehow, having Charlie's confirmation gave her the courage she needed to perhaps actually go to him. And oh, how she longed to see Reb again, to talk with him, touch him, kiss him!

"I'm back," Sage called, setting the sage sprig down on the kitchen counter. "Anybody home?"

"Sage! There you are!" Rose said, entering the kitchen. Her face was pink with delight, her eyes wide as saucers.

"What is it, Miss Rosie?" Sage asked. She couldn't help but smile at the woman. She looked so pleased with herself.

"I've let out the empty room, Sage!" Rose exclaimed. "Just this mornin' while you were gone! I've let out the empty room! And to a young lady, too! You know how we always worried that some filthy old man would want to let it? Well, I've let it out to a nice young lady. Now, she won't be here long. I guess she's in town just a short while until she's married. Says her intended is close by or some such thing. Still, I've let out the room and that should help cheer things up a bit. Right?"

Sage stood, eyes wide with astonishment, attempting to navigate Rose's babble. Rose had helped Sage so many times throughout the years since her parents' deaths. In fact, it had been Rose who found Mary and Olivia, finally convincing them to let rooms at Willows'. Sage trusted Rose, and yet, she gave pause, not entirely happy about a stranger infringing on the intimate, happy life she shared with the widows.

Still, life hadn't been as happy of late. Sage knew she could never be happy without Reb. But hope was rekindled in her and she smiled at Rose. Perhaps a new tenant wouldn't be so bad.

"Well that's wonderful, Miss Rosie," Sage exclaimed, feigning delight, still distracted by her conversation with Dugger and the prospect of seeing Reb. "Is she here now?"

"Oh, yes!" Rose exclaimed. "Come and meet her! I know you'll just adore her. She's just the sweetest little thing." Taking hold of Sage's hand, Rose began leading her toward the parlor. Sage reached up, smoothing her hair with her free hand. She was anxious about meeting the new tenant at Willows' Boarding House. Yet, she couldn't fathom why, until the moment she stepped into the parlor to see a young woman, golden-haired and beautiful as a sunrise.

"Sage," Rose began, "This is Ivy, our new resident."

"Oh, I'm so pleased to meet you, Miss Willows," the young beauty greeted. With a smile sparkling like sunshine, the young woman reached out, clasping Sage's hand in her own.

"I . . . Ivy?" Sage stammered in a whisper. Surely the young woman's name wasn't Ivy? Surely she didn't share the same name as the woman from Reb's past, Ivy Dalton?

"Yes," the lovely young woman answered. "Ivy Dalton. And I am just tickled pink to have found such a charmin' place to stay while I'm here! Your boardin' house is simply the sweetest little place I've ever seen!"

Sage couldn't breathe. She was certain she would faint, or simply drop and die where she stood.

"Ivy Dalton?" Sage repeated.

"Yes," Ivy said, frowning just a bit. No doubt she was puzzled by Sage's reaction.

"You all right, Sage honey?" Rose asked. "You look as white as a—"

"Ivy Dalton!" Eugenia interrupted, entering by way of the front door. "What're you doin' here?"

Ivy turned around, and Sage fancied the pink faded from her cheeks slightly as she said, "Eugenia?"

"I asked you a question," Eugenia nearly growled. "What do you think you're doin' here?"

"Eugenia!" Rose exclaimed. "Why . . . why you're bein' positively rude! What's the matter with you? This is our new resident here at Willows', Ivy Dalton, and she's just come in from—"

"From hell, I'm guessin'," Eugenia said.

"Eugenia!" Rose exclaimed.

"There's no reason for discourtesy, Eugenia," Ivy began. "However, if you happen to be livin' here . . . well, then I'll just find other accommodations elsewhere."

"You certainly will!" Eugenia confirmed.

"Eugenia!" Rose exclaimed again.

Sage still stood, too stunned to react. Ivy Dalton, Sage's greatest fear, stood there before her in her own parlor. Sage was sick to her stomach, thought she might vomit. How could it be? She was so beautiful! All dressed in lavender and lace, long blonde curls cascading from her perfectly coifed hair.

"Thank you for your kindness, Mrs. Applewhite," Ivy said, taking

Rose's hand in her own. "But I'm afraid I didn't know what type of people, other than yourself of course, are stayin' at this establishment. I'm afraid I simply can't lower myself to—"

"Get out!" Eugenia demanded. "Don't you ever set foot near this house again!"

"You might be thinkin' on changin' your manners pretty quick, Eugenia," Ivy said. "You wouldn't want any family rifts, considerin' things are about to—"

A knock on the front door interrupted Ivy's scolding of Eugenia. As Eugenia and Ivy continued to glare at one another, Rose looked to Sage. Sage could only shrug her shoulders, uncertain as to what to do. She felt paralyzed with fear, doubt, and every other negative emotion.

"Well, I suppose, since I'm the only one with my head still on straight . . ." Rose mumbled as she started for the door.

"I . . . I'll go, Miss Rosie," Sage choked, quickly brushing past her. She had no desire to look at Ivy Dalton for one more moment. Any visitor would be a welcome distraction. Sage found herself hoping it was Forest Simmons. Even he was preferable to the woman who might still own Reb's heart, or at least his memory.

Sage opened the door. She gasped as she looked up to see Reb standing before her.

He removed his hat, nodded at her, and said, "Hello, Sage."

"Reb," Sage managed to breathe. In that moment, she was certain she heard her own heart break. No doubt she felt it, for the pain in her bosom was at once excruciating. He'd come for Ivy. Sage had known something had changed between her and Reb. The mountain lion attack had somehow changed his feelings toward her and, though she didn't understand why, he'd changed his mind about her, about even being her friend. Somehow Reb had reconciled with Ivy! That was the only explanation for Ivy's presence, the only explanation for Reb's.

"Sage . . . I . . . I . . ." he stammered. He was uncharacteristically lacking in confidence. Sage knew why, glad he at least owned a little guilt for breaking her heart, though the knowledge did nothing to ease her pain.

"I know why you've come," she interrupted.

"You do?" he asked. He sighed, a slight grin relaxing the harsh expression on his face. "Sage, I'm sorry. I've been . . . I've been afraid to . . ."

"Reb?" Ivy exclaimed, suddenly appearing at Sage's side. "Rebel, darlin'!" Sage watched as the young beauty threw her arms around Reb's neck. Jealous fury washed over her like molten iron! Hurt, anger, fear all worked to paralyze her where she stood.

"Ivy?" he exclaimed. He looked to Ivy, an expression of utter astonishment on his features. He looked to Sage, frowning, then back to Ivy.

"Yes, darlin'!" Ivy exclaimed, still embracing Reb. "I came the moment I got the telegram!"

"Telegram?" Reb asked.

"You could've warned us, Reb," Eugenia said, coming to stand in the doorway as well.

"Warned ya?" Reb asked.

Eugenia stepped forward, dropping a large carpetbag on the porch. "We'll have anythin' else you might have brought sent over to the roomin' house at the other end of town. It's a more appropriate place for the likes of Ivy Dalton."

"What's goin' on?" Reb asked.

"Oh, don't mind them, Reb," Ivy said, linking her arm through his. Sage studied Reb. He seemed almost as surprised to see Ivy as she was. As he stood frowning at her, Sage wondered if she should say something to him, smile at him, offer some sort of gesture indicating her joy at seeing him. Yet, he said nothing to her, only continued to glare at her in a manner unnerving her all together. "Don't mind them at all," Ivy continued. "I heard this was nothin' but a boardin' house for widows and spinsters. Still, it looked so much nicer than the place down the road that I thought . . ."

"Hush up, Ivy!" Eugenia demanded. "Rebel," she said then. "Do you have somethin' to say to Ivy?"

Reb looked to Ivy, then back to his aunt, then to Sage. His eyes narrowed, his jaw tightening as he asked Sage, "Do I?"

Sage inhaled deeply. He had seemed so surprised to see Ivy. But was he surprised to see her or just surprised to see her at the boardinghouse? He made no move toward Sage. Not one. He did not reach out to touch her in any way. He didn't even smile at her. All he did was repeat, "Do I have somethin' to say to Ivy?"

"I . . . I . . . I'm sure I wouldn't know," Sage stammered.

"Sage!" Eugenia exclaimed.

❧

REB FELT HIS heart go cold. Like a heavy, frozen stone it settled hard in his chest. For a moment he felt empty, void of every emotion. He looked at Sage, beautiful, soft, wonderful Sage. Sage, who he'd come to apologize to. He'd found his courage and come to town to apologize for failing her, to apologize for the injuries inflicted on her tender, beautiful body by the old mountain lion. He'd failed her, and in failing her, she'd obviously seen his weakness. Still, he'd hoped he could win her back, push thoughts of Charlie or any other man from her mind. He'd worked hard to convince himself that what he'd seen between her and Charlie outside the boardinghouse a short time before was simply a misunderstanding on his part. He'd managed to convince himself Sage wasn't like Ivy, that she and Charlie were only friends, just like he and Charlie were friends. But from the look of indifference on her face as she stood before him, he realized he'd been wrong.

He'd been so afraid to face her, afraid his weakness would cause her to see what a worthless piece of flesh he was. He'd hoped she would forgive him, wrap her lovely arms around his neck, press her soft body to him, kiss him the way she had in the pastures on the way to the ranch that day and whisper forgiveness into his ear. He'd hoped she would understand he had simply not known the cat was lurking in the old barn, simply not been prepared, even though he should have been. He'd dreamt of her forgiveness, her smile, her sweet delicious kiss. Yet, standing before her now, he could see she did not trust him. She did not find him attractive, could not forgive him for what had happened to her. Otherwise, she surely would not have let Ivy overtake him the way she had. Perhaps, she had already settled on giving her heart over to someone else, someone more capable, someone like Charlie. The thought wounded him deeply.

What was it about him that caused women to feel unsatisfied, go looking elsewhere for something more?

He glanced at Ivy, Ivy? Why was she there next to him? How had she arrived? Why had she come? Reb studied her stunning eyes, her lovely poisonous smile. When he'd left to ranch for his aunt, Ivy had sworn she would follow him anywhere, search for him to the ends of the earth, and never let him go. It looked as if she was capable of making good on some promises, just not the ones which mattered most. He looked at her and felt nothing. Not even hate or resentment. Rather, the only emotion he could feel for her was indifference to her existence.

As he looked at Ivy, Reb felt his heart harden further, felt colder within than he'd ever felt before. Oh, Ivy Dalton had trodden on him, angered him, hurt his pride and wounded his soul. There was no doubt of it. But it was Sage Willows who had crushed, abused and broken his heart, torn his spirit into shreds and tattered remnants.

He looked back to Sage, still standing in the doorway looking at him, not a tear in her beautiful eyes. She no more wanted him than she did old Forest Simmons. Yes, it was Sage Willows who had finally ruined Rebel Lee Mitchell, just as he'd feared she would from the moment he'd first seen her.

The pain, throbbing in his chest, almost took his breath away. Reb wished it would, wished he could lose consciousness and be free of the misery stretching out before him. But he did not lose consciousness. Sage had spurned him. She did not want him. And if Sage Willows did not want him, then he wanted nothing. Nothing. Life held nothing for him without her.

∞

"ALL RIGHT THEN," Reb said, reaching down and picking up Ivy's carpetbag.

"Sage!" Eugenia whispered, taking hold of Sage's arm. "Do somethin'!"

"I'm . . . I'm sorry for the misunderstandin', Miss Dalton," Sage said.

"It's of no consequence, Miss Willows. How were you to know

Eugenia Smarthing and I had crossed paths before?" Ivy said, tightening her hold on Reb's arm.

"Rebel . . . don't you dare walk away like this," Eugenia warned.

"I'm just takin' Ivy over to the roomin' house outside town, Auntie," Reb said. "Miss Rosie," he said, returning his hat to his head and nodding at Rose. "Miss Willows," he said then, glaring at Sage. He turned and left, Ivy clinging to his arm. They walked across the porch, down the steps and into the road.

Sage watched him go, frozen with pain and heartache, disbelief and confusion. She couldn't move, couldn't speak, couldn't cry out to him that she loved him.

"For cryin' in the bucket, Sage!" Eugenia exclaimed. "Run after him! What is wrong with you?"

"Ask him," Sage breathed as tears filled her eyes.

"What on earth is goin' on?" Rose demanded, stomping a foot like an angry child.

"Sage!" Eugenia exclaimed again.

Sage turned, running through the house and out the back kitchen door. She didn't go to the barn to saddle Drifter. She simply ran—ran toward the clouds gathering in the distance and the loneliness of Ruthie's pasture.

Chapter Eleven

❧ ☙

Sage took the biscuits out of the oven. She opened the cupboard door and removed a jar of strawberry preserves. Taking the cloth off the top of the jar, she inhaled the sweet scent of sugar and strawberries. The bacon was nearly finished frying and Mary was already sitting at the table wearing her ratty, red nightgown.

"I suppose Rose and Livie are primpin' and primpin'. Can't they smell the bacon?" Mary grumbled. "And where in tarnation is Eugenia? I ain't waitin' around all day for them to get down here. I'll just have my breakfast alone."

Sage smiled. Mary was so cranky at times, especially before she'd had her breakfast.

"There's a herd comin' through town," Eugenia said, entering the kitchen. "Must be the new herd Reb's bringin' to the ranch."

At the mention of Reb's name, Sage held her breath for a moment. As was the case every time she heard his name, a sickening wave of heartache washed over her. Still, she tried to appear unaffected and, after a moment, she released the painful breath.

"Well, let's get a look at 'em," Mary said. The old woman rose from her seat at the table and left the boardinghouse by way of the front door.

"What on earth are you doin', Mary?" Sage heard Rose exclaim as she descended the stairs. "Do you want every man in town to see you in that raggedly ol' thing you call a nightgown?"

Sage held her breath once more as she heard the rumble of the approaching herd. She could hear the cowboys whistle as they drove the cattle, smell the dust the animals kicked up as they moved closer. The memory of the day Reb's main herd went through town poured over her, the memory of how happy he'd been and the kiss he'd taken from her in the barn.

Sage winced and held back her tears. It was too early in the day to run to Ruthie. She'd begun to accept she would have to go on, live some sort of life. She'd tried not to cry over Ruthie's grave every day. So far, she hadn't been able to go through a day without doing so, but she had to try.

Reb hadn't been to the boardinghouse, not even to see his aunt, since that day more than a week before when he'd shown up to collect Ivy Dalton. Every moment of every day Sage longed for him, yearned to see him. Even if he had chosen Ivy, even though Sage had not been able to capture his attention beyond a flirtation, she loved him and longed for his presence.

Yet, she knew she must get used to not seeing him. She would have to accept he would never again wink at her, flirt with her, hold her in his arms and kiss her. His smile would never be for her again. He'd never come to dinner and stay for a game of cards, placing ridiculous bets with the widows.

Mr. Getcher had told Sage only the day before that Ivy Dalton was the talk of the town! Word was she was Rebel Mitchell's intended and that they meant to be married before the summer was through.

Reverend Tippetts, however, having been to dinner that very night, said he knew of no such information from Reb. Scarlett was certain this Ivy Dalton woman had made up the entire story, though it was sure enough true Ivy was acquainted with Reb. He'd been seen with her, briefly, several times over the past week.

Winnery said very little on the subject, stating only, "That Ivy Dalton . . . she puts me in mind of a cowpoke I knew once. Never seen a man get throwd from a horse more'n that one."

"I'd rather have bacon and biscuits than watch a dusty bunch of cows wander down the street," Livie said, entering the kitchen and sitting down at the table. "Wouldn't you, Sage?"

"I'm always in the mind for bacon," Sage said, forcing a friendly smile.

"There's some good cattle in that herd," Mary said as she entered the kitchen again.

"Yes," Eugenia agreed, sitting at the table across from Livie. "They'll grow Reb's herd nicely."

"Well, I for one think it's high time we had some fun around here," Rose said, as she sat down. "Things have been too awful glum of late."

"How about some cards later," Sage suggested, again forcing a smile. "After lunch. We can sit down for hours!" She turned back toward the stove as four sets of skeptical eyes lingered on her.

So far, her friends had been very kind and understanding. Since the day Ivy had arrived and left the boardinghouse on Reb's arm, not one of them had pressed her. Not one. Not even Eugenia. Sage was grateful to them for it. Her tears were close to spilling over often. One word from any of them would've caused the dam to break, and she wasn't ready for that. Even though she'd begun to cry without the rain to hide her tears, Sage wasn't ready to allow anyone to see her so overcome with weeping. Only Ruthie. She didn't mind if Ruthie knew.

"Cards sound perfect," Rose said, at last. "But let's do wait 'til after lunch. I . . . uh . . . I have some errands to run."

"Yes. Yes, let's wait until after lunch," Livie agreed. "I have some things that need tendin' to as well."

"And . . . and I promised Gareth Getcher I'd look over his money books this mornin'," Mary added.

"I thought I might make us some cookies. If that's all right with you, Sage," Eugenia added.

Sage looked at the widows, suspicion thick in her mind. They seemed guilty somehow, quite guilty, as if they were up to no good.

"Are you ladies up to somethin'?" she couldn't help but ask.

"Whatever would give you that idea, Sage?" Rose asked, fiddling with the broach at her collar.

Sage frowned for a moment, then smiled and sighed. *Let them have their secrets*, she thought. They were probably up to no good at all. Just like the time they'd gotten mad at ol' Forest Simmons for proposing to Sage. They'd sneaked into his house one day when he was out and sewed the flies and trapdoors shut on all his long underwear. Sage giggled at the memory. Still, it had been some time since they'd gotten into that much mischief. Best to let their silliness stay a secret. They enjoyed it more that way.

Sage heard one of the cowboys whistle out in the street. Her thoughts immediately went to Reb. She, too, wished she could ride out to the ranch with the widows and watch this herd come in. But those days were behind her. She was the proprietress of Willows' Boarding House. That's what she was, and it was a far better life than some women knew.

Still, as she lifted the bacon out of the frying pan with a fork, her mouth began to water. Not from anticipation of the tasty meat, but from the memory of Reb's kiss the day his first herd had come in. She swallowed hard, trying in vain to push the memory from her mind.

"Here you go, ladies," she said, plopping a plate of bacon down in the middle of the kitchen table. "Breakfast is served."

ℜℛ

"WALK ON DOWN to the general store with me, won't ya, Sage?" Mary asked. Sage smiled, noting Mary had changed from her ratty nightgown into a pretty blue dress she usually reserved for church and social gatherings.

"On your way to see Mr. Getcher, Mary?" Sage asked.

"That man couldn't add two and two if his life depended on it," Mary grumbled. "I don't know how he ever roped me into helpin' with his books. I oughta be gettin' paid for my time and trouble."

Sage smiled. She knew Mr. Getcher rather doted on Mary. Furthermore, no matter how much Mary moaned and grumbled, Sage knew Mary was very fond of Mr. Getcher. In her own aching heart, Sage hoped

Mary's "goin' over the books" meetings with Mr. Getcher were secretly romantic rendezvous in disguise.

Mary's legs had been giving her more aches and pains than usual. Sage suspected the walk to the general store would be a little easier for Mary if she had a companion to link arms with.

"I'd be glad to walk down with you, Miss Mary," Sage said. "I could use a bit of fresh air myself."

It was a lovely day, warm and bright with sunshine. The slight summer breeze carried with it the comforting aroma of cattle and pasture grass. Sage sighed as she walked with Mary, pleased by the wildflowers growing along the side of the streets and between the buildings.

"The paintbrush is fiery this summer," Mary said. "And the columbine seems more vibrant than last year, too."

"Yes," Sage said. "It's a lovely summer, makes me dread winter."

Before long, Sage had delivered Mary to Mr. Getcher. He'd offered the old woman his arm and she'd smiled at him, slapping it away playfully. Sage smiled. Mary deserved a little attention. She'd lived a hard life, become a hard woman. She deserved a little romance in her life. However little it was.

Stepping out of the general store, Sage surveyed the goings on in town. Three little boys were tormenting a bull snake in the middle of the road, using a stick to move the reptile this way and that. Sage giggled when one of the boys paused, pulled a frog out of his pocket and tossed it into a nearby watering trough.

Forest Simmons was leaning against the outer wall of the dress shop across the street, nodding as he listened to something Winnery and Reverend Tippetts seemed to be discussing. Milly Michaels, Katie Bird and Dotty Benten were nearby giggling and whispering to one another as they watched a young cowboy walk down the street.

It was a good place to live, with good people. Sage sighed, glad for that at least. Glad she had a way to provide for herself. Thankful she had the widows.

"Well now, we meet again, at last."

Sage tried not to frown as she glanced to her side to see Ivy Dalton smiling at her. She carried a pink parasol which perfectly complemented her pretty pink dress. Her hair was lovely, her smile dazzling, her eyes spitting fire, however.

"Good mornin'," Sage greeted, forcing a friendly smile.

"I've been hopin' I'd run into you, Miss Sage Willows," Ivy said.

"Really?" Sage asked. She wanted nothing more than to run, run as fast as she could. Escape was her only hope as she felt tears welling in her eyes.

"Why, of course," Ivy said, still smiling. "After all, I'd like to know exactly what it was that happened between you and my Reb."

Sage frowned. She had no desire to talk to Ivy Dalton at all, let alone tell her anything about Reb. Yet, a sort of hateful pride rose in her at the knowledge Ivy knew something had happened, whatever it was.

"What do you mean?" Sage asked.

"Well," Ivy began, "And don't get me wrong . . . I know there's not a woman in this world who could outshine me in Reb Mitchell's eyes, but to hear Charlie Dugger tell the story . . . it seems you gave it a good try."

Sage frowned. "Is that so?"

"Well, to hear Charlie tell it, it is," Ivy said. "Seems there's somethin' about it bein' your fault Reb was hurt by that mountain lion. And I'm sorry, but that upsets me somethin' terrible."

Sage felt her eyes narrow. What a "chili pepper in the maple syrup" the woman was! Sage knew Charlie would never say such a thing! Furthermore, she sensed Ivy was worried. She'd twisted the story of the mountain lion attack, and for what purpose?

"Charlie told you about it, did he?" Sage asked. She'd play along with Ivy's game. She was curious as to what the woman was up to.

"Well, yes he did," Ivy answered. "And to be honest with you, Miss Willows—it is 'Miss,' isn't it? I have heard you've never been married, even for your obvious experience and years."

Sage seethed with anger, but did not let it show. What a vindictive woman! She wondered what Reb possibly saw in her! What he ever saw in her!

"Yes, *Miss* Dalton," Sage answered, emphasizing Ivy's own lack of a husband, or at least, current lack of a husband. "It is, 'Miss' Willows."

"Yes, of course," Ivy said. Her eyes narrowed, even though her sweet smile remained. "As I was sayin', Charlie was tellin' me all about how you rode out to the ranch one day, apparently to try and—well, how can I say this—apparently you intended to . . . to try and seduce my Reb."

"Is that so?" Sage asked. The woman was unbelievable!

"That's how Charlie tells it," Ivy said. "He says the old mountain lion went after you, and Reb had to put himself in harm's way to save you. Charlie says that's how Reb got so torn up . . . that it was your fault. And . . . and well . . . I was just wonderin' what in the world would make you think Reb Mitchell would look twice at the likes of you?"

Humiliation, shame, heartbreak and anger ran through Sage's veins as thick as gravy! Oh, she knew full well Charlie Dugger would never say such things about her. No doubt Charlie had told Ivy about the mountain lion attack, and Ivy had spun her spider's web to create her own story in an effort to discourage Sage. Unfortunately, it had worked. Still, Sage wasn't about to give Ivy the satisfaction of knowing it.

"Why don't you ask Reb?" Sage said, fairly trembling with anger and hurt. "In fact, why don't you ask Reb what went on between us before we got back to the ranch that day."

"Why don't you tell me yourself, Miss Willows?" Ivy asked, her sickeningly sweet smile fading at last.

"Well, I'd like to," Sage began. "I really would. I'd like to tell you all about how Reb gambled with me over a game of cards. How he gambled to either whitewash my boardin' house if he lost, or to 'have his way with me,' as he put it, if he won. And he did win that day, Miss Dalton. He won and took me out to the ranch house. Unfortunately, the mountain lion arrived before he could . . . shall we say . . . collect his winnin's." Sage felt her bosom rising and falling with the labored breathing of fury and hurt. She'd lowered herself to Ivy's level, to spiteful, hateful exaggeration. Yet she hadn't been able to stop herself! She wanted Ivy to know, whether or not all the rumors were true, whether or not Reb had taken the woman back into his life, back into his arms. She wanted Ivy to know she'd tasted Reb's kiss, too, been the object of his attentions.

"That's a lie," Ivy nearly growled. "I've been out to that ranch house. I've seen Reb's blood stainin' the floor, heard what you caused to happen to him."

"Believe what you want," Sage said. "But I think you know I'm tellin' the truth."

Ivy continued to glare at Sage. Sage continued to fight the need to cry, continued to try to drive the pain from her heart.

Suddenly, the sound of approaching horses, coupled with Ivy's exclamation of, "Rebel!" drew Sage's attention away from the villainess. Following Ivy's startled gaze, Sage turned around to see three horses approaching at a mad gallop. A man, unfamiliar to Sage, rode the first horse. Reb sat the second, riding hard, obviously in pursuit of the first man.

Charlie Dugger rode the third, shouting, "Reb! Reb! Don't do it, Rebel!"

As the riders and horses approached, Reb rode up next to the first man. Reaching out and taking hold of the reins of the man's horse, Reb pulled his own horse and the man's to an abrupt halt.

Reb leapt from his saddle, reaching up and taking hold of the stranger's shirt and dragging him to the ground.

Charlie reined in, dismounted and shouted, "Reb! Hold yer head there, boy!"

Sage gasped, stunned, as Reb clutched the man's shirt in one hand, landing a powerful fist to the man's face with the other.

"You dirty son of a . . ." Reb growled a moment before his fist met with the man's face again, knocking him to the ground. Only momentarily dazed, the man swiped his leg across the ground, knocking Reb's feet out from under him. Reb stumbled backward, falling to the ground himself. Instantly, the stranger stood, kicking Reb square in the stomach. Sage screamed, heard Ivy scream as well, as Reb doubled over in pain.

Still, he reached out, grabbed the man's leg and tripped him, sending him sprawling to the ground once more.

Reb was at the man instantly, punching, smashing the man's face into the dirt. He paused long enough to stand, pulling the stranger with him.

"That's enough, Reb! That's it! That's enough!" Charlie shouted, trying to take hold of Reb's arm. Wrenching his arm free of Charlie's grasp, Reb hit the man again, landing a fist to his ribs, then another and another.

"I trusted you, Retch!" Reb growled as he punched the man again. "I paid you to drive them cattle, trusted you with my herd. But you got burned by the devil's purty face, didn't ya, boy?"

Sage was astonished! She didn't know what to do! She couldn't believe the scene playing out before her eyes! Reb was a man gone mad with anger! Furthermore, he appeared so unkempt, as if he'd just gotten out of bed, hadn't shaved in a week. She worried he was ill. She wanted to run to him, beg him to stop beating the man, and plead for him to love her. But the sound of Ivy's voice stopped her from doing any of the things she thought.

"Reb! Darlin'! Have you lost your mind?" Ivy cried.

The sound of Ivy's voice seemed to penetrate Reb's anger, pull him from his mad attack on the stranger. Sage felt tears welling in her eyes as Reb looked up. He looked to Ivy, ceasing his assault on the man and striding toward her.

"I told you, Ivy," he growled, seeming unaware Sage stood before him as well. "Get on the next stage and get out of my sight!" Sage was confused, breathless, felt an ache begin in her head so painful it threatened unconsciousness. Had she heard him correctly? Had he just told Ivy to leave?

"Now Reb, Honey," Ivy began, reaching out and brushing at the dust on his shirt. Reb pushed her hand away. She continued, "I've told you, if you'll just take some time to think on things . . ."

"You paid him?" Reb shouted. "You paid Retch Williams to send you a telegram and tell you where I was?" The fury on Reb's face was frightening. Sage had never seen such anger in a man, such barely restrained aggression. "I told you we were through, Ivy. I told you that over and over. Did you think your showin' up here would change my mind?"

"Now, Reb, you settle down a piece," Sheriff Lambson said as he approached from across the street. "Settle yerself down, you hear?"

"Reb," Ivy said. Dropping her parasol, she reached out with both hands, clutching at Reb's shirt. "Reb! We belong together! I've loved you ever since I can remember! Ever since I started walkin' on this earth I've loved you."

"You don't love me, Ivy," Reb growled. "You love the idea of lovin' me." Reb looked to Sage then, his eyes smoldering with anger. Sage was trembling. Every inch of her body trembled with fear, hurt, even desire as he looked at her. She wanted to reach out and touch him, throw herself against him and beg him to love her.

Reb continued to stare at Sage, even though he spoke to Ivy. "Still, I'll give you this, Ivy Dalton," he said. "You didn't give up easy."

Sage felt the tears brimming in her eyes. Did he mean to say she did? Was he implying she should've chased after him the way Ivy obviously had? In truth, if she'd had an ounce of hope that it would've worked, she would have.

"Simmer down, Reb," Sheriff Lambson said, walking up behind Reb and placing a hand on his shoulder.

"Don't you touch me!" Reb shouted. Turning around he shoved the sheriff hard, sending him tumbling backward to sit soundly on the ground.

Reb turned and faced Sage. He was infuriated! His eyes burned with anger and frustration. Sage leaned back, intimidated by his countenance.

"And you," he growled at her. "You're as cold-hearted as she is, ain't ya? Unforgivin' as the devil."

Suddenly, Reb reached out, taking Sage's face firmly between his hands. His lips crushed her own, driven, hot, angry! He kissed her with a violent passion, willing her to meet his fevered attack on her tender mouth. His kiss was powerful, moist, unrelenting. The kiss exchanged between them was brief, but frenzied! And it *was* an exchange, for Sage had longed for his touch, and she accepted his angry kiss, returning it as best she could, considering the aggression with which it was applied.

"Reb!" Charlie shouted then. "Rebel!"

The sheriff had gotten to his feet, and he and Charlie pulled Rebel away. Sage gasped as Mary suddenly stepped in front of her and dumped a bucket of water over Reb's head.

"You cool off, boy!" she scolded. "You cool off now, ya hear me?"

Reb stood, dripping wet, his chest rising and falling with the labored breathing of residual anger.

"A night in jail oughta cool him off a bit," Sheriff Lambson said.

Charlie held Reb by the shoulders as the sheriff pulled his hands behind his back and bound his wrists to keep him from fighting any further.

Reb looked at Sage, then to Ivy, then back to Sage. "Two peas in a pod," he grumbled. "That's what the two of you are. Just two peas in a pod."

"Come on now, Reb," Sheriff Lambson said. "Cool off now."

"He's just out of his mind with bein' angry, Miss Sage," Charlie said. "He don't mean nothin' by any of that."

"Help me out here, will ya Charlie?" Sheriff Lambson said, struggling to push Reb across the street toward the jailhouse.

"I can walk on my own!" Reb growled, wrenching his arm free of the sheriff's grasp.

Sage stood, watching the sheriff and Charlie urge Reb toward the jailhouse. Her entire being trembled, her body burned with confusion and heartache. She put a hand to her mouth, covering her tender lips, still able to sense Reb's delicious kiss. She felt a sharp pain in her bosom as his hurtful words echoed in her mind. *"Two peas in a pod. That's what the two of you are,"* he'd said.

Sage looked to the stranger, still struggling to catch his breath as he stood in the street. His face was bleeding, he was breathless. She recognized him then as one of the cowboys who had ridden in with the first herd Charlie had driven to the ranch for Reb.

Realization washed over her. Reb hadn't wanted Ivy. Ivy had wanted Reb, sought him out, and bribed the cowboy to send her a telegram telling her where Reb was. Reb had been as surprised to see Ivy as Sage had been that day at the boardinghouse. But why then had he let everyone believe he wanted Ivy? What was the real reason he had arrived at the boarding-house that day?

Sage buried her face in her hands for a moment, fighting to keep the tears from spilling from her eyes. She should've gone to him! She should've ridden out to the ranch to see him after the attack. If she had, perhaps . . . perhaps . . .

And if he loathed her so completely, if he thought she was the shallow, heartless woman Ivy was, why then had he kissed her just now? Why had she sensed a wanton desire in him like nothing she'd imagined?

"He never kissed me like that," Ivy said. Sage looked over at Ivy, loathing the very sight of her.

"What?" Sage asked, still trying to absorb what had happened.

"Never," Ivy repeated, her expression that of complete astonishment. "He never kissed me like that. Not even . . . not even when he planned to marry me."

"You all right, Sage?" Reverend Tippetts asked as he approached.

"I'm . . . I'm fine, Reverend," Sage stammered. "I'm fine. Th . . . thank you."

"Seems to me Reb Mitchell's got himself in a bit of a bind," Reverend Tippetts said.

"He'll cool off, Reverend," Mary said, placing a comforting arm around Sage's shoulders.

"He . . . he never kissed me like that," Ivy repeated. The woman seemed entirely awe-struck. But Sage didn't care. She didn't care about any of it, only the fact Reb somehow thought of her in the same loathing regard as he did Ivy.

"I 'spect that oughta tell you somethin' then, miss," Winnery mumbled.

"Come on, Sage," Mary said. "Let's get home."

Sage shook her head. "I . . . I need a walk, Mary," she said. "I . . . I just need a little walk."

"All right, honey," Mary said. "All right."

As Sage turned to leave, Ivy caught hold of her arm. Sage looked at the vile beauty, repulsed by her touch.

"I hate you," Ivy growled. "I hate you for the way he kissed you just now."

Sage drew in a deep breath. "Then we're even, Ivy Dalton," she said. "Because I hate you. I hate you for ever hurting him."

Sage turned then, turned and walked away. She wasn't certain at first that her legs could support her. She wasn't certain she wouldn't collapse in a sobbing heap right there in the middle of town. Yet, somehow, she managed—she managed to keep walking. Somehow, she managed to make it to Ruthie. And when she did, she wondered what it would be like to lie quiet and peaceful beneath the sweet green grass of the pastures. She imagined it would be cold and lonely, as cold and lonely as her heart felt now. Only her heart couldn't ascend to the glories of heaven. Though her lips still burned with the fire of Reb's kiss, her soul felt abandoned and cold. Though her heart still ached with the pain of being in love with a man who was so far out of reach, her arms and legs were numb.

As Sage lay down in the grass next to Ruthie's grave, tears spilled from her eyes at last. As she cried out the aching of her wounded heart and soul, the clouds drifted silently overhead. As she sobbed for want of being in Reb's arms, simply in his company, meadowlarks nesting in the piñon trees nearby called out their happy summer songs. As she drifted into a sad slumber, exhausted from her tears and heartache, the breeze played among the wildflowers and cattle grazed nearby, careless of the world.

Chapter Twelve

❧ ❧

"Never thought I'd see the day that nephew of mine would spend a night in jail," Eugenia said. Sage sighed. She reached down and drew a wet petticoat out of the basket at her feet. Shaking it out, she took two clothespins from the pocket of her apron and attached the garment to the clothesline.

"Did you . . . do you get to talk to him then?" Sage asked. Though she'd cried herself to sleep near Ruthie's grave the day before, Sage had been unable to sleep soundly through the night. She could think of nothing but Reb, his anger at the cowboy who betrayed him, the beating he'd given the man, and his ordering Ivy to leave. Most of all, however, her thoughts lingered on the way he'd looked at her, accusing her of being just like Ivy. The kiss he'd given her had been administered with a brutal passion, an angry desire. Yet his eyes held more hurt and anger than she could ever imagine.

All through the night, Sage had tossed and turned, replayed every event, every moment she'd ever spent in Reb Mitchell's presence. The angel on her right shoulder whispered Reb cared for her, was hurt that she'd broken his heart by not going to him after the mountain lion attack.

The devil, perched on her left shoulder, however, murmured Reb saw every woman having as black and as selfish a heart as Ivy's, and that it wouldn't have mattered if she'd gone to him.

"Yep," Eugenia said. "Went down to the jail yesterday right after it all happened, thinkin' I could talk some sense into Sheriff Lambson and get Reb out. But . . . but after I saw the way that boy was still carryin' on . . ." Eugenia shook her head. "Well," she continued, "I got to thinkin' a night in jail might be just what he needed." Eugenia sighed. "It seemed to do him some good, 'cause when I saw him just now, he was settled down and on his way home like a whipped dog with its tail between its legs."

"He's all right then?" Sage asked, pinning a white shirtwaist to the clothesline.

"Well, he's out of jail, at least," Eugenia said. "As far as him bein' all right, well . . . that remains to be seen."

CƷ

EUGENIA DID NOT miss the moisture in Sage's eyes. The girl had been crying for more than a week! Each time she'd come home from her walks or her rides out on Drifter, her eyes would be red, her cheeks swollen and puffy. Eugenia knew Sage's heart was breaking, knew Reb's was, too! Confound it! She wanted to take them both, plop them over her knee and paddle their behinds good and hard! But a body couldn't force people to let go of what frightened them. A body could only love and encourage.

Rebel and Sage were both stricken with fear. Reb was afraid Sage wouldn't forgive him for the mountain lion attack, couldn't love him forever. He feared she was like Ivy, only loving him on the surface. He feared he'd let himself love her, only to find she'd toss him away one day, having lost interest in him somehow.

Sage on the other hand, was afraid to take a chance, afraid to show any emotion. Fear kept her from running to Reb, kept her from confessing she loved him, from seeing he loved her. It was as if Reb stood on one side of a river and Sage on the other, both afraid to cross for fear of drowning. Therefore, they both simply stood gazing at each other, dreaming of what each wished would come true, each one certain they'd drown if they attempted to swim out and capture the dream.

It was the most frustrating, infuriating and heartbreaking situation! Eugenia wanted to scream with exasperation at Reb's guilt and mistrust and Sage's blindness and inability to express herself! Still they were each wounded. She must keep that in mind, use sympathy, patience, and compassion as her tools. Yet her resolve to remain calm and patient was quickly thinning.

☙

"DO YOU LOVE him, Sage?" Eugenia asked, suddenly.

Sage began to tremble, yet tried to appear unaffected. Draping the waistband of another petticoat over the line, Sage secured it with several clothespins. Eugenia knew the answer to her own question. As sure as Sage stood there right next to her, Eugenia knew. So why then did she ask it? Yet Sage knew she would be a fool to deny it.

"It doesn't matter if I love him or not, Miss Eugenia," Sage said. "He's . . . he's obviously lumped me in with Ivy." Sage fought the tears begging for release.

"He's afraid, Sage. Surely, you see his fear. Surely, you know he doesn't really think you're the likes of her," Eugenia scolded. "And you're just afraid, too! It's plain and simple." Eugenia, rather huffed, shook her head. She reached out, taking Sage by the shoulders. "Now, you look me in the eye and tell me you think Reb really still has any feelin's for Ivy. Look me in the eye and tell me you really think he doesn't care for you. I heard tell, from not just a few folks in town, that boy gave you quite the kiss there in front of God and the entire world a moment before Sheriff Lambson hauled him off to jail yesterday. So you look me in the eye and tell me he doesn't care for you."

Sage swallowed hard, willed the tears not to leave her eyes for want of traveling down her cheeks.

"Tell me, Sage. Do you really think Reb feels the same way about you as he does Ivy? I think you know he doesn't. I think you know he cares for you and I think you're just afraid to let him know you care for him," Eugenia said.

Sage couldn't confess to Eugenia, however. She couldn't tell Eugenia she loved Reb more than she did her own existence! She couldn't tell her she'd never know one happy moment for the rest of her life without him. She couldn't tell her anything! Not about the peach cobbler kisses in the kitchen, not about the kiss in the barn or in the pastures on the way to the ranch. She couldn't explain how the sun had warmed her that day, how wearing Rose's scandalous dress had freed her mind, allowed her to accept and, indeed, return the passion Reb had rained over her. At that moment, the enchanting memory still caused her flesh to prickle with goose bumps.

Sage closed her eyes, clinging to the memory of being in Reb's arms, remembering the feel of his lips to hers. Her stomach sickened, nearly heaving at the thought of Reb ever holding Ivy or any other woman in his arms, ever taking any other woman's mouth with his the way he had taken hers.

Sage opened her eyes as she felt Eugenia firmly take hold of her chin. An unfamiliar frown puckered Eugenia's brow, her teeth seemed tightly clenched, and her eyes narrowed as she looked at Sage.

"Now you listen to me," Eugenia began, "I don't know what went on between the two of you before that infernal cat started all this mess! I don't know what went on before that wicked Ivy Dalton stirred the soup pot further. But I do know that, whatever Reb's plans were for you the day he took you out to the ranch, whatever the two of you might have shared over these past couple of months, it's worth fightin' for, Sage. Every bit of it!"

"How . . . how can you be sure?" Sage whispered. "How can I be sure he wasn't just . . . just . . . just havin' a bit of fun?"

"He wasn't," Eugenina stated. She sighed, releasing Sage's chin and lovingly caressing her cheek. "And you know him well enough to be certain of it in your heart. That cat gettin' at you scared him, Sage. Scared him nearly to death. Then Ivy shows up and reminded him fresh what heartache can do to a man. Reb knew Ivy wouldn't ever own his heart, wouldn't ever break his heart again. But he knows *you* can."

"Then he's a coward," Sage said, leaning down to retrieve another petticoat from the basket. She shook her head, reminding her tears they could not come. Reb Mitchell was anything but a coward. Sage knew it.

Yet Eugenia's words were harsh and accusing, hurtful.

"You're right," Eugenia said. "You're right. Forget the fact he fought a mountain lion to save your life. Forget he tended to your wounds, sewed you up first before takin' care of himself. Forget all of it. And you're still right. He is a coward."

Sage shook her head again, held her breath. She could not cry, not until she was alone. She thought of the wounds to Reb's body, the deep, painful wounds inflicted by the cat. She thought of his attention to her wounds, how careful he must've been. She shivered at the knowledge that he could've been killed for her sake. The mountain lion could've killed him, but it didn't, just as it hadn't killed her because of him.

Sage thought of his beating the cowboy in the street, the way he'd shoved the sheriff, told Ivy to leave. She thought of the way he'd kissed her right there in broad daylight for all the town to see. Reb Mitchell was no more a coward than she was a loose saloon girl.

"He's a coward all right," Eugenia continued, "an idiot, too, to think you'd blame him for that cat. But he's more of a coward for not reaching out and takin' what he wants for fear of losin' it," Eugenia said. Sage nodded. "But then, he's no more of a coward than you are."

"What?" Sage exclaimed.

Eugenia raised her eyebrows, shrugged her shoulders, tipped her head to one side as she said, "You're pointin' the finger awful straight at a man who's been badly wounded. By "wounded" I'm talkin' about the wounds that devil-girl left on his heart and soul. The wounds that cat gave him were nothin' compared to it. And you're pointin' the finger awful hard, Sage. You've never had those kinds of wounds. You've had your own, and I'm not sayin' you haven't, but how can you stand there judgin' that boy when you didn't have the courage to claim him yourself?"

"What?" Sage exclaimed again. "What do you mean? Claim him? How could I ever have . . ."

"The day Ivy arrived," Eugenia interrupted. "You were shaken up and I understand that. It shook me up somethin' awful, too. But when Reb came to the door, you didn't make one move to claim him. You didn't make one sound to let Ivy know he was yours."

"But he wasn't!" Sage exclaimed in defense of herself.

"Oh, pig snot!" Eugenia grumbled. "He's been yours for the takin' since the day Bullet wound the two of you up on the front porch! You just haven't given Reb any sign whatsoever that you even want him. You just stood there next to Ivy Dalton, stood there with your mouth glued shut, not a tear in your eye. What was a man in Reb's situation to think? Hmmm?"

"But . . . but he's so . . . how could I have hoped . . . You saw her . . . You saw how beautiful she was," Sage stammered. It was a fierce fight to hold onto her tears.

"She's beautiful, all right. Like a snake in the grass," Eugenia said. "And Reb knows that. Oh sure, he's been an idiot, but only because he's been through a world of hurt. And I don't mean this to sound as heartless as it does, Sage, but he's been hurt worse than you ever have. At least up until now. So quit bein' so selfish. Quit bein' so scared of life and the disappointment that comes with it. And you go on . . . You keep callin' Reb a coward, but I'll say it again, I haven't ever seen you do one thing to let him know you love him, to let him know you want him. And I still don't see you doin' anythin' to let him know."

"But I . . . But I . . ." Sage stammered. Sage's mind was whirling with confusion. Was Eugenia blaming her for Reb's unhappiness? What was she supposed to have done the day Ivy had shown up at the boarding-house? When Reb had arrived? Should she have thrown her arms around him, smothered him with kisses? Yesterday in the street, after he'd beaten the cowboy, should she have wrestled him to the ground and confessed her undying love? What good would that have done? Would he have then suddenly confessed an endless love for her? Would he have swooped her up in his arms and demanded the Reverend Tippetts marry them then and there?

"That boy put a mountain lion down for you, Sage! Put his very life in jeopardy without one thought the other way!" Eugenia shook her head, her expression pleading. "Can't you find enough courage to fight for him now? It seems to me, if Reb can best a mountain lion for you, you oughta be able to best that Ivy, drive out the poison she spit in his heart and fill it up with sweet sugar again."

Somehow Sage still managed to choke back her tears. Closing her eyes she saw Reb's handsome smile, his easy manner and fiery eyes. Rebel Mitchell was more than she could ever have even dreamed a man to be.

"Sometimes," she whispered, "sometimes . . . sometimes I wonder if he's even real, Eugenia. Sometimes I think . . . I think I just dreamed him up. Sometimes I think I dreamed all of it up. Him, his smile, and the way he laughs when Miss Rosie is being silly. Sometimes I think I dreamed up that entire day . . . the trip out to the ranch, dreamed up the mountain lion and all that happened before it." Sage forced a smile and shook her head as she looked at Eugenia. "I'm . . . I'm just Sage Willows, Miss Eugenia," she said. "I'm just the woman who runs the boardin' house in town."

Eugenia smiled and put a hand to Sage's cheek. "But that's not true, Sage. You're not just the woman who runs the boardin' house in town. And Reb's not just the cowboy who runs the old Smarthin' ranch." She took Sage's hands in her own, squeezing them with reassurance. "You're the girl who loves Reb Mitchell. And he's the man who loves you."

"That's not true," Sage said, shaking her head. "Please don't say it."

"It is true!" Eugenia exclaimed. "You know it's true, Sage. You're just afraid, afraid of feelin' the way Reb did when Ivy did him wrong. You're afraid of heartache, but doesn't your heart ache already?" Eugenia paused, seeming to choose her words carefully. "Your life has had a bit of disappointment, Sage. No one would fault you for feelin' fearful. But don't let fear win. Don't let fear keep you from happiness. Fear is the devil's saddle pal, Sage, and he depends on it. Fear wants you to stay disappointed. It wants to break you. It's breakin' the man you love right now. Right now, while you're standin' here hangin' out your underwear, fear's whippin' Reb. Fear of not havin' you is whippin' him down. And when a man feels whipped, that's when he's at his weakest. That's when he gives up, gives in, and settles for what feels easy and safe. I think you know that."

Sage closed her eyes, willing herself not to cry. She thought of running, running to her escape in Ruthie's pasture. She inhaled deeply, holding her breath, envisioning Reb again, his frown, his angry behavior in the street the day before. Again, she envisioned him sitting in the ranch house, blood streaming from the wounds the mountain lion had inflicted on his powerful body. She thought of his eyes, the expression of anger and hurt in them the day he'd come to the boardinghouse and found Ivy there. She thought of the way he'd looked at Sage, the day before, accusing her of being the likes of Ivy Dalton.

Releasing her breath she thought of other things then, of his smile and playful manner. She thought of the mischievous grin he wore, the bright twinkle in his eyes as he teased her or the widows. She thought of his kissing her in the barn when she'd only just touched him, the slightest of gestures. She thought of his preying on her in the kitchen, taking a bite of the juicy peach she offered and then brushing her hand aside as he kissed her. She thought of the delighted look on his face when he'd entered the boardinghouse to see her dancing on the table, the way he'd carried her off to the wagon. She thought of his lifting her down from the wagon on the way to the ranch, remembered the emotion in his eyes a moment before he'd kissed her. She thought then of the fear, the undeniable fear in his expression as he'd looked at her in the kitchen after the mountain lion attack. Only then did she remember and finally recognize the fear, the agony of guilt, apparent in his eyes in those moments before she fell unconscious again.

"What if he . . . what if he hates me now?" Sage whispered, looking to Eugenia. "What if it's too late?"

Eugenia smiled, lovingly cupping Sage's cheek in one hand.

"He doesn't," Eugenia said. "And it's not too late. I promise."

❧

REB HUNKERED DOWN before the small tombstone.

"Well, good mornin', Ruth States," he said aloud. "Sage been out to see you lately?"

Rubbing at his week's worth of whiskers, Reb sighed and looked around him. Ten or fifteen head of cattle were grazing close by, and two jack rabbits sat a ways away, seeming anxious about his presence. The pasture grass was green and fragrant, the wildflowers brilliant with color. It was truly a place of serene beauty.

"Spent me my first night in jail," Reb said. "Sure hope it's my last."

He frowned then. Reaching out he traced each letter engraved on the tombstone. "It's mighty peaceful out here, little Ruth," he said. "I wonder if any of your kin ever thinks on what a peaceful spot you're restin' in."

Reb closed his eyes, drawing in a deep breath of discouragement and fatigue. He felt grimy, still covered in the dust kicked up by the fight he'd had with Retch Williams the day before. His hands were sore, too. He looked at them, stretching his fingers and grimacing at the pain in his bruised and bloodied knuckles. No doubt he had a couple of nice bruises on his ribs as well. He'd forgotten what a good fighter Retch Williams was.

"She ever said much about me to you, Ruth?" Reb asked, sighing. He plucked a foxtail from the grass, placing the stem between his teeth. "You don't tell her about our little talks now, do ya? I wouldn't want her knowin' we'd struck up a friendship of our own. Might get her dander up." Reb frowned again, shaking his head. "Still, it don't seem she gets her dander up too awful much anyhow." He nodded and rubbed at his whiskers again. "Me, on the other hand, seems my dander's been up for a month of Sundays of late. I beat the waddin' out of ol' Retch yesterday. And he deserved it, too, so don't go scoldin'," he said, wagging an index finger at the tombstone. "Still, it was bad what I said to Sage, comparin' her to the likes of Ivy Dalton. Guess I nailed my own coffin shut with that, didn't I?" He glanced at the tombstone, quickly adding, "I didn't mean no disrespect with that, Ruth. I'm sure you know what I meant to say. What was I thinkin' kissin' her that way, then yellin' at her more harsh than I'd yell at Bullet for chewin' on my good boots?"

Reb reached down, brushing the soft grass and sage with one palm. He pinched a sage leaf from one plant, bending it, rubbing it with his fingers and drawing it to his nostrils. Closing his eyes, he inhaled deeply, intoxicated for a moment by the fragrance of the plant. In his mind, he could see Sage, smiling up at him, drawing a sage leaf or two up to her own nose the way he'd seen her do so many times. The flesh on his arms prickled with goose bumps as he remembered the flavor of her kiss, the soft feel of her body in his embrace.

"What I wouldn't give to taste her now, Ruth," Reb mumbled. He raised his face to the sky, squinting into the sun. "What I wouldn't give to have her touch me, have them sweet, sage-scented fingers soft on my face." He shook his head. "So what's she thinkin' about me now, Ruth?" he asked. "She's thinkin' I'm the devil for sure." He sighed, tucking the sage leaves into his shirt pocket. "But she was sweet when I did hold her, Ruth. The sweetest pleasure I ever had."

Reb stood, stretching his aching fingers again, studying the purple of his knuckles. "I'll see you another day, sweet girl. You say 'hey' to Uncle Buck for me, okay?"

It was a long walk back to the ranch. He'd better get started. Taking the sage leaves from his shirt pocket, he inhaled their fragrance once more before tossing them in the direction of the two jack rabbits still curious about his presence.

With a heavy sigh, Reb Mitchell started out for the ranch with the scent of Sage still fresh in his nostrils, the taste of her still sweet in his mouth. It was the touch of Sage he most longed for at that moment—so soft, so wildly wonderful to his flesh. He longed for the touch of Sage.

Chapter Thirteen

"*T*here goes the stage!" Rose said as she entered the kitchen later that evening. "And Ivy Dalton was on it! You girls shoulda seen the sour pickle-pinched pout on her ugly ol' face!"

Sage tried not to think hateful thoughts, tried not to be absolutely elated Ivy had gone. Still, she couldn't help it. The woman was her worst enemy, pure and simple. Who wouldn't be glad to see their worst enemy go? Perhaps it would ease Reb's pain a bit as well. Perhaps with Ivy gone, he could go on living his life as well.

"Now that there ain't very nice to say, Rose," Mary mumbled. "That ain't nice at all." Eugenia, Livie and Rose looked to Mary, puzzled frowns puckering their brows. Sage was rather astonished at her uncharacteristic defense of anyone, let alone Ivy Dalton. "And that's good it ain't nice," Mary continued, "'cause that little poison ivy plant don't deserve nothin' nice!" Sage smiled, glad to see Mary was still as cantankerous as ever.

Rising to her feet, Mary began to swish her skirt this way and that, the way Rose often did when she won a hand of rummy.

"Poison ivy, poison ivy," Mary sang, still swishing her skirt. Sage couldn't help but smile when Rose danced over next to Mary and joined in singing, "Poison ivy, poison ivy! Sour pickle, poison ivy!" Eugenia and Livie giggled when Mary and Rose each turned around, flipped their skirts and petticoats up over their hind ends, displaying their bloomer seats to the world.

Sage laughed, too, astonished that Mary Farthen owned a piece of clothing even rattier than her red nightgown.

"You're in sad need of some new bloomers, Mary," Rose said, standing up and bending back to inspect Mary's bloomers.

"Do ya really think so?" Mary asked, craning her neck to take a look herself.

"Sage is in need of a little brightenin' up, too," Livie said. She smiled lovingly at Sage and put an arm around her shoulders. "It's been such a rough ride, the past few weeks since . . . since that mountain lion, Ivy Dalton and all, Sage. Let us fiddle with your hair and such for a while. Let's put you in a pretty dress and get that smile back on your face."

"Oh yes, let's!" Rose exclaimed, excitedly clapping her hands together. "I've still got some other dresses upstairs, the ones I drug out of the trunk a while back. Oh please let us, Sage."

Instantly, Sage began shaking her head. She had no desire to dress up and pretend to be happy. She had no desire to put on another one of Rose's old dresses and have the delicious and sweet, yet painful memories of Reb toting her off in his wagon overcome her again.

"No, no, no," she said. "Not . . . not now. I've got . . . I've got so much to do."

"Oh, please, Sage," Mary pleaded. "I never did get to dress up all purty and soft the way ya look when ya let the girls fiddle with yer hair and all. It makes me happy to see ya that way, to imagine how it must feel."

Sage's head ached. She was still very preoccupied by the conversation she'd had with Eugenia earlier in the day. She was frightened and anxious. Thoughts had been bouncing around in her head ever since, of Reb, going to him, and facing him again. One moment she felt determined to go to him, throw herself at his feet and confess her love for him and beg for his love in return. The next, she would begin to tremble, fearful, terrified of ever seeing him again, perhaps again seeing the hurt and loathing she'd seen in his eyes the day before. The struggle caused her to feel greatly fatigued. So much so she'd barely managed to fix up some biscuits and gravy for supper. She certainly was in no frame of mind to entertain the widows at her own expense.

Yet Mary's plea had caused a sympathetic pinch in her heart. As she looked at Mary's pleading expression, trying to imagine the kind of life the woman had endured—a life lacking so much in joy and silly fun—how could she refuse?

Rose nodded her encouragement to Sage, smiling the smile of a woman desperate to dote.

Livie smiled as well, mouthing "Please" at her. And when Sage looked to Eugenia, it was to see her soft, encouraging smile as well.

"Have some fun with us, Sage," Eugenia said. "Tomorrow's another day, a fresh day filled with hope and maybe a little courage to boot."

"Oh, please, Sage," Rose begged. "Please let us dress you up all pretty."

Sage sighed, certain she would regret agreeing to their antics. Yet, how could she refuse? She always did feel a little better, a little fresher, a bit happier when she let the widows dote on her and mercilessly primp her. Maybe it was just what she needed to find a bit of courage within herself as well.

"Oh, all right," Sage relented. Reaching up, she pulled the pins from her hair, letting it fall down around her shoulders. "I guess it couldn't hurt. Right?"

She was a little suspicious, however, as all four women simultaneously agreed, "Right!"

ᘓ

"NOT THAT ONE, Mary!" Rose whined. She pointed an index finger, bouncing it in the direction of the pink and black satin dress strewn across Sage's bed. "The pink and black one, Mary. Not the orange."

"Well, for cryin' in the bucket," Mary grumbled. "One saloon girl's dress is the same as the next to me." Mary gathered the garment from the bed, studying the purple ribbons and black lace adorning it.

"I was not a saloon girl, Mary," Rose corrected, snatching the dress from Mary. "I was a dancer."

"Now," Livie began, twisting a long strand of Sage's hair around the hot curling iron in her hand. "I think ringlets all down the back here. Your hair is so pretty when you wear it pulled up soft like this, Sage. I wish you'd give up that old widow's knot."

"Yes, Sage," Eugenia agreed. "Men like to get their hands in a woman's hair, curl a length of it 'round their finger."

"Do they now, Miss Eugenia?" Sage asked. "So you think ol' Forest Simmons will find me more attractive with my hair up like this?"

"Maybe," Eugenia said, shaking her head at Sage, "though I think one woman's no different than the other in Forest Simmon's squinty old eyes."

"Here now, Sage," Rose began holding up the dress. "Slip into this pretty little thing."

"This is positively scandalous!" Sage exclaimed. "How do I let you ladies talk me into such nonsense?" Still, she felt happier, a bit cheerier than she had before. As Rose and Livie helped her into the dress, Sage remembered the last time she'd donned one of Rose's costumes. "It's a wonder I trust you at all, after the no good trick you played on me last time."

"Oh, we was just havin' some fun that time," Rose said. "This time, we're serious." Rose tugged at the corset laces, tightening the outer corset of the dress.

"Oh, ya look so purty, Sage!" Mary exclaimed, smiling at Sage.

"Do I?" Sage asked, gazing at her own reflection in the oval standing mirror in one corner of the room. Sage couldn't help but smile as she studied her reflection, her hair gently coifed, with long, soft ringlets cascading over her back and shoulders, ruffled lace capped sleeves cupped her shoulders and the dress's outer corset pulled in her waist nicely. The hemline of the dress dipped low in the back, tapering up to just covering her knees in the front.

She turned to study the bow bustle at the back of the dress. Instantly, however, her eyes were drawn to the scars left by the mountain lion's bite.

"Even for these?" She asked, running her fingers over the small scars. The claw scars weren't visible, too far down her back to be evident above the corset and purple shirtwaist beneath it, but the puncture wounds from the cat's bite were there. They looked dark and ugly to Sage.

"They ain't even noticeable, Sage," Mary assured her. "And besides, ain't nobody gonna see them but Reb."

"What?" Sage exclaimed, spinning around to face the four women.

"Mary!" Eugenia scolded. "You got a mouth as big as a trout!"

"What are you all up to?" Sage asked, panic rising over her.

"Nothin', Sage," Rose said. "Mary was just funnin'." But Sage was uncertain as to who was telling the truth. Rose looked sincere enough, but there was a familiar twinkle in her eye. Sage knew that twinkle as well as she knew the mischievous grin now blazoned on Livie's face, the look of determination on Mary's, and the expression of delighted misbehavior on Eugenia's.

"Get me out of this dress!" Sage exclaimed, reaching back, her fingers fumbling with the corset stays. She was trembling, suddenly shaking with anxiety. She glanced up to the door, certain the widows had tricked her again, certain Reb would enter at any moment to find her looking as ridiculous and gullible as before.

"Grab her, Mary! Eugenia!" Rose shouted. "Reverend! Winnery! You better get in here!"

Before Sage could move to elude them, Mary had taken hold of one of her arms, Eugenia the other. She gasped, mortified with embarrassment, as Reverend Tippetts himself entered the room, Winnery close behind.

"Reverend Tippetts!" Sage exclaimed, horrified to be found by the reverend in such a scandalous state of dress.

"Evenin', Sage," Reverend Tippetts said, offering a calm, friendly smile.

Scarlett entered the room as well. She gasped, smiled and shook her head in awe as she looked at Sage.

"Oh, Sage!" Scarlett exclaimed. "You look so lovely! How I loved that dress when I wore it. I knew it would fit you perfectly. Doesn't it fit her perfectly, Rose?"

"Oh my, yes!" Rose agreed. "You bein' taller and all than me, it's more fittin' for her than mine was."

"What?" Sage asked, confused, frightened, and horrified at what was happening. "What . . . what are you all doin' here? What's goin' on?"

"Go on ahead and tie her up then, Winnery," Reverend Tippetts instructed.

"Mind her hair!" Rose said as Winnery approached, carrying a length of rope in his hands.

"What are you doing?" Sage cried out. It was like waking up from a nightmare only to find the nightmare was real.

"Now, you hold still there, Miss Sage," Winnery said. "Give me her hands," he instructed Mary and Eugenia.

"No! No!" Sage exclaimed, trying to pull free.

"Settle down, Sage," Reverend Tippetts said, smiling at her. "It's for yer own good."

"What?" Sage breathed. She couldn't believe what was happening. As Winnery secured her arms at her sides and bound her wrists, she was sure she'd wake up at any moment. Surely, she'd only fallen asleep in Ruthie's pasture. Surely, this wasn't really happening.

She blushed to the tips of her toes as Winnery bound her ankles next, then her knees. She hadn't finished dressing, no stockings whatsoever! It was disgraceful! Winnery lifted her then, tossing her over one shoulder like a sack of flour.

"Put me down! What are you doin'" Sage fairly screamed.

"Hush now, Sage," Mary ordered, "else we'll have to bind yer mouth up, too."

"The wagon's waitin' out back," Reverend Tippetts said. "Let's get goin'."

"All right, reverend," Eugenia said.

Sage's eyes widened, disbelief striking her dumb as, one by one, the widows each pulled a length of red fabric from the front of their shirt-waists. Simultaneously, they tied the bandanas around their necks, pulling the cloths up over their mouths and noses. Sage could not believe it! They looked like a band of gray-haired bandits! Female bandits! They looked like a bunch of mad banditas!

As Winnery carried Sage down the stairs, Scarlett followed, calling out instructions to Sage. "Now, just keep your head and stay calm," Scarlett said. "Calm and confident. We all know how he feels about . . ."

A loud knock on the boardinghouse front door caused every imp in the room to stop cold.

"Help!" Sage yelped a moment before Reverend Tippett's hand covered her mouth.

"Be quiet, Sage," he ordered. "Get the door, Livie."

"All right," Livie said, skulking toward the door like a prowling outlaw.

"Livie!" everyone whispered in unison.

"What?" Livie asked, turning to face the others.

"Yer scarf, Livie," Mary whispered. "For cryin' in the bucket! She don't have one wit in that empty skull of hers. I swear I can hear her brain a rattlin' around in there like a dried out pea in a wooden bucket!"

"Shhh!" Rose demanded. "Everyone, hush! Especially you, Sage."

"Good evenin'," Sage heard Livie greet. There was silence for a moment and then Livie said, "Well, certainly! I'm delighted to meet you. Do come in. Please."

In another moment, Livie returned. She went to the ink well and pen sitting on a nearby desk, quickly removed a piece of paper from the desk and scribbled something on it.

"Here, Eugenia," she said, folding the paper and handing it to Eugenia. "Be sure he gets this. I suppose I'll need to stay here."

"I'll stay with you, Livie," Scarlett said, pushing past Winnery and his captive to stand near Livie. "You all go on ahead. We'll entertain the guest."

Sage tried to scream, tried to cry out for help, tried to scold them all for torturing her so. But the Reverend Tippetts had a firm hand over her mouth, adeptly muffling any noise she made.

"Get her in the wagon before anybody else shows up," Eugenia whispered.

"Yes, ma'am," Winnery said, nodding.

Reverend Tippetts kept his hand firmly over Sage's mouth as he opened the back kitchen door for Winnery.

The warm light of dusk softened the appearance of everything as Winnery carried Sage out of the boardinghouse and toward a waiting wagon. The softness of the onset of evening did nothing but heighten Sage's anxiety. Oh, she'd certainly figured where they were taking her . . . to Reb! She was horrified! The full extent of the tom-foolery the widows had concocted this time she did not know. She did know, however, that it meant humiliation and further heartache for her. She was dressed in a confounded saloon girl's dress, for pity's sake! No stockings or even shoes! It was indecent!

Winnery rather roughly dropped Sage into the wagon's bed, hopping in after her before she had the chance to struggle.

"Now, no screamin' or carryin' on, Sage," Reverend Tippetts instructed. He climbed up on the wagon seat, taking hold of the lines to the team. Sage watched as Eugenia, Mary and Rose, still looking like wild cattle-rustling banditas, scrambled into the wagon with her as well. If it hadn't been for the absolute absurdity of the situation, Sage could've giggled at the sight of the three old women awkwardly bumbling into the wagon bed. But she did not for the heartache and panic owning her then.

"Miss Eugenia, please!" she pleaded.

"Hush now, Sage," Eugenia said from beneath her bandana. "It's for your own good!"

"I'll set in to screamin'," Sage threatened.

"And who's gonna come for ya with the Reverend Tippetts at the lines?" Mary said. Her eyes burned with excitement above her bandita's mask.

"Now, just you settle in, Sage," Rose said, tucking a stray strand of soft white hair behind one ear. Her eyes twinkled with mischief above her bandana. "We got it all planned out. Keep a hand on her, Mr. Winnery," Rose added. "We don't want her tryin' to throw herself from the wagon or some such nonsense."

"Nonsense?" Sage nearly shrieked. "Nonsense? This entire situation is nonsense! I can't believe you would do this to me!"

Shaking her head, Rose reached down the front of her shirtwaist, producing another bandana. Quickly she folded the bandana into a triangle, then into a length.

"I'm sorry, Sage," Rose said, handing the folded bandana to Winnery. "But we just can't have you causin' such a fuss."

Sage gasped, wriggled like a worm on a hook, attempting to avoid the inevitable as Winnery tied the bandana around her mouth.

"Mind her hair!" Rose said, shaking her head with annoyance.

"Yes, ma'am," Winnery said, adjusting the bandana at Sage's mouth. "Is that comfortable enough for ya, Miss Sage?" he asked.

Sage's eyes widened as she looked at him. What a ridiculous question! Of course it wasn't comfortable! The entire situation was anything but comfortable!

Sage closed her eyes for a moment, inhaling deeply, trying to calm herself. She couldn't believe what was happening! She couldn't believe Reverend Tippetts was involved!

"She'll get a chill," Eugenia said.

Sage opened her eyes to see the three old banditas looking at her.

"Winnery," Mary instructed. "Get that old horse blanket there," she said, pointing to a folded blanket in the bed of the wagon. "Put that around Sage's shoulders, would ya?"

"You will not, Winnery!" Rose argued. "You want us to deliver her smellin' like a sweaty ol' horse, Mary?"

"Yer right," Mary agreed, nodding at her friend. "Winnery, just take off yer shirt and put it around her shoulders then."

"Mary!" Rose exclaimed. "Then she'd smell like a man. We can't give her over smellin' like a man."

"Are ya cold, Sage?" Mary asked then.

Sage shook her head. If anything she was hot, aflame with indignation, fear and disbelief.

"Leave her be then, I suppose," Eugenia said.

Sage frowned. It was so odd to hear their voices when she was unable to see their mouths moving. It all felt like a dream, and she wished so badly it was. Then she could giggle, break into uproarious laughter, and enjoy the amusement of the scene playing before her. She thought about how strange it would all look to any passerby: a clergyman driving a team pulling a wagon with one man, one tied-up saloon girl and three white-haired banditas in the bed. It would be delightful, hilarious if it weren't for the fact she was one of the players.

She couldn't let Reb see her this way! She couldn't! How could the widows, Winnery, Scarlett, even Reverend Tippetts . . . how could her friends conspire to do this to her?

"Isn't it a lovely night for a ride?" Rose said, sighing. Sage frowned, amazed they could all be so calm. They each acted as if nothing whatsoever out of the ordinary was happening.

"Yes it is," Eugenia added. "Look at the fire of those wildflowers at dusk."

"It puts one to thinkin' on restful things, don't it?" Mary said.

Sage was undone then. She began to struggle, thrash around, attempt to scream. Though the bandana bound her mouth, muffling any sound she made, she yelled at them, demanding to be set free.

"Settle down, Sage," Rose said. "You'll muss up your hair."

"And it does look so nice," Eugenia added. Her eyes smiled above her bandana. "Doesn't it look nice, Mr. Winnery?"

"It looks very purty. Indeed it does," Mr. Winnery agreed.

Sage released a heavy sigh, let her head drop forward. She was defeated. It didn't matter what she did. Tied up the way she was, with Winnery so strong and capable as her captor, it didn't matter what she did. She would simply have to wait for a future, more opportune moment to escape.

She slumped back against the wagon wall, suddenly very tired.

"You did hear Katie Bird is plum peached over Charlie Dugger, didn't you?" Rose asked Mary.

"Oh, I like her!" Mary said. "She's a nice girl. The only one in the bunch with any gravy to her taters."

Sighing again, inwardly admitting she was in for a long night, Sage looked out over the landscape. The sun was low in the west, spilling soft light over the pastures. Sage thought of the truth of what Eugenia had said, for the Indian Paintbrush dotting the landscape was beautiful! It seemed to burn wherever the fading light of day touched it. She inhaled deeply, savoring the fragrance of the grass, the piñons, and the wildflowers. The warm breeze of evening caressed her skin and played with her hair. The squeak of the wagon seat, the sound of the leather harness and trace chains, the rhythm of the wheels as they traveled, all combined to miraculously soothe her.

Somehow, incredible as it seemed, Sage slowly began to feel a surprising sense of excitement at the prospect of seeing Reb again. All at once, his handsome face fresh in her mind, she could almost feel his touch on her skin. Perhaps utter humiliation would be endurable for the chance to be in his company once more.

She closed her eyes, remembering the last wagon ride she'd taken out to the ranch. She thought of the way Reb looked at her that day, the way he'd kissed her, the things he'd implied. She thought also of everything that had transpired since that day, all the anguish, heartache, confusion, and grief. She thought of the things Eugenia had told her only that morning, of Reb's fears and of her own. She knew it was fear which had kept her from going to Reb after the mountain lion attack, and she knew it was fear which had kept her from him since. Still, she found it so very hard to believe Rebel Lee Mitchell was afraid of anything.

Reverend Tippetts drove the team fast and hard, and soon the ranch house was in view. Upon seeing it, Sage instantly began to tremble again. What would he do? How would he react to seeing a wagon full of crazy people arriving at his door?

Sage shook her head, mumbling, "No, no, no," beneath the bandana covering her mouth.

"Now, don't be nervous, Sage," Eugenia said. "You look lovely."

"Ya do look so purty, Sage," Mary added.

"Like a lovely little bird," Rose sighed.

Sage rolled her eyes, sighing with exasperation at the sweet sound of Eugenia's voice. A body would've thought tying up a friend and dragging her off to certain humiliation and heartbreak was the most natural thing in the world.

As Reverend Tippetts pulled the team to a halt, Winnery stood up. He took hold of Sage's elbow, helping her to her feet.

Reverend Tippetts climbed down off the wagon seat and the widows scurried out of the wagon like a group of startled chipmunks.

As Winnery took hold of Sage's arm, urging her toward the side of the wagon, she struggled, wrenching her arm out of his grasp and sitting down in the wagon. She knew he wouldn't be able to throw her over his shoulder and climb down from the wagon. She'd sit hard, refuse to cooperate. That way they couldn't get her into the ranch house. That way maybe Reb would never see her in such a compromised and ridiculous state.

"Get 'er outa there, Winnery, would ya?" Reverend Tippetts asked.

"'Course," Winnery said. Reaching down, he picked Sage up, cradling her in his arms. "There now, Miss Sage," he began, "this'll all go down a might easier if ya just accept that it's so and do what ya need to."

"Give 'er to me," Reverend Tippetts said. Winnery dropped to his knees in the wagon, lifting Sage over the wagon wall and into Reverend Tippetts' arms. Reverend Tippetts dropped Sage's feet to the ground, allowing her to stand on her own, but keeping a tight hold on her all the same. Winnery jumped out of the wagon and lifted her over one shoulder.

"It's dark," Mary said, looking in the direction of the house. "Dugger's done his job, but we ain't got long."

"Hurry," Eugenia said, skulking toward the house. "Let's get in there and get out quick!"

Sage began to struggle. Her screams, though muffled, were audible enough.

"Hush, Sage!" Rose ordered. "Be quiet. We're sneakin' here!"

Winnery tightened his hold around her knees. Sage was caught and she knew it. She wouldn't get away before they reached the house. Yet, hope burned within her, for the house was dark, indicating Reb was not there.

All at once, Forest Simmons' lady dog came out of the barn, loudly barking. In a moment, four wobbly-legged puppies followed her, yipping with excitement.

"Oh for cryin' in the bucket!" Mary grumbled. "Here girl! Here lady!" she called to the female dog. "That's a good girl," Mary cooed as the dog ceased barking, licking Mary's outstretched hand.

"Get them pups back in the barn, Mary!" Eugenia ordered in a whisper. "Reb could ride up at any moment."

"Yes, ma'am, bossy Betty," Mary grumbled, leading the mama dog and her pups back to the old barn. "I'll shut 'em in so they can't bother us."

Winnery followed Reverend Tippetts, Rose and Eugenia up onto the front porch of the house. Eugenia pushed the door open and stepped inside.

"Okey-dokey, Winnery," she said. "Bring her in."

Winnery stepped into the house and, instantly, the lingering smell of bacon filled Sage's senses.

"Let's tie her up on the bed," Rose suggested. "We don't want Reb too startled when he first walks in?"

What? Sage exclaimed to herself.

"Yes," Eugenia agreed. "That way he'll find her when he's all tuckered out and relaxed, stead of before he's had his supper."

Sage began to struggle, frantic to escape! But Winnery held her tight and followed the others through the house to one of the bedrooms.

Eugenia lit a lamp and turned up the flame. Sage fought to hold back her tears as she looked about the room.

The bed was large and comfortable looking. It also looked as if it hadn't been spread up in a month. The quilts and sheets were twisted and rolled every which way.

"Men!" Eugenia sighed with exasperation. Sage watched as Rose and Eugenia quickly spread the bed up.

"Now, sit her right there, Winnery," Eugenia ordered, pointing to the bed. "Don't you think that's the best place, reverend?"

"Sure enough," reverend Tippetts said. "He oughta find her just fine there. Eventually, anyway."

Winnery rather indecorously dropped Sage on her sitter in the middle of the bed. Instantly, Sage began to struggle, but Winnery drew another length of rope from his pocket. Weaving the rope through the others around Sage's body, Winnery secured her to the slatted headboard of the bed. Sage squirmed and tried to twist, but Joss Winnery was good with a rope. Sage knew she was still trapped, would be until someone else came along. She wanted to cry, knowing that that someone else would be Reb.

"That's good enough. Looks to hold her fine," Reverend Tippetts said.

"Let's just take this off . . ." Rose began, reaching out and removing the bandana from Sage's mouth, ". . . and fluff her up a little."

"Miss Rosie, please," Sage pleaded.

Rose's eyes sympathetically smiled over her bandana.

"You'll be just fine, sweet pea," she said as she twisted a lock of Sage's hair around one finger to dress up the ringlet.

"Here, darlin'," Eugenia said. Reaching into the pocket of her skirt, she withdrew the piece of paper Livie had given her before they left the boardinghouse.

"Ya better quit fiddlin' around, Eugenia," Mary said, entering the room. "He oughta be ridin' up any minute."

"Yes, yes, I know, Mary," Eugenia mumbled. She reached into her skirt pocket again, rummaging for something. "I need a safety pin," she said. "Do you still have one holdin' your camisole together at the shoulder?"

"Yes I do, Eugenia," Mary grumbled, reaching inside the shoulder of her shirtwaist. "But I wish ya wouldn't mention such things in front of the rever'nd."

Mary quickly produced a rather bent up safety pin, handing it to Eugenia. Using the pin, Eugenia attached the piece of paper to the bodice of Sage's dress.

"Now, you be sure Reb gets this, Sage honey," Eugenia said.

"What does it say?" Sage asked. What had Livie written on the piece of paper for Reb to read? And how was she supposed to give it to him when she was tied up?

"Oh, just stuff and nonsense," Eugenia said. She reached into her skirt pocket once more, producing a piece of hard candy. Popping it into Sage's mouth, she said, "Here's a peppermint to hold you over 'til he comes home. All right?"

"How could you all do this to me?" Sage mumbled, hurt and frightened.

It was Reverend Tippetts who answered. Sitting down next to her on the bed, he patted her hands and said, "The Lord is love, Sage. I'm on the Lord's side, the side of good and right and true. The devil is hate, hate and unhappiness and fear. The devil's usin' fear here, Sage. He's tryin' to interfere with love, the good and right love and true love between a good man and a good woman. I'm out to stop the devil cold in his tracks. And if it means tyin' ya up and leavin' ya here so Reb'll find ya so the two of you can beat the devil together, then than that's what I mean to do."

Sage felt tears brimming in her eyes. She was so apprehensive and so very anxious!

"But . . . but . . . reverend..." she stammered. "I'm . . . I'm here now. If you just untie me . . . I promise . . . I promise to face him on my own."

Reverend Tippetts reached out, cupping her face in one hand. "Oh, ya'll be facin' him on yer own all right, Sage. And won't this just make the story all that more interestin'?"

He stood then and walked out of the room.

Winnery touched the brim of his hat as he grinned at Sage and said, "Ya have a nice evenin' now, Miss Sage." Then he left too.

Sage looked to Rose, then to Mary and Eugenia, still wearing red bandanas over their faces but standing with hands clasped and slouchy shoulders like two guilty children.

"I'll never forgive you for this," Sage said, fighting back tears.

"You'll thank us for it one day, Sage," Eugenia told her. "I promise.

Trust us, Sage. Trust us and trust Reb, too. And trust yourself."

"You look so pretty, Sage," Rose sighed. "You know we love ya, Sage. You know we do. And you look so pretty. Reb's gonna feel like a toddler on Christmas mornin'!"

"Just cinch up yer corset strings and hang on for the ride, Sage," Mary said, nodding with encouragement.

Eugenia breathed a heavy sigh and said, "Well, girls, let's get goin'." She looked back to Sage as they turned to leave. "I do love you, Sage. I love you as much as I do my own children. It'll all be fine."

They were gone. Sage closed her eyes, allowing some of her tears to travel over her cheeks. She couldn't let them all escape, however. It was bad enough Reb was going to come home and eventually find her. She couldn't let him find her dressed like a saloon girl, tied up to his bed and red-faced and puffy-eyed from crying, too.

Leaning her head back against the headboard, she sighed. She closed her eyes and listened. Through the open window, she could hear the rumble of the wagon as her friends abandoned her. The rumble grew fainter and fainter until it was too distant to hear. Soon, only the soothing music of crickets and the far off burping of the frogs down by the creek reached her ears.

Sage opened her eyes and looked around the room. The dim light of the lamp cast soft shadows, the flicker of its flame causing them to dance along the walls. There was a wash basin and pitcher on a nearby table. An old trunk with blankets and clothes strewn across it sat in one corner. A mirror hung on one wall above a chest of drawers, and a framed painting of a cow hung over the wall above the headboard of the bed.

She couldn't help but smile as her eyes fell on another corner of the room where a pile of boots, shirts and worn blue jeans lay in a heap. She sighed, all at once delighted by the idea of being in his room, of witnessing the place where he slept.

Her smile faded instantly, however, as her ears caught the sound of approaching horses. For a moment she thought, actually hoped, the Reverend Tippetts, Winnery and the widows had experienced a change of heart and were returning to free her. As the sound grew louder, however, she recognized the rhythm of the gait, of horses bearing riders.

She heard a sharp whistle, heard Reb call, "Here! Bullet!" Suddenly her body was awash with goose bumps, trembling with nervous anticipation.

"I'm bunkin' in early tonight," she heard Charlie Dugger say.

"Ya feelin' all right, Charlie?" Reb asked.

"Oh, yeah," Charlie said. "Just a bit more tuckered out than usual."

"Don't ya want some supper?" Reb asked.

"Nope," Charlie said. "Had me some jerky 'fore ya rode out with me. I'll take care of ol' Ned for ya, though. Ya look as tired-out as an ol' dog tonight."

"Well I won't thank ya for that, Charlie," Reb chuckled. "But I will thank for ya takin' care of Ned for me. I'm a bit tired out myself tonight. Looks like I left the lamp burnin' inside when I left this mornin'. I gotta start makin' sure I'm wide awake when I ride out from now on."

"Well, it has been a long couple of days," Charlie said.

"It's been a long week," Reb said.

"Good night then, Reb," Sage heard Charlie say.

"Good night, Charlie," Reb replied.

Sage held her breath as she heard Reb's boots on the front porch, held it even longer when she heard him open the door and walk through the kitchen, the click click and soft padding of Bullet's paws as he accompanied his master. She heard the sounds of the pump handle working in the kitchen, heard water splashing in the sink.

"There ya go, boy," she heard Reb say. "Yer a good dog, Bullet. A good dog. You eat hearty, okey-dokey? I'm turnin' in."

Sage began to breathe again, the rapid breath of fearful anticipation. What could she do? What could she possibly say? She closed her eyes for a moment, willing herself to disappear. But when she opened them again, nothing had changed. She still sat dressed in Scarlett Tippetts' old saloon dress, tied to Reb Mitchell's bed and unable to do anything to change it.

Anxiously, she watched the bedroom door, waiting for him to appear and burst into angry questions. In the next moment he did appear, pausing in the doorway as he yawned, pulling his shirt off over his head. Tossing the shirt to join the pile of others in the corner, he closed his eyes tightly, stretching long and hard. He seemed overly tired, completely worn out, and Sage felt all the more fearful and anxious for intruding on his private existence.

He still did not see her as he looked down, fiddling with the button at the waist of his blue jeans. Sage gasped, realizing he might continue his routine of undressing if she did not make herself known, but fear silenced her voice. What could she say? How could she possibly speak?

He glanced up for a moment, but looked back to his hands, working the button at his waist, as if his mind hadn't quite noticed Sage tied to the bed.

Slowly, he looked back to her, a puzzled frown puckering his handsome brow.

"Sage?" he asked. Sage felt tears of humiliation and panic filling her eyes and she looked away from him for a moment. Reb turned and looked back over his shoulder as if he half expected to see someone standing behind him. He looked at her, still frowning, and asked, "Sage, what're ya doin' dressed up like a saloon gal and tied to my bed?"

Chapter Fourteen

✶ ✶

"It wasn't me, Reb!" Sage began to explain. "I swear . . . it wasn't me. I . . . I . . . I didn't do it. It wasn't me."

She could only imagine what Reb must be thinking as he stood there staring at her. Yet, the sight of him, his mere presence in the room, caused a breathless sort of thrill to rise in her bosom.

Still frowning, Reb walked toward her. Sage felt more tears fill her eyes as her gaze fell to the painful-looking scars blazoned on his chest. The scars on his body were far more severe than the ones on her back. She was suddenly awash with guilt, self-blaming for their existence.

"I didn't figure ya did it yerself, Sage," he said as he approached. His eyes narrowed as he studied her. "That's a mighty good job of ropin' and tyin', though," he said.

Sage's heart pounded violently. He was so near, standing there so close! If she hadn't been tied up, she could've easily reached out and touched him. Oh, how she wished she could touch him and throw herself into his arms.

"It was Mr. Winnery!" Sage exclaimed. "The widows . . . the widows put him up to it! Reverend Tippetts even! He helped! All of them! They tied me up back at the boardin' house and Winnery carried me out to the wagon. Reverend Tippetts drove it here!"

"Winnery tied ya up?" Reb asked. His expression hadn't changed. He still frowned at her, eyes narrowed as he listened.

Sage was desperate to absolve herself from any wrong-doing, however, and babbled on.

"It was the widows! I don't mean for you to take me for a liar, Reb," she continued, "But I think your Aunt Eugenia was at the heart of it! They . . . they had masks, too! The widows, they . . . they wore red bandanas around their faces like they thought they were rustlers or somethin'! They all threw me in the wagon, drove me out here and . . . and . . . and . . ."

"And tied ya up to my bed," Reb finished for her.

"I swear, Reb . . . I didn't do it," she repeated.

He was silent for a moment, still studying her, his frown softening as he asked, "How'd they get ya in that dress?" Sage blushed from the top of her head to the very tips of her bare toes. She felt so ridiculous, foolish for being so gullible. "Did Winnery do that, too?" Reb asked.

"No! Of course not," Sage said, her teeth clinching with indignation. "I . . . I was stupid enough to fall for that myself," she admitted. She continued to fight tears of humiliation, continued to wish she could reach out and touch him.

All at once, his face broke into a smile. Sitting down on the bed next to her, he began to laugh. Shaking his head, he looked at her and continued to laugh.

"I can just see it," he said, tipping his head back, shaking it in disbelief. "Them four old ladies dressed up like bandits." He looked at her then, eyebrows raised as he chuckled. "They talked the Reverend Tippetts into this?" he asked.

"He drove the wagon," Sage reminded him. "This dang dress even belongs to Scarlett."

"Does it now?" he asked, his gaze falling to her bare legs. He placed his hand on her ankle, caressing it and sliding it up her leg to her knee. Sage's entire body broke into goose bumps at the pleasing sensation of his touch. "And no stockin's or shoes?" he asked.

"They . . . they didn't give me time," Sage said.

Reb shook his head, chuckling again. "Looks like I really missed out on the fun this time."

"Please, Reb," Sage begged. "Please . . . please just untie me. I'm sorry . . . I'm sorry they . . ."

"Untie ya?" he said, frowning again. "Well, how do I even know yer tellin' me the truth, Sage?" he asked.

"What? Of course I'm tellin' you the truth!" she exclaimed. Certainly she knew how ridiculous the entire story sounded, how far-fetched. But Reb knew the widows as well as she did. He knew they were little mischief-makers. Furthermore, he knew she couldn't have possibly tied herself up the way she was.

"But what if yer lyin'?" he asked. "What if . . . what if Santy Claus just came early on this year? What if yer my Christmas present and Santy Claus just had to drop ya down the chimney a might early? Ya know, 'fore ya spoiled, or went bad or somethin'?"

"Please, Reb," Sage whispered. He was teasing her now, not maliciously, but she still felt all the more foolish.

He seemed to ignore her plea, however, saying, "Looky here." He reached out, unpinning the note from her dress. "Seems Santy Claus me left a note. Maybe this'll explain why he's come by so soon, so unexpected." He tossed Mary's bent-up old safety pin on the lamp table next to the bed. "I mean, Christmas don't often come in August."

"Reb," Sage begged.

"Hush now, Sage," he mumbled. "Ain't often a man gets a note from Santy Claus hisself."

Sage sighed. She felt so very defeated, so very tired, so very uncomfortable. If she hadn't known better, she'd have thought Reb was in cahoots with the widows, Winnery and Reverend Tippetts. He did not seem the least bit angry. He only seemed amused. She wondered then, wondered if perhaps what Eugenia said was right. Perhaps Reb did care more for her than he let on. She studied him as he read the note from Livie, happy to see his face again, delirious to be in his presence. All at once, she didn't care so much she was dressed up in some ridiculous get-up, helplessly tied up to his bed. All at once, all she cared about was being with him.

It was all worth it, she thought. *Just to be with him again. All this was worth it.*

She watched as he finished reading the note. Folding it once more, he tucked it into the pocket of his trousers.

"Yep," he said, grinning at her. "Ol' Santy says he just had to deliver early this year." He chuckled, taking hold of her ankles and running an index finger over the bottom of one of her feet. Sage flinched, trying to pull her ankle from his grasp before he could tickle her again. "I'll say this 'bout ol' Santy, though," he began, "I sure like what he's leavin' off for me these days a darn sight better than them toy soldiers he brung a few years back."

"You . . . you don't seem very angry," Sage stammered. Oh, he was beautiful! For a moment Sage was so lost in the alluring fire of his eyes she almost forgot she was still tied up. He'd cleaned up his whiskers since she'd seen him the day before. His mustache and goatee were once again perfectly manicured. His hair, however, was mussed and tousled, the way she preferred it. Oh, how she wished she could reach out and run her fingers through the softness of his hair.

"Why would I be angry?" he asked. "What kind of fool would be mad about findin' you all gussied up and helpless?" He frowned and added, "Even so, I do wonder what they were thinkin' I'd do with ya when I found ya this way. Reverend Tippetts must trust my self-restraint a bit more than I do myself."

Sage blushed, delighted at his teasing inference. In that moment, she wished she could sit and stare at him forever, stay tied up if it meant she could do so. She sighed, realizing the widows had been right. She was glad they'd tortured her, for Reb was speaking to her again.

Reb's smile faded, however, and he reached down, drawing a knife from his boot.

"More'n likely they're all just callin' me out as coward," he mumbled, cutting the rope binding Sage's ankles.

"What?" Sage asked, remembering the conversation she'd had with Eugenia. She felt hot, disgusted with herself. In her anger and hurt, she'd called him a coward, too. She knew, as she knew when she'd said it, Reb Mitchell was no coward. It was heartache that had caused her to say it. Heartache and the fear the devil had put in her.

"Ain't I?" he asked, cutting the rope at her knees. "Wasn't bad enough I was ignorant and let that cat get to ya," he began, "I had to go and let it nearly tear ya to bits." He cut the ropes which bound her hands, then the ones binding her arms.

Sage rubbed at her sore wrists with her hands as she said, "That wasn't your fault. None of it. You couldn't have known that cat was . . ."

"I couldn't even face ya after," he said. He reached up caressing the bareness of her shoulder with one hand, his fingers lingering on the scars left by the mountain lion's teeth. Every inch of her flesh tingled because of his touch. She wanted so desperately to throw herself into his arms. Yet fear, coupled with the need to remain strong and to restrain her tears, kept her from it.

"I was sick to death about it. I knew ya musta thought I was the weakest man ya ever did come across."

"How could I have thought that?" she asked. "You saved my life."

"Maybe," he said, shrugging his shoulders.

"Maybe?" Sage asked in a whisper. How could he even think for one moment that he hadn't literally saved her life? The gruesome scars on his chest were proof enough!

"And then that mess with Ivy," he mumbled, rising from the bed. He returned the knife to its place in his boot. "I shouldn't a . . . I shouldn't a said the things I did to ya yesterday in town."

Sage was trembling, tears brimming in her eyes, begging for release, but she held them back. She couldn't let Reb see her cry. He'd think she was weak. Wouldn't he? Yet, he still believed she thought he was weak because of the mountain lion attack and she didn't. Maybe, maybe he wouldn't think her tears were weak either. Still, she held them back.

It was all wrong somehow. He wasn't angry for finding her tied up in his house. He didn't seem angry about anything. He only seemed defeated, calm, tired and defeated. He didn't even seem fearful. Eugenia said he was afraid, but Sage did not sense it in him. Eugenia had been wrong.

As Sage sat, trembling, so desperately holding back her tears, confusion washed over her. She had expected Reb to be angry at finding her there, irritated that his privacy had been breached. But he only seemed amused by the widows' antics. Sage had expected, even hoped for an angry outburst from him, something to perhaps provoke her into her own confessions. She was unprepared for his composure.

Reb smiled at her, his eyes warm and fascinating. He held his hand out to her. "Come on, you brazen hussy," he said winking at her. "Let's haul ya on home."

As Sage placed her hand in his and allowed him to help her stand up from the bed, she fancied the life was draining from her. She was dazed, unable to believe the entire experience, all the widows' planning and mischief was all for naught. The ebb of dying hope throbbed through her body as the familiar pain of heartache stabbed at her heart. As he led her toward the door, she relented—relented and freed her tears.

Ruthie was nowhere near, there was no rain, but she could no longer stop her pain from manifesting itself through her tears. She made no noise, no sniffle or sound to indicate her tears had begun. Glancing up quickly, she was grateful Reb was looking forward as he led her toward the bedroom door, thankful he had not yet seen her weakness.

When he reached the door, however, he paused. He still did not look back at her, only paused, casting his gaze to the floor for a moment. Unexpectedly, he reached out and closed the bedroom door, shutting them in the room.

Sage's tears increased as she stood behind him. She was the coward! She was! Why couldn't she just open her mouth and tell him she was sorry for being so guarded? Why couldn't she just tell him she loved him, and that she knew she would die if he did not love her in return?

Reb did not speak at first, only continued to face the door. He lowered his head as he mumbled, "I can't take ya back." He shook his head and added, "Not without tastin' ya one more time first. I swear, Sage Willows, whenever yer around, I feel like I ain't had nothin' to drink in a month."

Sage gasped as he suddenly turned, taking hold of her shoulders, spinning her around and rather roughly shoving her back against the bedroom door.

His head still bent before her, he began, "Sage, I . . ." but when he looked up at her, his words were silenced.

ଔ

REB HAD MEANT to steal one last kiss from her, determined to savor her mouth once more before freeing her. But as he looked upon her, he was awe-struck at the vision before him. He wasn't certain he was awake at first. He knew he must be dreaming, for Sage Willows never cried! Never! Not without the benefit of the rain to mask her tears. Yet, she stood before him, tears spilling from her eyes and over her cheeks in astounding profusion.

Had he hurt her when he'd turned her to face him? Had she been hurt during the widows' kidnapping scheme? He looked her up and down quickly. He didn't see any injuries

Sage turned her face away form him then, turned her head to one side as if she were ashamed he'd seen her tears. Reb's heart began to race. He felt his breathing increase. Could it be? Could it possibly be she meant to forgive him for his weakness with the cat, for his asinine behavior where Ivy was concerned? Reb felt hope building in him, felt strength returning to his limbs. Perhaps his Aunt Eugenia had been right that day she'd scolded him for not going to Sage after the mountain lion attack. Perhaps, just perhaps he'd misread Sage's reaction the day he'd gone to the boardinghouse to apologize to her and found Ivy Dalton there. Was Sage as afraid as he was of disappointment and heartache?

His mouth watered for her, but there were things to be said between them first. He swallowed his desire and let hope lead him.

ଔ

"ARE . . . ARE YOU thinkin' on forgivin' me, Sage?" Reb asked. Sage was embarrassed by her tears, but his words stunned her so completely she could not help looking at him again.

"What?" she asked in a broken whisper.

"Are . . . are you thinkin' you can forgive me?" he asked again.

"Forgive *you?*" she cried. "Forgive you for what? For walkin' up to my front door one day and makin' everythin' so wonderful? For savin' my life when that cat came after me? For thinkin' I was . . . for thinkin' I was as cold-hearted as Ivy Dalton when I . . . when I was too afraid to tell you . . . when I was too afraid to tell you . . ." Her breath caught in her throat for a moment, the result of so much restraint built against emotion. "I'm . . . I'm the coward," she whispered. "I'm the coward the widows called out tonight. I'm the one who . . . who . . ." She raised her hand to wipe her tears, but Reb caught her hand in his.

"Are ya cryin' for me, Sage?" he asked. His voice was low, something in the intonation of it hypnotically alluring.

"The day Ivy came," Sage began, "I . . . I thought you . . . I thought you sent her the telegram. I thought . . . I thought you didn't want me and only wanted . . ."

"Are these my tears, Sage?" he interrupted. "Are they for me?" Sage gasped and held her breath as he kissed her cheek. She raised her hand again to wipe her tears, but he only caught it in his again, whispering, "These are *my* tears, Sage, and I'll take care of them *my* way."

Sage felt her body erupt into a nervous trembling, a delightful wave of goose bumps breaking over her as Reb kissed her cheek several more times in succession. Moistening his lips, he moved to her other cheek, and she felt the soft, moist touch of his tongue on her skin as he kissed her, tasting her tears.

"I'm . . . I'm sorry," she whispered in his ear, breathless from his kisses.

He raised his head, looking at her, frowning. "What could you ever have to be sorry for?"

Sage closed her eyes for a moment, struggling to keep from melting into a sobbing puddle at his feet and struggling for the courage to speak the words to him.

"I'm . . . I'm sorry I couldn't find the courage to . . . to tell you . . ." As she spoke, as she stammered, her emotions and residual fear causing her speech to be broken, she reached out to touch him. Somehow she hoped if she could touch him, simply feel he was really standing before her, that she could tell him what her heart so desperately needed to tell him. Tentatively, for fear she was dreaming and touching him would somehow awaken her and cause him to disappear, she let her fingertips travel over one of the fresh scars on his chest. He inhaled deeply, his chest rising as she pressed her palm against his skin, feeling the scars on his body, the scars inflicted there because he'd saved her life.

"Sage," he breathed. She looked up to him as his hand suddenly encircled her throat. "Don't touch me unless ya intend to let me . . ."

"I love you," she breathed, sliding her hand upward from the scars on his chest, over his shoulder and along his neck, finally resting her palm against his cheek. "I love you."

Reb's brow puckered. He winced as if some sort of wonderful ache had just gripped his heart.

More tears spilled from Sage's eyes as his hand moved from her throat to cup her face. As his thumb traveled over her lips, he breathed, "I love you, Sage," a moment before his mouth crushed hers in a driven, passion-drenched kiss.

There was no measured, careful kiss between them, only the heated storm of amorous fervor! With the searing intensity of fiery affection barely restrained, desire ignited and burned!

Reb drew Sage into his arms, against the strong, powerful protection of his body. Sage melted into his dominant embrace, careless of anything else in the world around her. She did not care that his loving aggression on her mouth took her breath away. She did not care that his powerful embrace crushed her ribs or that his hands tangled her tender tresses.

Pressed against him, she desired only to be closer to him. Held by him, she wanted only to be held tighter. Kissing him, she wanted him to kiss her more aggressively, never separating their lips.

Suddenly, however, he broke the seal of their affection, holding her against him and breathlessly whispering, "I love you. I love you."

"I love you," she told him, resplendent in the feel of the back of his neck beneath her palms, the breadth of his shoulders in her arms.

Suddenly he reached behind her, opening the door.

Sweeping her into his arms, he said, "I gotta get ya home."

"But . . ." Sage began to argue, reaching out to hold his face between her hands.

"Don't argue with me. Please," he said, striding out of the bedroom and through the kitchen. "It ain't safe . . . you bein' here with me like this."

"You mean it isn't proper," Sage said, smiling at him.

"I mean it ain't safe," he corrected.

"Really?" Sage asked, still smiling.

"Really," he chuckled. "I don't know what them old hens were thinkin', droppin' ya off, lookin' like ya do with nobody left to protect ya from me."

"They knew *you* would protect me," Sage told him, wrapping her arms around his neck as he carried her. "They knew I didn't need anybody else."

Dropping her feet to the kitchen floor, Reb opened the front door to the ranch house.

"Well, they shoulda known I'd have a hard time protectin' ya from myself!" he said. "Wait here while I get the horses saddled. We'll ride home quick. Before I change my mind." He kissed her once, so deliciously it caused her to sigh as he broke from her and headed toward the barn.

Sage watched him go, wishing she could stay, wishing she never had to leave him again. Love had chased the fear from her heart. Reb's love. He loved her. His eyes, his kiss, his words told her so, and she knew it was true.

ᘓ&

WHAT THE DEVIL was his Aunt Eugenia thinking? Reb shook his head, amazed by the mischief those old women could get into. Bless their little impish souls for working the mischief that tore down the walls between Sage and him. Dang, she was delicious! So soft and beautiful and tempting! Reb knew he had to get her home quick before he lost his head and proved Reverend Tippetts a fool for trusting in Reb Mitchell's self-restraint.

As he entered the barn, Charlie looked up, smiling.

"I see ya found the present them ladies at the boardin' house left for ya," Charlie said.

"You knew it all along, didn't ya?" Reb said, taking the horse blanket Charlie held in his hands and throwing over Ned's back. "I dare say you were in on it."

Charlie chuckled and nodded. "Well, somebody had to get the two a you to talkin'," he said.

Reb nodded, offering a hand to his friend. Charlie took hold of Reb's hand, squeezing it tight.

"I thank ya for all ya done for me, Charlie," Reb said. "Yer a true friend."

"Yer welcome, Reb," Charlie said with a smile. "Now get that little filly on home 'fore ya do somethin' the Reverend Tippetts regrets." Charlie nodded his approval once more and left the barn.

Reb chuckled. Charlie was a good friend, the kind a man only had once in a whole lifetime.

He saddled Ned and his new gelding. Leading them out of the barn and toward the house, his resolve to get Sage home was almost vanquished. She stood on the front porch, gazing up at the moon, her hair loose, a strand of it blowing in the breeze. For a moment he stood, just looking at her. He couldn't believe it was true. He couldn't believe Sage Willows was in love with him. He felt excess moisture in his eyes as his heart swelled near to bursting with his love for her.

It's too soon, he thought. Even with the revelation waiting for her back at the boardinghouse, it was too soon to hope Sage would consider what he had in mind. Wasn't it?

Chapter Fifteen

໕ ໖

The wind in her hair as they rode gave Sage an indescribable sense of freedom and joy! Something about her hair being free, even the lack of stockings and shoes on her legs and feet, liberated her soul.

She looked at Reb riding next to her. He had completely forgotten to grab up a shirt to wear on their way back. He was so handsome, so perfect!

"What a pair we make," she said as they slowed their horses' gaits to a walk for a moment.

"Must look like a couple of mad bandits ourselves," he chuckled. The fire in his eyes was evident even with the low light of the moon and stars. "Hold up," he said, reaching over and taking hold of Ned's bit. "Whoa there, Ned," he said, reining in the gelding he rode.

Chuckling with mischief, Reb led his mount around in front of Ned 'til he was right up beside Sage, facing the way they'd just come.

"Just give me one more kiss 'fore we get there, darlin'," he said, leaning over and putting an arm around Sage's waist.

Sage giggled and leaned toward him, placing one palm against his rugged jaw. "What if I can't keep it to just one?" she teased.

Leaning forward, she met his mouth with her own, warmth flooding her being like the summer sun.

"Mmmm," he sighed as he pulled away from her. "That's why I'm takin' ya home." Slapping Ned smartly on the flank, he hollered, "Get her home, boy, 'fore the Reverend Tippetts tans my hide!"

◌ʒ

REB LIFTED SAGE down from the saddle, pulling her against him and kissing her. Still kissing her, he reached behind her to open the back door of the boardinghouse. Sage wrapped her arms around his neck, returning his playful kisses as he tightened his arms around her waist and lifted her over the threshold.

Sage sighed, letting her fingers comb his soft, tousled hair.

"Well for cryin' in the bucket!" Mary exclaimed. "Reb Mitchell! Ya know we got company."

Sage giggled as Reb kissed her once more before releasing her.

"I know it, Miss Mary," Reb said, smiling at the older woman.

"Well, then why're ya carryin' on like some hungry animal?" Mary scolded. "We been waitin' half the night for you two."

Only then did Sage remember. Someone had arrived at the boardinghouse while the widows were about their shenanigans. Livie had gone to greet whoever it was, returned, and written the note Eugenia pinned to her dress bodice for Reb to find.

"Well, Mary," Sage began, "I can't possibly meet anybody lookin' like this."

"Yes ya can," Mary said. "We been tellin' her the whole story."

"What story?" Sage asked.

"The story 'bout you and Reb," Mary answered.

"Well, who exactly have you been tellin', Miss Mary?" Sage asked. "Who arrived just before you all drug me off?"

"Ya best be askin' Reb that question, Sage," Mary said.

Sage looked to Reb. His face had softened, his eyes burning with deep emotion.

"I thought . . . I thought if I could do somethin'," he began, "somethin' meanin'ful . . . somethin' that would show ya how deep I been thinkin' of ya and for how long. I thought maybe then ya might . . . I thought ya might see somethin' in me worth carin' for."

"All you have to do is exist, Reb Mitchell," Sage said, caressing his cheek lovingly.

"Oh, the sweet's thicker in here than syrup," Mary said. Sage looked at Mary to find her smiling, however. With a nod, Mary added, "And if ya weren't in love with the boy already—which the girls and I knew ya were—well then, this would sure have done it."

"Will you two get in here?" Rose exclaimed, appearing behind them suddenly. "She's been waitin' half the night."

Sage felt the hair on the back of her neck prickle. It was a good feeling, however, with nothing ominous or frightening in the sense of it.

"My goodness, Reb!" Rose exclaimed. "You might at least have taken the time to put your shirt back on."

"I wasn't thinkin' about what I was or wasn't wearin' when I came into my house to find my lover kidnapped and all tied up," Reb teased. "Way I hear it, three wild-eyed, white-haired banditas are to blame."

"Oh, go on with you, Reb," Rose giggled. "Now get in there. The poor woman's gotta be beat to death with fatigue."

Reb smiled at Sage, taking her hand in his. "This is for you," he said. "And our little friend."

Sage frowned, puzzled. Reb led her into the parlor where she saw Livie and Eugenia sitting on the sofa. Another woman, a lovely elderly woman with snow-white hair, sat in the chair next to them. Sage did not recognize the woman, she was certain.

"My stars and garters, Reb!" Eugenia exclaimed. "Dahlia will think you're nothin' next to a heathen!"

"Nothing in all the world could make me think badly of this young man," the woman said, rising from her chair. Slowly, she walked toward Reb, her lovely blue eyes radiant with emotion as she approached him.

"I'm Dahlia," she said, offering her hand to Reb.

"Reb Mitchell, Miss Dahlia," Reb said, taking her hand in his and covering it with his other. "It's a pleasure to finally meet you."

"Your letters meant everything to me, Mr. Mitchell," the woman said. "You'll never know the healing power of those sweet letters."

"I'm glad to hear that, ma'am," Reb said. "I'm real glad to hear that."

Sage frowned, completely confused, entirely bewildered. Before she had a chance to ask a question, inquire about whom the woman was or why Reb had been writing letters to her, however, the woman looked to Sage and smiled.

"And is this your Sage?" Dahlia asked. "Is this the girl who has captured your heart?

"Yes, ma'am," Reb said. Taking Sage's hands in her own, Dahlia's eyes brimmed with tears as she gazed adoringly, gratefully at Sage. "Sage Willows," Reb began as tears spilled from Dahlia's eyes and over her cheeks, "Meet Dahlia."

"Hello, Dahlia. I'm very pleased to meet you," Sage said. So distracted by what had previously transpired that evening, what had transpired between her and Reb only moments before, Sage could not understand who the woman might be. She could not understand why Reb would have gone to all the trouble of finding her. Was she a long lost relative? A great-aunt she had not been aware existed?

"Oh, you lovely girl!" Dahlia exclaimed in a whisper, tears still trickling down her wrinkled cheeks. "God bless you for your kind heart and heavenly goodness."

Sage smiled, still perplexed. She looked to Reb, but he only grinned, his eyes holding excess moisture as he looked at her.

"I'm . . . I'm afraid I don't understand," Sage said.

"Wait!" Dahlia said, holding up a hand. "I've brought something for you, my darling."

"Reb?" Sage whispered as Dahlia hurried back over to the chair she'd been sitting in.

Reb only smiled at her, mouthing a silent, "I love you."

Dahlia reached behind the chair, producing a rather large, oval object wrapped in brown paper secured with twine. Returning to Sage, Dahlia held the package out to Sage.

"It's for you, Sage," Dahlia said. "She would want you to have it. I want you to have it."

Sage frowned. She looked to Eugenia whose eyes were filled with tears, to Livie who seemed to be holding her breath, to Rose smiling resplendently. Even Mary's face was pale with emotion, her weathered eyes bright with moist sentiment.

Sage was entirely bewildered. The soft fire in Reb's eyes told her that what was wrapped in the brown paper pleased him.

"Go on, dear," Dahlia said. "Open it up."

"But, Miss Dahlia," Sage began, "I can't possibly . . ."

"It was meant for you, dear," Dahlia interrupted. "I know that now."

"Go on, darlin'," Reb urged. "I believe it's meant for you, too."

Sage sighed, still puzzled. She glanced at Reb again, wanting nothing more than to be in his arms. Yet every other person in the room was watching her expectantly. Even Reb.

She tentatively tugged on one loose end of the twine. The twine's bow gave way and Sage began carefully removing the brown paper. Almost at once, she realized the object beneath was a frame encircling a painting. She smiled at Reb, an inquisitive frown puckering her brow, a broad grin spreading across his face.

Pulling the paper away from the painting, Sage gasped. Her breathing stopped, her mouth dropping open in astonishment. The painting was a portrait, the image of a young girl of perhaps five or six. The child wore a simple blue dress to match the sky blue of her piercing eyes. Her hair was dark, parted in the middle and styled in pin-curled ringlets hanging to her shoulders. Her lips were the softest pink as were her cheeks, and donning the sweetest soft smile, she bore the overall appearance of happiness.

"Who's . . . who's this?" Sage asked in a whisper, though her heart had already answered the question of her soul.

She felt the tears in her eyes as Reb asked, "Who do ya think it is, sugar?"

Sage looked to Reb and he smiled at her, a thick sense of joy mingled with melancholy about him.

"Here . . . on the back, darling," Dahlia instructed, helping Sage to turn the painting over. "Right there . . . on the lower edge. Can you make it out?"

Sage studied the back of the painting. Indeed there was worn ink, handwriting on the back of the painting. Tears instantly springing to her eyes, Sage covered her mouth with her hand, overcome with emotion.

"R . . . Ruth Anne States," she read in an awed whisper. "Ruth Anne States—aged 5 years—1839," she repeated, tears spilling from her eyes. Turning the painting over once more, Sage gazed into the angelic face of little Ruth States. "Ruthie?" she whispered, reaching out to trace the lines of the painting with her fingers. She could not believe it. To know what Ruthie looked like in life, to see her eyes, her smile—it was something she'd only dreamed of. "Ruthie," she whispered again.

She looked up to Reb, his countenance so strong, so loving . . . so loving of her. She looked to the widows, all weeping and dabbing at their eyes with various handkerchiefs and apron hems.

"Where did you get this?" Sage whispered, entirely awed by what she held in her hands. Looking to the woman, looking to Dahlia, she asked, "Where . . . where did you get this? How did you come by it and . . . and why would you give it to me?"

Dahlia smiled at Sage, tears still streaming down her face. Her slight size and height gave her an air of being imaginary, like a fairy or other mythical creature. "It was mine," Dahlia said, tracing Ruth's sweet face with trembling fingers. "And so was Ruth."

"What?" Sage breathed.

"I'm Dahlia States," Dahlia said. "I'm Ruth's mother. I know she would want you to have her portrait, Sage. I know with all my heart she knows who you are and how you've watched over her."

For a moment, Sage couldn't breathe. She looked to Reb, overwhelmed with the knowledge he had found Ruthie for her.

"Reb," Sage whispered, feeling suddenly light-headed and weak, overcome with emotion.

"It's all right," he said, putting a supportive arm around her waist. "Yer just tired from the goin's on tonight."

"Your Rebel wrote to me," Dahlia explained. "He wrote to me of the girl he loved, the girl he wanted to love him in return. He told me about you and how you've kept my Ruth safe and happy, well cared for and . . . and how you've never let her be lonely."

Sage put a hand to her temple. Her head ached with trying to take in everything she was being told, with trying to comprehend the lengths to which Reb had gone for her sake.

Dahlia smiled and reached up, taking Sage's face in her hands. "That's quite the beau you have there, darling. And it's quite the girl he has here. Thank you, Sage. Thank you for caring for my little girl."

"But I only . . . I only kept her grave," Sage explained. "I only . . . I only talked to her . . . to the wind."

"She knows you're there, Sage," Dahlia said. "My very soul knows she does."

Sage looked to Reb. She could not believe it! She could not believe Reb loved her! She held in her hands the very image of the little girl who had once played in the sweet pasture grass.

"But . . . but how did you . . . Reb?" Sage asked. "How did you find . . . all this? How did you find it?"

"I loved ya, Sage," he said. "From that . . . well, maybe Ruthie led me. Ruthie and ol' Forest Simmons."

"Forest Simmons?" Sage asked.

"Seems ol' Forest Simmons has been keepin' secrets all these years," he said. Reb's smile was warm, filled with loving emotion. "When I picked up his lady dog and her pups a while back, we got to talkin', and he told me he knew Dahlia and her children when they lived here. He knew where Dahlia had gone after Ruthie passed. All these years he'd known where she settled. Did ya know yer daddy bought that acreage, the land with Ruth's grave on it? Did ya know yer daddy bought that acreage from ol' Forest back before ya were born?"

Sage shook her head, saying, "No. No, I never knew that."

"I sold the land to Forest Simmons . . . asked him to look after my Ruth's little resting place for me," Dahlia explained. "I asked him to take care of her for me . . . asked him to make certain someone always took care of her until I could come back and be with her myself."

Sage's mind was still spinning. She could not believe it! Ruthie's mother, standing before her! How could it be real? She looked back to the lovely painting of sweet little Ruth States. She fancied the painting smiled at her, Ruth's eyes shining with love and happiness. She looked up to the handsome, wonderful man she loved, the man who'd found Ruthie for her. Whatever had she done to deserve the heart of such a man as Reb Mitchell?

"I wrote to the sheriff in the town ol' Forest told me Miss Dahlia here had moved to," Reb explained. "I told him the situation . . . that I was lookin' for the mother of a little girl buried here. He knew right where to find her."

"The sheriff . . . well, he's married to my granddaughter," Dahlia added, a quiet sort of laughter escaping her throat. Her eyes narrowed with merriment. "When Mr. Mitchell's letters began to arrive, I knew the time had come. Then, when his telegram arrived last week, asking if I would come here, come to see you and tell you about my Ruth . . . well, then I knew it was time for me to go back to my little girl . . . make certain she knew I was here . . . make certain she wasn't alone any longer."

"But I've been here, Miss Dahlia," Sage began. She wanted the woman to understand her daughter had always been cared for, never forgotten. "I made sure she was never alone long."

"I know, sweetheart. I know," Dahlia said, cupping Sage's cheek once more. "The ladies here, your good friends at the boardinghouse, took me out to see her only just this evening, just as the sun was beginning to set. It's a beautiful space, Sage. Just beautiful! And . . . and your handsome cowboy hero has also assured me that, when my time comes . . . and I won't be lying to you . . . I've been ill and my time is near . . . your Reb assured me in his letter that he can extend the range of the fence he built around Ruth so as to include my resting place next to her when I do go. If . . . if that's all right with you."

"Oh, don't say such things, Miss Dahlia," Sage began, "I'm sure you have a good long time yet before . . ."

"I want you to keep her portrait, Sage," Dahlia interrupted. "I want you to have it. Ruth wants you to have it, so that you'll always have her face in mind to go along with her spirit that you already know."

Sage brushed the tears from her face as she looked again at the painting of the lovely little girl who had once laughed, lived, and was still loved. She closed her eyes, imagining the little dark-haired darling, running and playing in the green pasture grasses and beautiful wildflowers.

"She . . . she was my strength so many, many times," Sage whispered.

"Mine, too, sweetheart," Dahlia said, tears traveling over her cheeks. "Mine, too."

Sage threw one arm around Dahlia's shoulders, hugging her tightly, holding the painting safely in the other arm. Dahlia returned her embrace. Dahlia States—Ruthie's mother! It was a miracle.

"And I hear you have an empty room here at your boardinghouse," Dahlia said, once their embrace had ended, "a lovely little room perfectly suited for a woman in the winter of her life, awaiting the call of heaven."

Sage smiled, nodded and wiped more tears from her cheeks. "I do, Mrs. States. And . . . and nothin' would make me happier than to have you stayin' here with us."

"I'll write to my son . . . have him send some more of my things out," Dahlia said.

"And . . . and do you, perchance, play rummy, Dahlia?" Livie asked, dabbing at her tears with a pretty lace hanky.

Sage shook her head, smiling. She heard Reb chuckle and looked up to him, breathless at the sight of him so near to her.

"I do, indeed, Miss Livie," Dahlia said. "I do, indeed!"

"Then, what's say we get a lively game goin'?" Rose said. Rose walked to Dahlia, placing a friendly hand on her arm.

"Fair warnin' there, Dahlia," Mary said. "Livie here cheats, and she don't shuffle right at all, not at all."

"I shuffle fine, Mary," Livie said, sticking her tongue out at Mary.

"Just sit next to me, Dahlia," she said, taking Dahlia's other arm. "I'm the only one who doesn't try to sneak peeks at other people's cards."

"Now that's just a plain lie, Livie, and you know it!" Mary exclaimed.

"Girls," Eugenia began, "Dahlia is gonna think we're a bunch of cacklin' old hens if you don't stop your bickerin'."

Sage brushed the tears from her cheeks, carefully setting the portrait of little Ruth States on the mantel over the parlor fireplace. Once more, she gazed into the bright happiness of Ruthie's eyes, still unable to entirely grasp the reality of all that had happened.

Sage sighed, blissful, as Reb stepped up behind her, wrapping his powerful arms around her waist and pulling her back against him. As he pressed a tender kiss to her neck, Sage closed her eyes, breathless at his touch. Letting her arms cover his, she leaned back against him as he placed another kiss on her shoulder.

"She was a purty little thing," he said as he, too, gazed at the portrait a moment.

"Yes, she was," Sage said. "I expect she'd look a lot like her mother now."

"Sage? Reb?" Eugenia asked. Reb turned them around and Sage smiled at the four guilty expressions which met them. The widows looked like four children caught with their hands in the cookie jar. "We're . . . we're thinkin' that, by the looks of things . . ." Eugenia stammered.

"We're thinkin' now the two of you got past all that stuff and nonsense goin' on between ya," Mary finished.

"And . . . and that, since you obviously did get past it all . . . that perhaps neither one of you is holdin' any kind of a grudge against us for interferin'," Rose added.

"I missed out on all the fun, Sage," Livie added. "So you can't possibly be too angry with me. Now can you?"

Sage smiled at her friends. Her heart was so filled with love and joy she thought it might literally burst! She gazed for a moment at each one of them. She looked to Mary, her leathery old face so filled with emotion. She looked to Rose, her cheeks as over-pinked as ever. Livie still wore the expression of having just a smidgen less brains than any of the others, and

Eugenia . . . well, Eugenia wore the most sentimental expression of all, an expression of satisfaction, of love and happiness.

"Well, I ain't mad in the least," Reb said, releasing Sage and going to hug his aunt. "Can't think of one thing I'd rather come home to after a long day than Sage dressed like a brazen hussy and tied up to my bed."

"Oh, Reb!" Eugenia scolded, slapping him on the shoulder as he kissed her cheek.

"You were right," he told her. "You were right all along." Sage smiled as Eugenia brushed a joyous tear from her cheek. "My only regret is I didn't get to see you girls dressed up like bandits," he said kissing Livie on the cheek. "What a sight that musta been." Reb kissed Mary on the cheek, too. However, as he reached Rose, he took her face between his strong hands and kissed her soundly on the lips.

"Payin' up your debts, Reb?" Rose asked as he released her.

"Yes, ma'am," Reb said. "Though I still owe ya some waltzin'."

"You don't owe me a thing, sweet boy," Rose said, reaching up and caressing his cheek with the back of her hand and then her palm.

Sage giggled, going to Mary and embracing her. She smelled like bacon and old fabric, and Sage promised herself she'd remember the aroma of Mary Anne Farthen forever.

"Thank you, Miss Mary," Sage whispered. "Thank you for loving me."

"Oh, go on now, Sage," Mary said, brushing a tear from her leathery cheek. "Ya'll get me all hog-sloppy."

Throwing her arms around Rose then, Sage said, "Thank you, Miss Rose. I could never have survived everythin' without you. What would I have ever done if you hadn't been here when my parents . . .'"

"It's me who couldn't have survived, Sage," Rose said, tears trickling down her over-pinked cheeks.

"Miss Livie," Sage said, embracing Livie then. "Thank you. Thank you for touchin' my life, for makin' it better because you were in it."

"I'm a mess, Sage," Livie said, fanning her face with one hand, tears spilling from her eyes. "You know how I hate to be a mess."

Sage looked to Eugenia then. She was distracted for a moment, giggling as she heard Rose ask Reb, "Think you could part with one more of those kisses of yours, Reb? Maybe a little more lingerin' this time?"

Sage smiled, amused as Reb relented, letting Rose take his face in her hands and kiss him squarely on the mouth once more.

"I really do love you like my own, Sage," Eugenia said. Sage looked at the woman, smiling.

"I know," Sage said. "And you've been the mother I've needed."

Eugenia burst into tears, wrapping her arms around Sage and kissing her soundly on one cheek.

"Thank you, Sage," Eugenia whispered. "Thank you for loving my little Rebel."

Tears fell from Sage's eyes, her heart so full of love and gratitude for the women who had gifted her so much loyalty, love and affection.

"Thank you, Miss Eugenia," Sage whispered. "Thank you for bringing him here to love me."

"Have you forgiven them for their plotting, Sage?" Dahlia asked, coming to stand near her.

"I love them for their plottin'," Sage told her. She reached out, embracing Dahlia. "Thank you for comin' here, Miss Dahlia. Thank you for bringin' Ruthie to me."

"Thank you, darling," Dahlia whispered.

"Rose Applewhite!" Mary exclaimed suddenly. "Yer gonna smother that boy fer certain! Leave him be."

Sage released Dahlia, looking to where Rose stood, still holding Reb's face. The mischief in her eyes sparkled like the stars in the sky.

"Now, Reb," Rose began, "Two little kisses like that are hardly gonna hold me over."

"I'm sorry, Miss Rosie," Reb said, taking her hands in his and kissing the backs of them sweetly. "But you just got the last kiss I'm ever givin' to any other woman except my brazen hussy over there."

Sage giggled, then gasped, having all at once remembered the state of her attire.

"Oh!" she exclaimed, turning to Dahlia. "I want you to know, Miss Dahlia," she explained, smoothing her dress with her hands, "I don't normally dress like this. I . . . I . . ."

"I normally dress like this, though," Reb said. Turning from Rose, he gathered Sage into his arms and she sighed, breathless in his embrace.

"Oh, give her a big lickery kiss, Reb," Rose said. "Just for us."

"Yes, ma'am, Miss Rosie," Reb mumbled. Sage gasped, her entire being alive with excitement as he kissed her. The widows giggled with glee as Reb coaxed Sage into sharing a moist, heated, deeply impassioned kiss.

Suddenly, however, he broke the seal of their lips, swooped Sage into his arms and said, "Excuse us, girls. I'd like to finish this in private."

Sage smiled at him, caressed his handsome face with her hands. He loved her! Reb Mitchell loved her! She could see it in the fire in his eyes, had sensed it by the way he handled her, tasted it in his kiss.

"Where are we goin'?" Sage asked as he carried her. Oh, she didn't care a lick where he was taking her. She'd go anywhere with him. Still, the smile on his face told her there was mischief in his mind.

"Outside," he answered, kicking the back door open with one boot. Stepping outside, he pushed the door closed with one shoulder.

"Now then—," he began, dropping her feet to the ground. Leaning back against the door, he gathered her into his arms, pulling her snuggly against the warm protection of his body. He paused, however, his eyes narrowing as he gazed down at her.

"Now what?" Sage asked, resting one palm against the strength of his chest, the other softly caressing the back of his neck. "Aren't you gonna kiss me?"

"Do ya want me to kiss ya?" he asked, his voice low, alluring, fascinating.

"Oh, yes!" Sage breathed, excess moisture flooding her mouth in heavenly anticipation. "Please," she added, letting her fingertips lightly trace his lips.

Her simple touch seemed to instantly ignite him, for his mouth captured hers at once as white-hot passion blazed between them. Such love, such passion, such desire Reb evoked within her—Sage had never imagined before knowing him. She must belong to him! She had to have won him! A strange, almost frightening desperation began to rise in her and she tightened her embrace, wanting only to be his, forever.

He broke the seal of their lips suddenly. Pressing his forehead against hers, his breath quickened, labored, he asked, "Will ya marry me, Sage?"

"What?" Sage breathed, pulling away slightly in order to look at him.

His eyes were narrowed, filled with moisture. A frown puckered his brow as he said, "I . . . I know ya've been through a lot today, the widows' antics, seein' Ruthie, meetin' Dahlia and all."

"Rebel," Sage breathed. She didn't want him to say it again, not unless he truly meant it. Oh, how she longed for him to mean it.

"I know yer probably tired and that the last thing ya want to decide right now is . . ."

"Ask me again," Sage breathed. "But only if you meant it. I couldn't bear it if you didn't mean . . ."

"Will ya marry me, Sage?" Reb asked without pause. "I love you," he said. "I love ya and I can't do without ya. I need you, Sage," he continued. "I need ya to smile at me, laugh with me. I need ya to take long rides out with me, long rides out to Ruthie's pasture. I want ya to sleep in my arms. I want to wake up in the mornin' sun and see yer face first thing. I want my babies growin' inside you. I want ya to love me every minute of every day the way I love you. Sage I . . ."

"You'd marry me, Reb?" she asked in a whisper, tears streaming over her cheeks suddenly. "Would you really marry . . ."

"I love you, Sage," he interrupted. "I love you like I never imagined lovin' anybody. Say you'll marry me, Sage Willows. Say you'll marry me, be my wife. Say you'll love me forever."

"I already love you forever," Sage said. "I will marry you. I'll marry you and be your wife." She reached up, running her fingers through his hair. "And you'll be all mine."

"I've been yers," Reb said, softly kissing the corner of her mouth, "since the minute that fool dog wound ya up with me on the porch."

"I love you, Reb Mitchell," Sage breathed as he bent to place a lingering kiss on her neck.

"Then marry me," he said. "Marry me tomorrow and prove it."

"Tomorrow?" Sage asked smiling up at him. "Wearin' what? Scarlet Tippetts old saloon dress?"

"We've already got your weddin' dress finished, Sage!" It was Rose's voice.

Sage looked over to the open kitchen window to see five heads of white hair with five smiling faces peering out at her and Reb.

"We've been workin' on it all week!" Livie added with excitement as if there were nothing at all wrong with their eavesdropping.

"Now ya done it, Rose!" Mary grumbled. "Ya give us away."

"Shut that window and let me love on Sage awhile, ya naughty little banditas," Reb said.

"Now ya done it," Mary grumbled, as she closed the window.

Reb chuckled, shaking his head as he looked back to Sage.

"They love you so much, Reb," Sage told him.

"They love *you* so much," he reminded her.

"Will you kiss me, Reb Mitchell?" she asked. "Will you kiss me 'til I can't hardly breathe?"

"You bet," he mumbled a moment before his mouth found hers, "'til *we* can't hardly breathe."

And he did.

Sage Willows' Cornbread Stuffin'

Cornbread:
2 cups cornmeal
2 cups flour
½ cup sugar
2 tsp. salt
6 tsp. baking powder
1 tsp. black pepper
4 sage leaves (finely chopped)
2 eggs
½ cup oil
2 cups milk

Combine ingredients for cornbread and bake in greased 9x13 pan at 400° for 20–30 minutes. Allow to cool.

Stuffin':
1 chopped onion
5 chopped stalks of celery
2–8 fresh sage leaves (finely chopped)
Strip leaves from 10–15 fresh thyme branches
2 tsp. dried marjoram
salt to taste
warm turkey or chicken broth

Crumble cornbread into large bowl, add marjoram and set aside. Sauté onion, celery and fresh herbs in butter and mix into crumbled cornbread mixture. Add salt to taste. Then add ½-1 cup broth until stuffing is moist, but not soggy. Place in glass baking dish or bowl. Cover and heat thoroughly before serving.

To my husband, Kevin . . .
My perfect dream and own little *"Johnny Reb!"*

❧

And . . .
With endless gratitude, devotion and adoration to . . .
Mom and Kay-Ron (a.k.a. El Rabine),
Jeff, Ron, Coreen, Karen, Joyce, Jo Ann, June, Meriam,
Tammie and David.

About the Author

*M*ARCIA LYNN MCCLURE began writing novels as Christmas gifts for her closest friends, friends who longed for a breath of the past and missed the romance of bygone eras; friends searching for moments of distraction from the stressful, demanding times in which we live.

Knowing that it is the breath of the past and the "take me in your arms and kiss me" kind of moments that so many long to relive, Marcia spins her tales of love, life and laughter, adventures woven around those compelling, romantic instances that most appeal to a loving heart. Marcia feels that, if her readers close one of her books with a contented sigh and a delighted smile, feeling rejuvenated, cheerful and uplifted, then she has achieved what she set out to do—to shower refreshment and happiness on anyone having experienced the story.

Currently, Marcia lives in Colorado Springs, Colorado. There she writes her stories, surrounded by the spacious beauty of the high plains, blissful in the company of her family.

Marcia adores corresponding with her readers. You can write to her at P.O. Box 641, Monument, CO 80132.

Send e-mail to: marcialmcclure@cs.com,
or visit her website at www.marcialynnmcclure.com
also see: www.granitepublishing.biz

Also by Marcia Lynn McClure

The Heavenly Surrender
The Visions of Ransom Lake
Shackles of Honor
Dusty Britches
The Fragrance of Her Name
Desert Fire
To Echo the Past
An Old Fashioned Romance
Born for Thorton's Sake
Divine Deception
Sudden Storms

E-Books
by Marcia Lynn McClure

Daydreams
Saphyre Snow
Love Me
The Highwayman of Tanglewood
The Prairie Prince
The Rogue Knight
Weathered Too Young
The Windswept Flame
The General's Ambition
Indebted Deliverance
The Unobtainable One

Visit www.marcialynnmcclure.com for more information
about Marcia Lynn McClure and her books
www.granitepublishing.biz